SHADOWS OF DECEPTION

Gary Carmody

Dark-N-Stormies
An Imprint of Grace Abraham Publishing
Bristol, Virginia

GRACE ABRAHAM PUBLISHING
13335 Holbrook Street
Bristol, VA 24202

Manufactured in the United States of America

ISBN: 0-9741090-2-9

SHADOWS OF DECEPTION

TO MIKE,

ENJOY THE BOOK,

[signature]

Dedication

This book is dedicated to three extraordinary ladies:
My wife, Sareta; my mother, Bobbie;
and my daughter, Jennifer.
Their unwavering support, understanding and love
are more than I deserve.

Prologue

Jake Leighton sat in relative darkness nursing a scotch and fondling the silencer on his Beretta—his dark hair and attire melted into the shadows filtering in from the street outside. When he heard a key being inserted into the front door lock, he set his empty glass on the counter and focused his narrow eyes on the entryway. Now the fun began.

As the door opened, a large shadowed figure walked through the threshold. With the click of a switch the lights came on, revealing a big man in his mid-fifties with chalk-white hair and a round, smooth face. He was wearing a double-breasted suit with a green silk shirt and a Gucci tie. He walked across the room and tossed his keys onto a black marble kitchen table. When he turned towards the bar and focused in on Jake, his eyes grew wide and his mouth dropped open. Jake pointed his gun at the man and felt the corners of his mouth rise with pleasure.

"Who—who are you?" the man stammered. The pitch of his voice was much higher than Jake would have expected for a large man.

"My name is unimportant, Mr. Bentley. But what I want is very important."

Pursing his lips, Bentley glanced to his right towards the front door. "What's this all about?"

"Loyalty. Honor. Greed. Take your pick."

Bentley's eyes shifted from Jake to the empty glass on the bar. "I hope you're enjoying my scotch."

"Very smooth," Jake said.

"How did you get in here?"

Jake shrugged his shoulders. "It wasn't difficult."

Bentley licked his lips while his oval eyes searched the room like a cornered animal plotting an escape route. The sunken living room housed a white, chintz sofa with two matching wing chairs at either end, a sea of black marble tables adorned with assorted nick-knacks, alabaster lamps, a sculpture of geese in flight, several paintings of various subjects, and, along the far wall, a long paneled bar stocked with an assortment of liquors and crystal glasses.

Jake motioned towards the sofa and smiled. "Please, have a seat."

Easing down the steps into the living room, Bentley ambled over to the sofa, unbuttoned his suit coat and sat down. He crossed his legs. "So what do you want?"

"Information," Jake said.

"What kind of information?"

Reaching inside his shirt pocket, Jake produced a small notebook and a green pen. He walked to the cocktail table in front of the sofa and tossed them both on the table. "My client is extremely displeased with the way you've been handling his funds. He would like the matter resolved as quickly as possible."

"Client?" Bentley said.

"Yes, I'm what you call a professional."

"A professional what?"

Jake leaned his head back and gazed up at a white ceiling fan, its wooden blades rotating around three attached light fixtures like giant winged buzzards circling their dying prey. He nearly choked on the irony. Lowering his head he focused in on Bentley. "I like to think of myself as a professional problem solver."

After a moment of consideration, Bentley said, "This client of yours . . . he have a name?"

Jake shook his head, disappointed that Bentley was playing dumb. He had expected more from the man who had embezzled

2.3 million dollars from one of the leading crime families in the tri-state area. But when it came right down to it, they all acted innocent. It never failed. "Please," Jake said. "May we continue? I have a dinner date at six."

Sitting upright on the sofa, Bentley looked at the pad on the table. "What exactly does your client want?"

"Simply put, he wants the funds you've stolen from him."

"Stolen! I don't know what you're talking about."

Jake leaned against the arm of a wing chair opposite the sofa. "What does a CPA pull in now a days? Seventy, maybe a hundred grand a year?"

Bentley shrugged, ran his hand across his chin. "I do all right."

"Oh, I think you do better than all right. I'll bet that suit alone set you back at least three grand. And then there's the homes in Chicago, Florida and Cape cod, a long standing membership in the Miami Yacht Club with a fifty footer docked in slip number 28, a vintage Mercedes and a new Ferrari, and a very impressive investment portfolio. And I wonder, what would a simple CPA need with numerous off shore-bank accounts?"

Bentley's eyebrows rose. Perspiration dripped from his forehead. "How the hell do you know all that?"

"Impressive, isn't it?"

Bentley was quiet. He adjusted his position and looked at Jake. "What's it going to cost me for you to walk out of here and forget you ever saw me?"

"Far more than you can afford."

Running his hand across his chin, Bentley narrowed one eye. "You have any kids?"

"Never saw the need," Jake said.

"Well then, you have no understanding of how much it costs to raise a child these days. Private schools are outrageous, and public schools are a joke. Then you have piano lessons, dance recitals, and gymnastic competitions. And college . . ." He rolled his eyes and made a clicking sound through his teeth. "College tuition is skyrocketing. Do you have any idea what an

3

Ivy League education can run?" He paused, caught his breath, and then whisked his arm through the air like he was trying to rid himself of a pesky fly. "And on top of all that, my ex-wife is bleeding me dry. Her idea of roughing it is getting up before noon, missing her afternoon swim, and drinking domestic champagne."

Jake clenched his teeth, tipped his head to one side. It was the way the guy said it, with that pompous arrogance that seemed to dominate the offices of corporate America from Wall Street to Hollywood. If the fee for this meeting hadn't been so substantial, he'd be tempted to mix a little business with pleasure; maybe remove a couple of digits. He loved to watch their expressions the split second they realized there would be no tomorrow.

"I couldn't care less about your financial problems," Jake said. "I'm paid to obtain information, that's all. Now we can do this the easy way or the hard way." He paused, his contempt for Bentley swelling. "All I need are a few account numbers and the access codes and I'm gone. You'll never see me again. It's totally up to you how this plays out."

Bentley furrowed his brow. His right foot thumped the floor. Then he pointed to a pack of Nat Shermans on the table.

Jake nodded his approval.

Picking up the cigarettes, Bentley extracted one with a flick of his wrist. He lit it with a gold lighter he removed from inside a carved wooden bird on the cocktail table. He inhaled deeply and blew the smoke towards the ceiling.

"Those any good?" Jake asked, the smell of burning tobacco permeating the air.

Bentley snorted. "For six dollars a pack they'd better be." He tapped his foot faster, took another drag and looked at Jake. His eyes shifted to the pen on the table.

Jake waited patiently.

The air-conditioner kicked on and a blast of cool air filtered through the room. It smelled of pine, fresh linens and Musk cologne.

A moment later, Bentley picked up the pad and pen and began to write.

"A wise decision," Jake said.

While Bentley scribbled down the numbers, Jake glanced at his Rolex. Time was running short. In less than two hours he would be boarding a plane for Kennedy International. Chicago was a nice town if you liked fine dining and jazz and could overlook the blustery weather, but New York was still his home. Nothing beat Broadway on Saturday night, except maybe an expensive hooker after the show. His tastes ran to blue-eyed blondes with stout breasts. It didn't get any better.

When he had finished, Bentley tossed the pad and pen on the table. Then he sat back and folded his arms across his chest. "You've got what you came for, now get out."

Jake retrieved the notepad and inspected the numbers. Holstering his Beretta, he reached into his pocket and removed a cell phone. He punched the button that read — Memory One. "It's me," he said when the client came on the line. "I have the information."

Bentley took a deep drag from his cigarette and let the smoke out through his nose. Perspiration trickled down his face.

After Jake had given the account numbers to the client, he was instructed to hold. With the phone still to his ear, he strolled to the bar and poured another scotch into a clean crystal shot glass. He took a sip and felt the familiar burning sensation nip at his throat and stomach. It felt good. "First rate," he said.

Bentley's eyes flashed between the front door and Jake. He took another drag and exhaled. Smoke engulfed his head and drifted towards the ceiling. The whirling fan snatched it up and dispersed it throughout the room. "I'm so glad you approve. If you give me your address, I'll send you a case."

Jake was about to respond when the client came back on the line. "Everything looks good. You may continue."

"Gladly."

"Oh, one more thing. Have you ever been to Phoenix?"

Deep lines formed in the middle of Jake's forehead. "Yes. It was hot."

"Well, when you've finished with our friend, I have an associate out there who needs some assistance. If you're agreeable, your travel information will be forthcoming."

"I'd be glad to assist in any way I can."

After he hung up, he walked back over to Bentley, put a foot on the cocktail table and laid both hands across his knee. "You made the right decision."

"What," Bentley said. "Did you think I was going to do something stupid like give you the wrong numbers?"

"It's always a possibility."

"Look, tell your client he's made his point. Now you have what you came for, so get out and leave me alone."

Jake smiled. He loved this part. "Just one more little detail."

"No," Bentley said. He sat forward and glared at Jake. "You said you would leave if I gave you what you wanted."

"Honesty is overrated," Jake said. He took his leg off the table, pulled his weapon from the holster and leveled it on Bentley's forehead.

The moment Bentley opened his mouth to scream, Jake squeezed the trigger and pumped two bullets through Bentley's brain.

(1)

Brian Fogarty was seated behind the wheel of his '92 Taurus parked along the curb of a narrow street a mile south of downtown Phoenix. Weather-beaten warehouses lined the street as far as he could see; pale white, green, and gray buildings erected more for function than beauty. Tall weeds grew from large cracks in the sidewalks and shards of broken glass lay in the gutter. In the distance, Brian could see heat waves rising from the asphalt.

Pulling a handkerchief from his back pocket, Brian wiped the perspiration from his forehead. He wore his thinning brown hair a little longer than most men pushing forty and combed it straight back behind his ears. In the afternoon sun his gray streaks glittered like tinsel. His faded green eyes seemed lost in his pale Irish face: a sad face, he'd been told, that viewed the world with less fervor than in years past. On this particular occasion he was wearing faded Levis, a red t-shirt, and an Arizona Cardinals ball cap with a warped bill.

"I'm sick of this heat," Brian said, glancing over at his partner of six years seated beside him. "It's the middle of October, for Pete's sake. The rest of the country is enjoying fall colors and crisp mornings and we're still pushing triple digits."

Gabriel Bethencourt looked up from his hand-held video game and produced a mouthful of perfect teeth. He was one of those guys most men disliked, just on principal. He had a thick crop of black wavy hair, with every strand in place. His skin was tanned and flawless. The muscles on his arms rippled and bulged as he attacked the buttons on his video game. His large silver blue eyes never seemed to miss an opportunity to slip a peek at the finer sex, or notice when they returned the gesture. He wore a pair of white Dockers, a Hawaiian shirt, and a pair of Birkenstock sandals. A gold chain with a Saint Christopher's medal hung from his neck.

"Man, you're always griping about the heat," Gabe said. "The hotter the better I always say."

Brian shook his head. "You're a sick man."

Gabe grinned and returned to his video game.

Brian looked at his watch; five minutes to go.

Across the street was a two-story, gray and white stucco warehouse. The building had two rows of large, dirt-encrusted windows, four sets of tall, double garage doors, and a metal staircase along the side that led to an upper door. There were two rusty swamp coolers attached with wires and "L" brackets at either end of the building. One of them rattled and hissed as if it were trying to breathe life into the aging structure.

"I'll never get used to this," Brian said.

"Pull yourself together," Gabe said, looking up from the game. "I told you before; it'll go like clockwork. Ramone thinks he's about to make the biggest deal of his life. Our groundwork has been good. We played every scene perfectly. There is no way he's made us. Relax, this will be a walk in the park."

"Yeah," Brian said as his stomach began to churn. "I'm sure you're right."

"Of course I'm right. When have you ever known me to be wrong?"

Brian swiveled his head and gawked at his partner. "You've got to be kidding."

Gabe spurted out a wheezing laugh and Brian smiled. It seemed to ease the tension of the moment and for that, Brian was grateful.

The last few years had been tough and seemed to be getting worse. In his youth, he had wanted nothing more than to become a police officer. The glamour of wearing the uniform and commanding the respect of the public held a tremendous appeal. But when the stark realities of police work confronted him, he struggled to keep his doubts in check. For years this had worked, but the last few months had seemed unusually difficult. Every day was a struggle. He became aware of being dragged into spiraling depression and felt helpless to control it.

Almost without thought, Brian felt his back pocket to make sure his resignation was still there. It had been typed out for almost six months, and had rested in his pocket daily, waiting for the right time. The outline of the paper in his pocket gave him a strange sense of security. It was his safety line, his sanity check. As long as he carried it with him, he had an out. But his loyalty to Captain Albert Fernandez, his partner Gabe Bethencourt, and his oath to the force had been holding him back.

Then there was Christine: beautiful, ambitious, energetic, and more notably, concerned for her husband's welfare. Over the course of their seven-year marriage, Brian and Christine had seen some rough times, and understandably so. Marriage to a cop was anything but easy. In the back of Brian's mind he knew she had always hated it. The long hours, low pay, and constant danger had caused more than a few arguments; and the last few months the pressure to resign from the force and go to work for their neighbor, Bob Phillips, selling furniture in Bob's high-end store had intensified. But Brian continued to resist.

"Here they come," Gabe announced, shattering Brian's thoughts.

When Brian looked up, he could see a brown Chevy van rounding Second Street. At the same time, one of the garage doors rattled opened. The van pulled into the garage and the doors closed behind it.

"You about ready?" Gabe asked.

Brian nodded. "Ready as I'll ever be."

Gabe picked up the radio and pushed the button. "We're going in, Frank. Stay close and don't leave us hanging."

"Hey," Frank said, his voice crackling over the antique radio. "Don't you Scottsdale boys worry about us. You're in our neighborhood now."

"I don't want another incident like Sixty-eighth Street," Gabe said.

"That was three years ago," Frank complained. "Let it go, will you?"

"I just don't want any mistakes."

Frank's voice boomed over the crackling speaker. "Man, you're like a freaking mongoose, you never let go of anything."

Gabe flashed his perfect teeth. "That's why I'm so good at my job." He switched off the radio.

"Give him a break," Brian said. "He'll be there."

"He'd better be."

Brian climbed out of the car and closed the door. The street was nearly deserted with the exception of an ancient VW bus that rattled it's way down the narrow stretch of potholed asphalt, almost losing its bumper as it bounced over a railroad track that ran across the street a block down.

With Gabe right behind him, Brian crossed the street and worked his way around the side of the warehouse and up the metal staircase. When he reached the top, he pulled his derringer, checked the load, and returned it to the ankle holster. Then he turned and looked at Gabe. "Here we go."

As he rapped on the door with a clenched fist, he could feel the adrenalin pumping through his veins. From inside he could hear footsteps. A moment later the door opened, revealing a muscular hulk in his mid-twenties with a tattoo of Jimi Hendrix on his huge right forearm. He had an eyebrow ring that drooped down and touched his eyelashes. His hair was the color of grass.

"Yeah," Green Hair said.

"We're here to see Jerry," Gabe announced.

The man looked at Brian, then back at Gabe. "You must mean Mr. Ramone?"

"If Mr. Ramone's first name is Jerry, he'd be the one."

Green Hair made a ticking sound with his tongue. "We got ourselves a wise guy here."

Brian decided it was time to intervene. "I apologize for my friend. The heat's making him a little cranky. If Mr. Ramone is available, I believe he's expecting us."

Green Hair looked at Brian. "You I like." Then he glared at Gabe. "You I don't."

"He gets a lot of that," Brian said.

Green Hair took a step back and said, "Get in here and put your hands on the wall."

Brian and Gabe did as they were told. Green Hair frisked them and found nothing. Brian's derringer had once again gone unnoticed.

Green Hair motioned for them to follow, and they fell in behind. They were led down a long corridor lined with empty packing crates. The building was dark and musty smelling. A hint of cool air filtered in from a makeshift ventilation system consisting of white plastic tubes with small holes every three to four feet. The place gave Brian the creeps, as if he could hear the cries of animals being slaughtered. A blast of cool air made him shiver as he walked past.

When they stopped, they were standing in front of an open door with a light coming from the room within. Green Hair held up a hand and motioned towards the door.

Inside they found Jerry Ramone sitting behind a black, metal desk wearing a dark suit, purple tie and smoking a long, black cigar that smelled like an odor one might detect down-wind from a stockyard. Ramone's skin was the color of paste, his hair a bright orange. In his right hand he held two brass balls that he worked around in a nervous juggling act.

The tiny office contained a desk and chair, lamp, two upholstered client chairs, and a leather sofa against the far wall. Perched on the sofa were two of the largest human beings Brian had ever laid eyes on.

"Gabe," Ramone said. "It is good to see you again, my friend." He motioned to the two client chairs in front of the desk. "Please, sit down. Be comfortable."

After they had taken their seats, Ramone sat back in his chair and gestured towards the two hulks. "These two gentlemen are my associates, Mr. Borching and Mr. Camillo."

Borching was bald and broad with a neck as wide as his head. He sported a bushy moustache that was twisted into tight points at the ends. His suit was identical to Ramone's but several sizes larger. He folded his arms when introduced and stared at Brian with dark, narrow eyes.

Brian had a bad feeling about the guy.

Camillo was short and stocky with curly black hair and a bushy goatee. He wore tight slacks, a t-shirt and a tan sport coat. He chomped on a wad of gum, smacking and popping with every chew.

Both men had the unmistakable bulge of large caliber weapons under their jackets.

"So," Gabe said. "You have the merchandise?"

"You have the money?" Ramone countered.

Borching unfolded his arms, stood and sauntered across the room, his eyes never leaving Brian. He leaned down close to Ramone and whispered in his ear.

Brian waited for some kind of reaction, but Ramone's black eyes revealed nothing.

Borching returned to his seat and placed his hands on his thighs.

"What is this?" Gabe asked. His voice was stern and loud. "We gonna do some business or what?"

Ramone set down the brass balls and removed his hands from the desk. He placed them out of sight and sat forward. "I'm afraid we have a small problem."

"Oh," Gabe replied. "And what would that be?"

"I don't believe you two are who you say you are."

Brian felt his body flinch. His grip tightened on the arms of the chair.

"This is crap," Gabe said. "Look, if we can't do business, then we're out of here. There's always another supplier." He started to get out of the chair.

Suddenly Borching and Camillo were on their feet, grabbing for their weapons.

Ramone lurched out of his seat, opened his desk drawer and reached inside.

A loud thud and then something that reminded Brian of a metal tailgate slamming into pavement came from down the hall. Shouts echoed in the distance and then two shots rang out.

Brian seized the opportunity. He gripped the derringer with a sweaty palm, yanked it from its holster, and leaped to his feet.

Ramone pulled a forty-five caliber automatic from the desk drawer. Gabe sprang out of his chair, his eyes wide with panic. He opened his mouth to speak but nothing came out.

Brian feigned to his right, leveled the derringer on Ramone and pulled the trigger. The bullet hit Ramone in the shoulder. He let out a shriek and fell back into his chair.

Unable to free his gun from its holster, Camillo rushed forward, his sights on Gabe.

Borching leveled his weapon on Brian.

Brian swung his derringer towards Borching.

Footsteps pounded down the hall.

With a desperate snarl, Gabe ducked Camillo's advance. Borching fired, the blast deafening within the confines of the small office.

In Camillo's haste, he stepped into the line of fire and took the bullet in the back. His body flew forward, slammed into the desk, and fell to the floor.

Brian rushed a stunned Borching, planted a size ten boot in the big man's groin and sent him wailing to the floor. When he dropped his gun, Brian kicked it to the far side of the room.

Ramone sat in his chair, a stunned look on his face. His left hand clutched his wounded shoulder.

Ten seconds later, the door to the office burst open. Frank and his partner Bert Washington came in, brandishing their weapons. Both men were short and stocky, wearing khaki pants and t-shirts. Bert had a long narrow head like someone had smashed it in a vise. Frank took a look around and then stared at Gabe. "You guys okay?"

Gabe shook his head. "You still need to work on your timing."

"Hey," Frank said. "We were a little busy all right?" He held up a plastic bag full of white powder. "Unless I miss my guess, this ain't aspirin."

Gabe turned, looked at Ramone and smiled. "You have the right to remain silent . . ."

(2)

A bell sounded and a fraction of a second later, twelve horses mounted by brightly-clad jockeys, leaped from the chutes and galloped down the track, the roar of the crowd masking the sound of pounding hooves.

Vince Decker was watching all this from his luxury office box high above the track at Desert Downs. He was a towering man with broad shoulders, thin lips and curly flaxen hair he had trimmed by a private stylist every Thursday afternoon. He wore white, loose fitting Dockers, an apricot colored silk shirt and a pair of brown loafers, no socks.

As the horses made the first turn, Decker listened to the distraught voice on the other end of his cell phone. When he had heard enough of the man's whining he said, "I understand, Mr. Johnston. Now understand my position. I'm a businessman. I did you a favor when you were in need. And, I might add, you agreed to the terms. Terms, I'm sad to say, that have not been met. Now, this is really quite simple. Either you live up to the terms of our agreement, or I can't be held responsible for what happens."

Vince picked up a pair of binoculars from his desktop and held them to his eyes. As he watched the pack thunder down the far side of the track, he focused in on the horse named Mylo's Momma. She was a powerful chestnut sporting green and yellow and ridden by William Towler, the best jockey money could buy. A black stallion named, Birthstone, led the pack with Mylo's Momma close behind.

"No," Vince continued. "I'm not threatening you. I'm simply stating a fact." He paused, inspected his fingernails, frowned, held the glasses back to his eyes and watched Towler ease Mylo's Momma to the outside.

"You have until Tuesday, Mr. Johnston. No later."

He hung up the phone and leaped from his desk chair, both hands clutching the binoculars as Mylo's Momma closed the gap on Birthstone. "Come on baby," he whispered.

Birthstone's rider showed no mercy. His whip rose and fell with each stride. Saliva flew from the corners of the animal's mouth.

Towler reached out and laid his hand gently on Mylo's Momma's neck. He seemed to be talking to her. Her ears were erect, as if taking in her rider's instructions.

Birthstone began to slow as the gap steadily closed.

A moment later, Mylo's Momma thundered past Birthstone like she was fresh from the gate and crossed the finish line a full length ahead of the other horse. The roar of the crowd sounded like a high wind whipping across a barren plain.

"A magnificent animal," Vince said aloud. He looked up at a framed picture of Mylo's Momma on the wall opposite his desk. "You were expensive, darling, but worth every penny."

He strolled over to a mahogany bar nestled in the corner of the room and blended a pitcher of strong margaritas. After he had poured the mixture into a non-salted glass, he took a sip and smiled. *Perfect.*

When he had taken a seat behind his desk and had begun to go through the morning vouchers, the office door burst open. Two of Decker's men, clad in dark slacks and muscle shirts, came through the door with the young man Decker knew as Eric Aberst. Eric was short and stocky with blond hair. His mouth was too small for his wide face and he had the kind of fake smile usually associated with salespeople and politicians. He wore green shorts, flops, and a flowered sport shirt with the tails out. The larger of the two hulks hauled Eric across the room, placed him on a sofa and then sat down beside him. The other man closed the door, turned and stared at Eric.

Vince leaned back in his chair and fixed his gaze on the frightened young man. "I'm very disappointed in you, Eric."

Eric sat forward on the sofa and cleared his throat. "Look, Vince . . ."

In the time it takes to swat a gnat, the hulk on the sofa reached out and slammed the back of his hand into the side of Eric's head. "It's Mr. Decker to you."

Eric scrunched his face, reached up and rubbed his head.

Vince sat forward and placed his arms on the desk. "You owe me a substantial sum of money, young man. And at the interest rate we agreed upon, your bill is quickly becoming a serious concern."

"I know . . . Mr. Decker."

"So what do you plan to do about it?"

"If I could just get one good score."

Vince chuckled. How many times had he heard that one? They were all the same. They all had the ridiculous notion they would hit it big with the next race, or hand, or pull of the slot handle. What made them believe they were any different from every other loser who threw their paycheck on the table for another man's entertainment? But then it was hard to fault such people. If it were not for such blind pursuits, he wouldn't have a sixteen million dollar a year enterprise. Thank God for America.

Returning to the business at hand, Vince flashed Eric a stern, almost fatherly look. "I'm running out of patience with you, son. I need to know when I might expect payment."

"Please, Mr. Decker," Eric said. "If you could spot me another ten grand I know I could cover what I owe you."

Vince leaned back in his chair and wheezed long and hard. He placed his hand on his stomach. When he had composed himself, he peered at Eric. "You have nerve, boy, I'll give you that. What am I going to do with you?" He drummed his fingers across the desk, his eyes never leaving the terrified young man in front of him. "You're like an itch in the middle of my back that I can't reach. Very irritating."

The man standing next to the door adjusted himself. "You want I should handle this for you boss?"

"No!" Eric shouted. He licked his dry lips and swallowed. "I'll get the money, I swear."

"I *could* let Marcus take care of this," Vince said, nodding his head and pointing towards the muscular man by the door. "But that would only eliminate the itch and not the urge to scratch." He stood up, walked over to the window and gazed out at the track below. Rubbing his hand across his pronounced chin he said, "I don't know why, Eric, but I like you. I always have. That's one of my weaknesses, I guess. I've always been rather soft-hearted." He took a deep breath. "I tell you what I'm going to do. I'm going to give you another week; seven days and no more."

"But . . ." Eric sputtered.

"Seven days," Vince repeated. "After that time, I'm going to have to cut my losses and let Marcus have his fun. And I really don't want to do that. When Marcus gets involved, things get . . ." He paused, cocked his head to one side, "well . . . messy."

Eric sat quietly as perspiration dripped from his forehead.

"So do we understand each other, son?"

Eric nodded.

The man next to Eric stood up, leaned down, latched onto Eric's left forearm, and lifted him off the sofa.

"You won't be sorry you gave me the time, Mr. Decker," Eric said. "I'll get the money, I swear."

Vince nodded. "For your sake, son, I hope so."

(3)

Two hours after Brian and Gabe had made the Ramone bust, they were seated in the office of Captain Albert Fernandez. Brian shuffled in his chair in front of the captain's massive desk while Gabe twirled a cinnamon toothpick in his mouth.

Fernandez was seated behind his desk perusing the arrest report, gnawing at his bottom lip as he read. He was a short, powerfully built man with a balding head, large nose, heavy eyebrows and a graying goatee. Judging by his disheveled white shirt and wrinkled black tie, Brian assumed the captain had once again spent the night on the tattered sofa in his office. It was a habit Fernandez had developed after a massive heart attack took the life of his beloved wife, Alice.

Fernandez looked up from the report. "Good bust, boys. Very nice."

"Thanks, Captain," Gabe said, the toothpick bouncing up and down as he spoke. "But I can't take all the credit. Brian helped a little."

Brian shook his head.

Fernandez glared at Gabe and then turned his attention to Brian. "How long you two been working together?"

Since the captain had teamed them up in the first place, Brian was surprised by the question. But he also understood the captain well enough to know he was taking this somewhere. He decided to go along. "A little over six years. Why?"

Fernandez leaned back in his chair, stuffed one fist into the palm of the other and placed them under his chin. "I know you're a patient man, Brian, but I would think you'd have been brought up on assault charges by now. I mean a man does have his limits."

Brian let out a subdued snicker. Fernandez dropped his hands and looked down at his desk. Gabe shook his head as the line between his eyes deepened. He pulled the toothpick from his mouth. "You guys are a riot," he said. "You should take your act on the road."

Brian laughed uneasily. His mind wandered to the folded paper in his back pocket. He needed courage to forge ahead and now seemed as good a time as any. With his eyes fixed on the captain, Brian cleared his throat. "I have something I'd like to discuss with you, sir, if you have a few moments."

Fernandez was quiet. He shuffled through a stack of papers on his desk then looked up. "Get yourself a cup of coffee, would you Gabe?"

Gabe remained seated. He looked back and forth between Brian and the captain. Then he eased out of his chair, gave a narrow eyed glance at Brian and left the room.

"So what's going on?" Fernandez asked when they were alone.

Brian's hands were shaking as he removed his resignation from his pocket. He unfolded the paper and handed it to the captain.

Fernandez took it gingerly, as if it were something breakable. He scanned the resignation, his eyes darting back and forth across the page. When he had finished, he set the paper on his desktop and looked up at Brian. "Why would you want to do this?"

Brian had rehearsed this moment over and over in his mind. But with the moment at hand, words failed him. He felt as though he were in grade school being asked to give an impromptu speech on the meaning of life. His hands were sweating. Perfect words or not, he had committed himself. There was no turning back.

"I have my reasons," Brian said.

Fernandez was quiet, his attention fixed on Brian.

Brian waited, hoping the captain would jump in and help him out. It wasn't to be. Realizing there would be no reprieve, Brian forged ahead. "I don't know if I can do this anymore, Captain. When I get up in the morning and come to the realization I have to go to work, I get depressed."

"You and three-quarters of the world," Fernandez replied.

"Yeah, but I never used to feel this way. I used to love my job. It was all I ever wanted to do." He paused, scratched his palm and inspected a worn spot in the carpet at his feet. "Now I'm not so sure."

"How does Christine feel about this?"

Brian sighed. A short hum sounded from down in his throat. "She's never been thrilled with my choice of profession. She's been after me for years to give it up and go to work selling furniture for our neighbor, Bob."

Fernandez snorted, rolled his eyes and began to rock in his desk chair. "Is that what you want to do, sell furniture?"

Brian let out a quick burst of air, his lips fluttered like cards on bicycle spokes. "About as much as I'd like to work in a slaughter house."

Fernandez stopped rocking. "Then what's the problem?"

Brian shrugged his shoulders. "You said it yourself, Captain. A man can only take so much and Christine is wearing me down. And to be fair, you and I both know how hard it is on the spouses. The hours suck. The work is dangerous. And we can't even tell them where we are when we go undercover. It's tough."

Fernandez was quiet. He rubbed a hand across his shiny dome and pursed his lips. "Alice used to tell me she'd lay awake for hours watching me sleep, like she wanted to absorb the moment in her memory in case something happened to me."

"Did she ever ask you to quit?"

Fernandez sniffed and sat upright in his chair. "Never. But Alice was one of a kind. She was a very special person." He cleared his throat and coughed.

"Yes, sir," Brian said. "She was that."

They were silent a moment. Brian felt uncomfortable, like he was treading on hallowed ground. The captain had never spoken of Alice's death before, at least not to Brian. But then there had always been a mutual respect between them that was never discussed. There had always been an unspoken bond, like brothers-in-arms. Brian knew Fernandez was different from most high-ranking officers in the force. He'd been in the trenches, been wounded in the line of duty, lost a partner in a bust gone sour, and had battled a persistent drinking problem compounded by the loss of Alice.

Fernandez picked up the resignation and handed it back to Brian. "Hold onto this a little while longer. This is an important decision, one that should not be made lightly. Why don't you take some time off? Tinker around the house or finish a long overdue project, anything that will free up your mind and allow you to put things in perspective. You're a good cop, Brian. I'd hate to lose you. But in a week or two, if you still want to go through with it, then I'll accept your resignation."

Brian took the resignation, folded it, and stuffed it in his back pocket. "Thanks, Captain. I think some time off is just what I need."

Looking around the office, Fernandez said, "If you're anything like me, you've got a half dozen unfinished projects around the house just waiting for your attention."

"Yes, sir, that I do. But I was thinking of spending some time up in the mountains where I grew up."

Fernandez's thick eyebrows rose up on his forehead. "Greer, wasn't it?"

"Just outside. I haven't been up there in over a year. It would be nice to breathe some clean air and do some fishing. And if memory serves, it's very quiet at night . . . and very peaceful."

"Sounds perfect," Fernandez said. "Heck, if I wasn't so busy here, I'd go with you."

Brian felt his lips part. "I'd like that, Captain. You know how to fly fish?"

Fernandez paused, smiled. He leaned back in his chair, locked his fingers together and placed them on his stomach. "Now why on earth would I want to fish for flies?"

Brian felt his mouth drop as he stared at the captain. "That has got to be the worst pun I have ever heard."

Fernandez smiled. "Best I could do on short notice."

"Next time," Brian said, "I'll give you more warning."

(4)

As Brian emerged from the captain's office, he swung left and headed in the direction of his desk. Down the hallway, he spotted Gabe near the water cooler, twirling his toothpick in his mouth, and chatting with an attractive young brunette with the most form fitting police uniform Brian had ever laid eyes on. The brunette shuffled from foot to foot, her eyes looking up and down the corridor as if anticipating the arrival of an old friend. Gabe leaned against the wall, his eyes locked on the woman.

Brian hurried down the hall, the squish of his sneakers sounding as if he had just walked through a puddle of rainwater. Off to his right, a sea of desks and computers stretched across the room like ships at anchor. Conversations intermingled with clattering phones and squeaking chairs. On the far wall, a huge picture window separated the police station from the outside world. Through the glass, Brian could see a mulberry tree rocking with the wind, its browning and withering leaves indicating an extreme need for water.

When he was close enough to overhear their conversation, Brian heard Gabe ask the brunette to dinner. She winked, produced a startlingly broad smile, but said nothing.

Gabe looked up and spotted Brian hurrying past. "Brian," Gabe called out. "Come over here. I want you to meet someone."

Brian stopped, turned and walked over to greet them.

Upon closer inspection, he found the woman quite attractive. She was about five-six, with rounded shoulders, an oval chin, and full lips painted the color of cinnamon. Her hair was cut short and brushed back. Her blue eyes seemed to sparkle with mischief.

"Brian Fogarty," Gabe said. "This is Officer Sheila Kipler. She just transferred in."

They shook hands. Her grip was loose and unassertive.

"Very nice to meet you," Brian said. He cleared his throat.

She parted her full lips revealing a slight gap between her bottom teeth. "The pleasure's mine," she said. Her eyes roamed over Brian like a prospective buyer thoughtfully considering an expensive painting.

Brian felt his muscles tense. "Well, if you'll excuse me," he said. "I have a ton of work to do before I leave. It was nice to meet you."

"It was very nice meeting you," Officer Kipler said. "Perhaps we could all get together sometime and share a few laughs."

"I'm sure Gabe doesn't need my help with that," Brian said. He spun on his heels and walked away.

He arrived at his desk, via the coffee machine, and began the arduous task of weeding through mounds of papers, files, and reports spread across his desk. His thoughts were on the Ramone bust when Gabe arrived and planted himself at his desk facing Brian. As Gabe leaned back in his chair, it creaked like an old wooden porch rocker that had weathered too many storms. He plopped his large feet on the desktop and settled his gaze on Brian.

"So what did you think?" Gabe asked. "Is that one fine looking lady, or what?"

Brian looked up from his paperwork and took his first sip of coffee. It was hot and bitter. "She's very pretty, yes."

Gabe took his feet off the desk and leaned forward. "I know that disapproving tone, buddy. So what is it now? You don't like our new Miss Dish."

"I think she's a police officer. She should act like one."

Gabe's eyes went wide. "What, Mr. Prim and Proper, she's not allowed to have any fun because she's a cop? What kind of crap is that?"

"Forget it," Brian said. "I have a lot of work to do."

Gabe leaned back in his chair again, twirled his toothpick and studied Brian. "So what did you and the captain talk about that was so secret?"

Brian took another sip of coffee, wrinkled his face and tossed the cup in the trash. "I gave him my resignation."

"No way," Gabe said. His toothpick dropped from his mouth, fell to the floor and rolled under the desk. It disappeared among the veined design of the tile. "You can't do this to me, man. I just got you good and trained."

"I'm not doing anything to you," Brian snapped.

The shortness in his tone startled him. In years past, he'd prided himself on the way he had taken everything in stride. Nothing seemed to rattle him. But over the last few months, the slightest irritation seemed to set him off. He found himself seeking solitude more and more. And snapping at his best friend and partner only compounded the need for a vacation. Perhaps the time away from the city and the rigors of the job would bring back the old patience, but maybe not. He knew himself too well to think it could be that simple.

Gabe shuffled in his chair, his eyes fixed on Brian as if reading the lines on his face. He opened his mouth, started to speak, then put his hand over his mouth.

A phone rang somewhere beyond the desk. The fluorescent light on the ceiling flickered. Footsteps came from down the hall that sounded like the person had metal taps attached to his heals.

Gabe cleared his throat. "He didn't accept it, did he?"

"No," Brian said, realizing he had been shuffling papers and files without seeing one word. His mind was elsewhere, mapping the route to the mountains and trying to remember the last time he had set foot in the old cabin. He wondered how much house cleaning Christine would insist upon before he could steal away for some serious fishing.

"So, what did he say?" Gabe asked.

Brian looked up from his desk, placed both hands on the arms of his chair and eased back. The swivel mechanism made a loud squawking sound. He clasped his fingers together and placed them in his lap. "He asked me to wait awhile. Take some time off and think about it."

"Good," Gabe said with obvious relief. "It'll give me time to talk you out of it."

Brian looked back at his desk. His stomach seemed to sour. Paperwork had always been his least favorite part of the job. He felt more at home on the street than sitting behind a desk; at least until recently, when he found himself watching the clock, waiting for quitting time. But he could never leave the job behind. No matter how hard he tried, it was always present.

Then, beyond the papers, on one corner of the desk, he focused in on a 5 x 7 photograph of Christine standing by the front door of their south Scottsdale home. He had taken the photo himself the day they closed on the house. She had been so happy then . . . and so beautiful.

"So what happens now?" Gabe asked.

Brian smiled and said, "I think I'll go home and make love to my wife."

"Need any help?"

"Thanks, partner," Brian said, as he swept the papers and files into one tall stack. He stood, opened his bottom file drawer, tossed the whole pile in and pushed the drawer shut with his foot. "But I think I can handle this assignment by myself."

(5)

Captain Fernandez sat contemplating his retirement as he sipped coffee from an Arizona Cardinals mug. He ran his hands across his once smooth desktop, recalling with vivid detail how each and every scratch and gouge had come to be.

In his nineteen years on the Scottsdale police force, he had seen a lot of change and experienced a lot of frustration. The city had transformed from a modest-sized, friendly community, to a rambling suburban nightmare. When he had first signed on as a beat cop, it had been a policeman's delight. Crime was almost nonexistent. A rough day consisted of no more than five traffic stops and maybe a couple of young Marlon Brando wannabes stealing candy and pop from a convenience store. But lately, with a steady influx of people escaping bitter winters or earthquakes, crime was on the rise and growing worse every year.

Leaning back in his chair, he gazed around the office reflectively. On the wall behind him was a photo of a red, 1955 Chevrolet Impala, the vehicle he had purchased two days after high school graduation. Along side it was his bachelor's degree from Arizona State, and an old photo of himself and Alice taken at the Grand Canyon.

Alice had been gone less than two years now. The pain lingered. In a strange way, he didn't want it to fade. He felt that as long as the pain was present, so was her memory. He had adored her in life, and he would love her and her alone until his own passing.

Still, he was hesitant to retire. Since Alice died, the job had become his life. It was all he knew. He had thrown himself into his work as a form of therapy, neglecting everything else. At one point, some years after a fellow officer had discovered the game of golf and attempted to recruit him into the sport, he had contemplated joining the masses rising at the crack of dawn and heading for one of the hundreds of courses scattered around the Phoenix metropolitan area. But upon reflection, he found himself amused at the thought of wearing brightly colored pants, a sun visor, and two-tone shoes with spikes while chasing a little ball around a greenbelt. Somehow the idea seemed a little absurd and a horrific waste of time.

He was startled from his thoughts by a loud knock at the door. "Enter," he instructed as he lifted himself out of his chair.

A tall, fair-haired man in his mid-twenties with a tan face and a thin moustache came into the room. He walked over to Fernandez, shook his hand firmly, and introduced himself as Officer Jerry Travers of Internal Affairs. His shoes were polished to perfection and his suit, in Fernandez's estimation, must have run a good five hundred bucks. In his left hand he carried a brown briefcase.

Fernandez motioned towards one of the wing chairs opposite his desk. Travers sat down, placed the briefcase on his lap, and crossed his legs. He flashed the captain a hundred dollar smile.

"So what can I do for I.A.?" Fernandez asked, retaking his seat. He had a fairly good idea why Travers was gracing him with his presence, but he had no intention of making things easy on him.

Travers cleared his throat. He scratched his fingers on the arm of the chair as if he was petting the head of his favorite cat. "I'll come right to the point, Captain. We've received some information regarding two of your men." He turned his attention to the briefcase in his lap, flipped the latches open with his thumbs, and removed a large manila envelope. Unclasping the envelope, he slipped out a few sheets of paper stapled together at the upper left hand corner and flipped to the first page. "Officers Fogarty and Bethencourt."

Fernandez remained quiet. Years of experience had taught him when to talk and when to remain silent. With I.A., he had found it best to let them do the talking and only offer what information was requested, nothing more.

As he eased back in his leather desk chair, it squeaked under the weight of his two hundred thirty pound frame. He fixed his eyes on Travers and downed the remainder of his tepid coffee. "Must be some kind of mistake. They're two of my best men."

"No mistake," Travers said, tapping the report with the index finger of his free hand. "I have a signed report from one of your own detectives stating . . ."

"Who?" Fernandez interrupted. The muscles in his chest fluttered. He felt a surge of adrenaline as if he might have exceeded his daily caffeine ration.

"I'm not at liberty to divulge the officer's identity at this time." He looked down at the report, his mouth moving silently as he read. "The report states that detectives Fogarty and Bethencourt have been taking kickbacks from one Vince Decker in return for pointing any impending investigations in other directions."

"I don't believe it," Fernandez said.

Travers shrugged his shoulders. "Nevertheless, those are the allegations."

Fernandez stood, ambled over to the window of his third story office and clasped his hands behind his back. As he gazed at the street below, he could see north for several blocks. The pollution hovered over the downtown area like haze from a smoldering campfire.

"These are serious charges," Travers said, breaking the silence.

Fernandez spun on his heels and faced Travers. "Yes they are. And I assume you have some real evidence and not just the word of an ambitious, self-serving little jerk with a chip on his shoulder?"

"Reporting illegal activities within the department is not only a brave act, it's an officer's duty. I'm not sure you're looking at this from the proper perspective."

Fernandez felt a gurgling sensation in his stomach, and the muscles in his neck tensed. Fists clenched tightly, he strolled back to his desk and sat down. First and foremost on his mind was who had leaked this information, and what did they have to gain by doing so?

He looked over his desk at Travers, trying to at least appear calm as his insides rumbled and sputtered. "Well, you're right about one thing. Our perspective on the matter is very different. You want to ruin the reputation of two fine officers, and I intend to do everything in my power to see that doesn't happen."

"Internal Affairs expects your cooperation, sir," Travers said, with a smirk.

Fernandez slammed his fist on the desk. "I don't need you telling me what my duty is. I was doing this job when you were still wetting your pants."

Travers clenched his teeth. His face turned a brilliant shade of red. Then, with practiced skill, Travers closed his eyes and mouthed a few silent words. He exhaled slowly through his mouth and forced a smile. When he opened his eyes, he focused in on Fernandez and said, "Very elegantly put, sir. I'm impressed with your language skills." He returned the report to the manila envelope, slipped it back in the briefcase, stood, and turned to leave.

Fernandez bit back his pride, an act that did not come naturally or with ease. "I will, of course, cooperate."

Travers stopped and looked over his shoulder.

"But I'm sure," Fernandez continued, "you will find this is a wild goose chase. And when all is said and done, you'll owe my officers an apology . . . in writing."

Travers smiled and said, "We'll see."

"I suppose you'll want to interview them as soon as possible?"

Travers turned around and shook his head. "I don't think so. Not yet."

Fernandez stood and walked around to the front of his desk. He leaned on the corner, one leg on the floor and the other dangling and rocking. "My officers should be informed of any charges filed against them."

"Policy states," Travers said, tapping his briefcase with his free hand, "that we do not have to inform an officer he is under suspicion until we see fit."

"That policy is under review as we speak and should be changed within the next few months."

Travers grinned. "I know. But until such time as it is revised, I don't have to tell your boys a thing. Furthermore, it's easier for our agents to observe the suspects when they are unaware they're under investigation."

"I don't approve of your methods, Travers. You're not the Gestapo."

"Look, I appreciate your loyalty to your men; but if these allegations are true, we need to know for the good of the department. If they're not, then we look into the officer who filed the charges and see what's going on there. But it is Internal Affairs' responsibility to follow up on all reports of misconduct, no matter whose apple cart it upsets." He reached up with his free hand and adjusted his tie. Then he walked to the door, stopped, and turned to face Fernandez. "And I expect you to keep this under wraps until we inform you otherwise."

"The soul of discretion," Fernandez said.

Travers turned and walked out the door.

Fernandez returned to his chair and eased back. He could hear the sound of his heart beating in his chest and could feel his temples keeping time. He sat silently for a long time, considering the consequences of his actions. Time was running out. He had to act quickly. He picked up the phone and dialed. A man's voice picked up after three rings.

"I just got a visit from Jerry Travers of I.A.," Fernandez said, rubbing his hand across the side of his face. "He was asking questions about Fogarty and Bethencourt. You're going to need to speed things up. I don't want this blowing up in our faces."

"These things take time," the voice said.

"Time is a luxury we're running out of."

(6)

As Travers headed for his desk in the far wing of the building, he found himself feeling empathy for the captain. He could imagine the difficulty in knowing there were fewer days ahead than behind and having a sad realization that the last few years had been stagnant and unproductive. It reminded him of his own grandfather who had worked twenty-six years in the copper mines in southern Arizona only to die of emphysema at the ripe old age of 54. He could recall the funeral with extreme clarity: his mother boosting him up on her knee so he could see inside the coffin, his grandfather's sun wrinkled face resembling a piece of dried up pastry, and the piped-in organ music droning on and on. Afterwards, family and friends milled about eating and drinking and talking about the old man like he was a saint.

Years later, Travers had made a promise to himself. He would do better than his grandfather. And he had. After receiving his bachelor's degree from the University of Arizona, he enrolled in the police academy and graduated second in his class. He joined the force a month later and things had been smooth sailing ever since.

He lived in a beautifully spacious home in north Scottsdale with his wife, Margaret, and their three daughters, but spent every Wednesday and Friday afternoon at the west side apartment of a young redheaded woman named Deborah. His car of choice was a 1956 B.M.W. Spitfire, which he kept covered in the garage and drove only on special occasions. All in all, life was good.

While he made his way through a sea of ancient desks, he watched with amusement as uniformed and plain-clothes officers scurried around like squirrels gathering nuts for winter. Several phones rang at various intervals. A dozen voices blended into one swirling array of sound. Across the room, he spotted his partner Marty Kirkland. Kirkland was short and heavy and covered his hairless head with a hideous looking toupee. His graying yellow hair stuck out from under the tangled, woven mass like weeds invading a thick bed of dying turf grass. He had a long, narrow nose separating two unusually small eyes — which, at the moment, were fixed on the chest of a frumpy looking female detective sitting at a desk typing on a computer keyboard.

As Travers approached, he took in the woman's features. She was plain, had short brown hair, heavy eyebrows, a round face and dark brown eyes. Her thighs, Travers thought, were a little too chunky, and her breasts a little too small. She wore a large size shoe with fat, rounded toes that looked as if they had come from the clearance rack at K-Mart. Her nameplate read: Detective Marion Bantor.

Travers stopped next to Kirkland and watched him tip back a medium size package of Doritos and dump the last of the chips into his mouth. The bag crackled in his hand as he wadded it into a ball and tossed it in a nearby wastebasket. His grease-covered hands went directly to his pants, leaving a pair of glistening spots just below his front pockets. The noise stemming from his mouth sounded like someone walking on loose gravel with hard soled shoes.

Detective Bantor glanced over her shoulder, glared at Travers and said, "Is *this* with you?"

Under normal circumstances, Travers might have found the off-the-cuff remark rather witty, even funny. Had it been in his best interest, he might have even forced a mild chuckle, just for appearance's sake. But after the tense encounter with Fernandez he was feeling less than jovial. He ignored her question, turned to Kirkland and said, "Let's go."

"Duty calls," Kirkland said through a mouth of chips. A small piece shot out of his mouth and fell to the floor. He didn't seem to notice.

"Please," Detective Bantor said. "Don't let me keep you."

The two men turned and walked towards the elevators.

"What were you doing talking to her?" Travers asked, when they were out of earshot.

Kirkland swallowed the wad of chips and wiped his lips with the back of his hand. "I thought I might be able to get something out of her."

"You didn't say anything about the investigation, did you?"

They pulled up next to the elevators and Kirkland pushed the down button. "Give me some credit, would you? I made it seem casual, like I was hitting on her, making conversation. I was very subtle."

Travers made a clicking sound through his teeth. "Yeah, that's you. Mr. Subtle."

Kirkland's head jerked back. The lines on his brow deepened. "What got up your butt?"

Not wishing to pursue the current course of the conversation, Travers said, "They have a past, you know."

"Who?" Kirkland asked.

"Fogarty and the Bantor woman."

"No kidding. You mean they've been doin' the horizontal bop?" He smiled, shook his head.

"The way I heard it," Travers continued, "it was over a about a year ago but she keeps the flame burning and her calendar open, if you know what I mean."

Just then the elevator bell rang and the door opened. Two men in business suits and a solemn-looking young woman wearing a short skirt, white blouse and too much lipstick exited the elevator, turned right and headed down the hall. Kirkland watched the woman as she walked away. Travers entered the elevator and poked the first floor button with his index finger. As the door began to close, Kirkland jumped in and smiled. "Pretty nice, huh?"

Travers shrugged, watched the doors close, and then listened to the elevator creak and groan as it began its descent.

"So," Kirkland said. "Fogarty's old lady know about his little love mate?"

"They're still living together, so I doubt it."

"What about Bethencourt? He got anything going?"

Travers laughed. "That guy is a walking Viagra ad."

Kirkland tilted back his head, slapped his leg and produced a loud singular burst of air like a muffled foghorn. Travers simply grinned, amused at his own wit.

The elevator stopped and the door opened. Immediately, Travers heard a loud, irritated voice. They walked out of the elevator and headed towards the exit. Across the room, a heavy-set desk sergeant with close-cropped red hair was trying to calm a very excited man speaking in a foreign language. Travers thought it might have been East Indian, but he couldn't be sure. It all sounded the same to him.

Outside, they turned right and headed down the street towards Travers' car. As they negotiated the crowded sidewalk, the constant hum of traffic filled the air. Behind them a car horn blared. Someone with a low voice yelled something Travers couldn't make out. A mixture of car exhaust, fresh baked bread, and women's perfume floated on the air and burned his nostrils.

"So," Kirkland said. "What did Captain Fernandez have to say?"

Travers shook his head. "Not much. But I think he's hiding something. He definitely knows more than he is letting on."

"That's not surprising," Kirkland said. "He has quite a reputation as a hard nose."

"The guy may have let himself go physically, but mentally, he's still sharp. I've been reading his file. It's very impressive. He became the youngest man on the force to make captain. He was decorated three times for bravery. Had a bright future. But everything went to hell when his wife died . . . heart failure I think it was. Anyway, after her death, he started drinking and missing a lot of workdays. It almost cost him his job. But he had friends in high places and managed to hold on to his position. Still keeps a bottle in his bottom drawer, from what I hear."

"Yeah, so?" Kirkland said. "The story's not a new one. Lots of guys are boozers. Been known to slam a few myself from time to time. What's your point?"

"The old man is cruising, waiting for his retirement to come through. He only has a year and a half before he can retire with full benefits. He's not going to let anyone screw that up for him. Smooth sailing . . . that's what he's looking for. All the way out the door."

Up ahead, in the middle of the sidewalk, Travers spotted a bearded man with long black hair wearing a white robe and holding a sign that read: The End Is Near. From his perch on a milk crate, the man was shouting something about God and repentance. His dark, wide eyes zoomed in on Travers as he approached. The man pointed a long finger at Travers and shouted: "You, sir . . . have you confessed your sins?" Travers felt his stomach churn. He looked away, embarrassed at being singled out, and pretended not to hear. He picked up speed and hurried past.

Kirkland was laughing, holding his stomach. "He's got your number, Travers."

"He's a nut," Travers said.

They stopped at a red light. Travers watched the DON'T WALK sign, waiting for his cue.

The light changed and they started across the street.

"You figure Fernandez is in on the scam?" Kirkland asked, digging through his pocket and pulling out a small package of Planters peanuts. "Maybe pullin' in a little extra cash to fatten up his nest egg." He ripped open the package, tilted back his head and dropped some of the peanuts into his mouth.

"I don't know," Travers said. "Maybe."

"But you're sure about Fogarty and Bethencourt?"

"Oh, they're dirty all right. I'd stake my reputation on it."

"Okay. Where do you want to start?"

Travers shook his head. "Didn't they teach you anything at the academy, rookie?"

Kirkland snorted and chomped on his peanuts. "Yeah. They taught me how to kick ass."

As they came along side his car and stopped, Travers reached in his pocket and removed his keys along with a small remote dangling from a short chain. He pointed the remote at the car and pushed a red button; a loud, high-pitched double bleep erupted from under the hood.

Returning his attention to Kirkland he said, "You know it's funny. On paper they're model officers. Their service records are spotless. But something happened, probably within the last year, something that turned them. I want to know what it was."

"Where are *you* gonna start?" Kirkland asked.

"Besides the house he shares with his wife, Fogarty keeps an apartment on the east side. I think I'll start there."

"That's odd," Kirkland said

"Yes, it is. Especially since the office manager told me the lease is under Fogarty's name, but a young lady by the name of Elaine Taberhaun actually lives in the apartment."

"Man, everybody's getting some side action but me," Kirkland said. He tossed another batch of peanuts into his mouth as a shapely redhead in tight leather pants, a pair of four-inch spiked heels and a form-fitting halter-top sauntered past. The conversation stopped. Both men gawked at her. "Now there's some action for you," Travers said.

"Man," Kirkland said. "What I couldn't do with that."

Travers slapped Kirkland on the back and said, "Dream on, partner. Dream on."

(7)

Flight 319 out of New York landed at Phoenix International Airport at 8:37PM and pulled up to gate 12. As soon as the airplane had come to a stop, Jake removed his seatbelt, grabbed his baggage from the overhead compartment and exited the plane. Despite the hour, he could feel the intense heat radiating through the tunnel walls as he made his way to the terminal.

Then and there he decided to accomplish his task quickly and leave the heat of Phoenix to the fools who found it pleasurable to reside in a sweltering inferno. If he stayed true to his self-imposed goal, this would be his last assignment. The thought of retiring to a remote island full of dark skinned women, simmering pots of steamed clams and consuming gallons of fine liquor brought a smile to his pale and aging face.

Once inside the air-conditioned terminal, he breathed a sigh of relief. He collected a single Armani suitcase from the baggage claim area and went outside where he once again felt accosted by the sizzling heat. Within moments he had hailed a cab and instructed the young driver to take him to the downtown Hilton.

"Here on business or pleasure?" the young cabbie asked.

Jake smiled. "A little bit of both, I hope."

* * * * *

When Brian arrived home, he found Christine asleep on the sofa with the TV airing an old episode of Saturday Night

Live. He sat down in a brown swivel rocker across from her and watched her sleep. Her eyes fluttered as she dreamed. Her blonde hair glistened in the flickering light. She was so beautiful. And in that moment all his doubts and fears seemed to fade away like the vanishing light of a lingering sunset.

He took off his shoes and crept towards her. Her perfume smelled of spring flowers and aroused him. From her parted lips came a faint snore. Brian smiled. Then he knelt down, allowed her aroma to caress him, and kissed her cheek. She stirred. He ran his hands through her hair and touched her smooth, soft cheek. Then he eased his hand under her blouse and caressed her supple breast. She groaned and pushed against his hand. A moment later, with a gravelly voice she said, "Don't handle the merchandise unless you intend to buy, sir." She produced the killer smile that made him fall in love with her so many years ago. He pressed his lips to hers and she responded. A moment later he grabbed the remote from the table and switched off the set.

(8)

The first rays of light were beginning to filter in through the bedroom window. Brian smiled. The timing was perfect. Not wishing to disturb Christine, he eased out of bed, pulled on a pair of Levis and a t-shirt, exited the room and closed the door behind him.

Out in the kitchen, the automatic coffee pot had just finished. The smell permeated the air. Pouring himself a full mug, he slipped on a pair of flops, and went out into the backyard. After positioning a lawn chair in the middle of the grass, he sat down and faced east. As he sipped his coffee, he watched with wonder as orange and yellow clouds moved on the horizon, constantly changing with the will of the breeze. Above the clouds, the sky turned from black to a pale blue as stars began to disappear.

Brian smiled. This had always been his favorite time of day. The air was clear and clean. The noise of the world had not yet shattered the peaceful hush of night. And all the troubles and worries of the city seemed distant and unimportant. It was a time to clear the mind; a time of wonder and amazement that normally went unnoticed in a society revolving around wealth, power, and ambition. Brian sipped his coffee, wishing the moment could last forever and knowing all too well that like all things, it too must end.

The thought had no sooner crossed his mind when he heard Christine's alarm clock beeping from the bedroom and knew the race for the almighty dollar was about to begin. He stood, took one last glance at the morning sky, and went back inside.

While he poured himself another cup of coffee, he heard the shower come on. He grabbed a box of Cheerios and a half-gallon of milk from the refrigerator and placed them both on the kitchen table.

Outside, he found the morning paper in the front flower bed and wondered how it could possibly be so difficult to hit a twenty by thirty foot slab of concrete with a rolled up wad of paper, yet so easy to hit a three by five mound of mud and flowers. But then some things in life were meant to be a mystery, and the newspaper game would always be one of them.

Back in the house, he dried the paper with a towel and perused the headlines. Then disgusted and depressed, he closed the paper and pushed it across the table.

It occurred to him that everything around him seemed wrong. The world was beginning to look ugly and out of sorts. Or maybe the world was as it had always been, but his perspective was changing. Whatever the reason, he felt as though he was sinking into a deep pit, digging at the sides with his fingernails in a desperate attempt to free himself from what awaited him at the bottom.

Then he heard the shower turn off and a moment later, Christine's alto voice humming an unfamiliar tune. Her voice had always reminded him of Karen Carpenter, but with attitude.

A half-cup of coffee later, Christine walked into the kitchen, her short blonde hair styled to perfection. She had an oval face with large, deep-set green eyes, and a discreet, yet voluptuous mouth Brian felt was her best feature. She wore a pale blue suit with three-inch heels and a diamond necklace with matching earrings.

She scowled at Brian. "If you're going to be late, you're supposed to call. That's the rule."

"You weren't complaining last night," Brian said.

Christine smiled, strolled across the room towards the coffee pot. She glanced sideways at him with that seductive look she knew made him reel. "You caught me off guard."

"Perhaps," Brian said, "I should catch you off guard more often."

Christine blew through her lips so hard they fluttered. She crossed her eyes. Her face turned pink. "You wish." She poured a cup of coffee and sat down at the table.

"You want some cereal?" Brian asked.

She crinkled her nose. "No. I'll get something on the way to the office." When she glanced up at the clock above the stove her eyes went wide. "I'm late," she said, jumping to her feet. "Gotta run. I have a new client I'm going to show the Brickman place."

Brian sighed. The Brickman place was a 7000 square foot home in the foothills of Paradise Valley with a pair of three-car garages, seven bedrooms the size of some houses, nine baths, a 2000 square foot guest house, two swimming pools (one indoor and one outdoor), a tennis court, a putting green and a private deck overlooking the mountains. The asking price was four and a half million. Christine's commission alone would pay off the house and buy two new vehicles. She had been trying to sell the property for over a year and a half without much success. Two previous prospective buyers had found cheaper properties elsewhere and had backed out of the deal. Christine had pleaded with the Brickmans to come down on the price but the couple, with a summer home in Florida and a villa in Spain, refused to lower their asking price. They intended to wait it out. The Brickman place had become Christine's obsession. Every new client meeting the financial criteria had been subjected to her hard pitch sales tactic.

"How about dinner tonight at Mario's?" Christine asked. "If I'm lucky, we'll have something to celebrate."

"Mario's sounds good. It's been a long time since we've been there."

"Why don't you meet me there at seven."

"Seven at Mario's," Brian repeated. "I'll be there."

Christine downed the rest of her coffee and turned to leave.

"Before you go," Brian said. "I need to tell you something."

Christine stopped and faced him. "Is something the matter?"

He swallowed hard and felt his heart rate increase. "I gave the captain my resignation yesterday, but he didn't accept it."

"He can't do that," Christine advised.

"Technically no. If I pushed the matter he would have to accept it. But he suggested I take a few days off to think about it, and I think it's a good idea."

Christine put her hands on her hips. "What's to think about?"

Brian ignored the question. "I'm thinking about going up to Greer for a few days — sort of clear my head." He ran his fingers through his thin hair. "This is a big decision for me, and I want to be sure I make the right one."

Christine smiled. "If that's what you need to do," she said softly.

Something in her voice made Brian say, "I'd like you to come with me."

Christine sat back down at the table. A frown creased her forehead. "I'm really busy at work. Business is booming. I don't know if I can get away."

Brian cleared his throat and continued, "You haven't taken a vacation in over two years. You have lots of time built up, and it will only be for a few days." His words sounded desperate, even to his own ears.

Christine got up, poured a cup of coffee, leaned against the counter and took a sip. She studied him over the rim of her cup. "I don't know."

"Come on. It might be just what the doctor ordered." He stood, moved over to her and slid his arms around her. "We could sort of make it a second honeymoon."

"Second honeymoon," Christine said. She withdrew from his arms. "We never had a first one. I wouldn't call a night at the Hilton and then back to work the next day a honeymoon."

Brian suddenly felt awkward, like a schoolboy asking the prom queen for a date. He stuck his hands in his pockets. "All the more reason to go."

Christine sipped her coffee and looked up at the clock over the stove.

Brian stared at a group of dust particles floating on a sunbeam that stretched across the kitchen floor. "Please, hon," he urged. "This decision will affect us both. I'd like you to make it with me."

"Why can't we decide right here?" Christine complained. "Why do we have to go all the way up to Greer? There's nothing to do up there, and it's so quiet. It kind of drives me nuts."

"You're such a city girl," Brian teased. "A little peace and quiet is exactly what we need. We could do some fishing in the morning, take a little hike in the afternoon and end the day with a barbecue. I don't think a little fresh air would hurt either one of us."

Christine walked across the kitchen, put her hand on the back of Brian's head and began to stroke his hair. "If it's that important to you, I'll talk to Jimmy. You know the office will fall apart without me and it will take me a week to straighten out the mess when I get back, but I'll see what I can do."

Brian shook his head. "The things we do for love."

Christine glanced at the clock again and gasped. "Now I really do have to go. I'm really late. I'll see you at Mario's at seven."

After she had gone, Brian sat alone in the kitchen considering all he had to do before he could head up to Greer. There were supplies to buy, the newspaper to cancel, last minute bills to pay, and more importantly, he would need to make sure Elaine would be all right while he was gone.

As he stood up to go to the bedroom and dress for the day, he heard a noise from down the hall and sighed. A moment later, Brian's brother-in-law, Eric Aberst came into the kitchen. He was a stocky young man in his mid-twenties with dirty blonde hair, a two-day growth of beard, and a tattoo of a lion on his right forearm. He wore black shorts and a white t-shirt with the word B.U.M. written across the front. Brian found the irony somewhat amusing.

"Christy leave already?" Eric asked. He stretched his arms over his head and opened his mouth so wide his jaw made a grinding sound.

"Dressed and gone to *work*," Brian said. "How about you? Got any interviews lined up for today?"

Eric snapped his mouth shut. He turned and glared at Brian. "Give me a break, will you? I just got up."

(9)

Jake Leighton was sprawled across the king-size bed of his hotel suite; eyes closed, foot tapping. The radio was tuned to a jazz station, and a sax blared through the speaker as if the musician had accepted a challenge as to the amount of notes he could cram into one measure. A plump bleached blonde with a wide face and big eyes was snuggled up close, her head resting on Jake's hairy chest.

"You want a repeat, baby?" the blonde said, with a deep voice like something out of an old Garbo film. "No extra charge."

Jake put a finger to his lips, "Shhh."

A moment later, an erratic pianist replaced the sax.

When the song ended, Jake opened his eyes. "Now that's music."

"Sounds like a lot of noise to me," the blonde said.

Jake's beeper sounded on the bedside table. He retrieved it and checked the number. Climbing out of bed, he removed his wallet from his slacks pocket and threw two C notes on the bed. "You're overpriced, darling. Now get dressed and get out of here. I have to go to work."

After she had left, Jake pulled on the clothing he had purchased in the lobby gift shop the night before and then phoned the front desk. He asked the clerk if a package had arrived for him. When the clerk told him there was indeed a package, Jake smiled. The tools of the trade had arrived.

48

* * * * *

Jake was sitting on a wooden bench in Eldorado Park. He wore dark glasses, a Phoenix Suns ball cap, tan shorts and a white, collared shirt. The park was a sprawling mass of lush green lawn, acres of trees, picnic tables, ball fields, several lakes complete with paddle boats, ducks and swans, and a tiny creek that meandered through the trees.

The place was booming with activity. Bicyclists, in-line skaters, and joggers moved up and down a concrete pathway like rush hour traffic. Several basketball courts were filled with sweat-drenched players. Off to his right, a group of youngsters were kicking a mushy looking ball around. Young mothers pushed strollers. Starry-eyed couples held hands. A black lab pursued an orange Frisbee. And on a distant field, some men were playing a robust game of touch football.

A few yards down the path to Jake's right was a large brick building that housed the restrooms. There were two red doors on either side with brick partitions blocking the view of passersby. Between the doors were a water fountain and a large colored map of the park.

Jake had been observing the building, waiting for the constant activity to subside. After enduring the hard wooden bench for over twenty minutes, he watched the two young boys who had entered the restroom a few minutes earlier emerge and run off across the field towards the lake.

Jake stood, walked down the narrow path and into the men's room. It was empty. Water was spraying from one of the three sinks and splashing out across the floor. Jake shook his head as he walked past. He went to the rear stall, knelt down, and reached behind the tank. He removed a small manila envelope taped to the back, folded it, placed it in the front of his pants and covered it with his shirt.

Outside the restroom, he headed along the path leading to the east parking lot feeling the same sense of anticipation he always felt before a job. There was an erotic pleasure in taking a life. It was the power he liked, the ultimate control over another human being. He had first experienced the pleasure of death when he was a young boy, far up in the mountains near Calgary, Alberta, Canada. A wounded squirrel had managed to find its way into Jake's back yard. It lay there helpless, squirming in pain. Jake had watched it for over an hour deciding what to do. Then a bizarre, but intriguing idea popped into his head. He stood up, walked to the shed and emerged with a can of kerosene. After emptying the can's contents on the squirrel, he touched off a match, lit a cigarette, inhaled deeply, and threw the flame on the animal. The experience had changed his life.

At a bend in the path, he found a secluded area surrounded by thick brush on all sides. A dense canopy of intertwined tree branches hung over the path and blocked the sun's rays, creating a natural shelter. Beyond the trees out in the sunlight, he observed a young woman riding a mountain bike. She had on a green and black skintight athletic outfit and was working her way along the winding path towards him. Her long blonde hair had been pulled back into a ponytail and swayed from side to side as she peddled. She wore dark glasses that veiled her eyes. Jake wondered if they were blue.

He searched the ground, found a large branch and picked it up. As the young woman came around the bend, she slowed to make the sharp curve in the path. When she came along side, Jake jumped from the bushes and clotheslined her with the branch. She fell to the sidewalk with a grunt as her bike continued along the path and crashed into a thicket of bushes. The young woman groaned and struggled to get up. Jake grabbed a hunk of hair and slammed her head into the concrete path. The girl fell silent.

Jake stood, combed the area with his eyes. No one was in sight. He knelt down next to the unconscious girl and removed her sunglasses. Her young face was soft and beautiful, her body firm and muscular. Her open mouth sucked air as her chest heaved up and down. Fate had been smiling on him. He lifted the lid of one of her eyes and laughed. They were blue. He ran his hand across her smooth thigh and licked his lips.

"Very nice," he said.

* * * * *

Homicide detective Marion Bantor was seated at her desk typing an arrest report into the computer. Sitting at his own desk across from her was her new partner, Nick Carey. He had his feet on the desk and was leafing through a thick file when the phone rang. He dropped his feet to the floor and picked up the receiver.

"Detective Carey," he said.

Marion stopped typing. Sitting back in her chair, she clasped her hands behind her head and looked around the room. There were twenty plus gray metal desks in neat rows covered with papers, letters, vouchers, and open files. Some of the desks held photos of family members, favorite pets and sports legends. Beside one desk was a tall dieffenbachia plant. On the corner of another desk, an overgrown ivy plant wound its way up a nearby support post and touched the ceiling. There were knick-knacks ranging from coffee mugs to bowling trophies. Opposite Marion's desk, a line of file cabinets stretched across an entire wall. Scattered about the room were portraits of former presidents, mayors, and chiefs of police. They seemed to be hovering over the room like ancient Greek gods surveying their domain.

Across the room, a husky detective with short, black hair labored at his keyboard while a large, bald man with a crooked nose and part of his left ear missing sat nearby, handcuffed to a metal chair. When Marion's eyes stopped on the man, he smiled, stuck out his tongue and touched his nose with it. Marion shook her head and turned her attention back to Carey.

"Oh, yeah?" Carey was saying into the phone. "Where?"

Marion knew the tone well. She would be grabbing lunch on the run once again. It was becoming her regular routine.

"We'll be right there," Carey said and hung up the receiver.

"So what's up?" Marion asked, moving the cursor to SAVE and clicking the mouse button.

"Some kids found a stiff out at El Dorado." Nick stood up, grabbed his jacket from the back of his chair and flung it over his shoulder. "Time to go to work, honey."

Marion switched off the computer, looked up at Nick and glared at him. "I've told you before, don't call me honey. This is the last time I'm going to tell you."

"Woo," Nick teased, his mouth making a perfect O. "Aren't we touchy. I'm just trying to be friendly."

"Try another approach," Marion scolded. She grabbed her purse and suit jacket and headed for the door.

"I'll drive," Nick called out.

Marion bit her lower lip.

(10)

The Taberhaun Antique Shop was located on prestigious Fifth Avenue in Scottsdale's old town district. Various specialty shops ranging from art galleries, antique and dress shops, to jewelry stores specializing in turquoise and silver, lined the lavishly designed street. Several early risers were meandering down the walk gawking in the windows and chattering away like morning birds.

Brian pulled his Taurus into a parking spot not far from Taberhaun's and turned off the motor. As he climbed out of the car, he was engulfed by the scent of fresh flowers and pine. He put a quarter in the meter, walked down the street and went into the store.

Mark Taberhaun was standing behind the counter at an open cash register counting bills and placing them in their proper slots. When he looked up and saw Brian coming towards him, he rolled his eyes and frowned. "What do you want?"

"Is that any way to greet a customer?" Brian said, forcing a smile.

"You're no more a customer than that stray dog that's been hanging around out back for the last few days," Mark said.

Brian weaved his way through a maze of tables piled high with everything from comic books to knives to pieces of crystal. "Maybe the poor dog is just hungry?" he offered.

"Not for long," Mark said. "I had the pound pick him up yesterday. With any luck they'll be sticking that worthless, tick infested mongrel into a hole before the day is out."

"Your compassion is awe inspiring," Brian said, shaking his head.

"What are you doing here anyway?" Mark asked. He turned and walked to the other end of the counter and started leafing through a stack of invoices.

Brian followed him. "I came about Elaine."

"What about her?" he said, tossing the invoices on the counter. His face turned a bright red, accenting the deep lines between his eyebrows.

"I'm going to be out of town for a few days, and I thought you might look in on her for me while I'm gone."

Mark slammed his hand down on the counter. "Are you really as dense as you seem, or is it just some cop thing to catch people off guard?"

"Whatever works," Brian said.

Mark shook his head. "How many times do I have to tell you I'm not the least bit interested in any way shape or form in you or Elaine?"

Brian felt his hand twitch and his stomach flop. "Damn it, Mark, she's your sister. Doesn't that count for something?"

"She is not my sister," Mark shouted, his eyes nearly bulging from their sockets. "Not as far as I'm concerned."

Brian struggled to corral his intensifying rage. "Look, Mark. The past is just that . . . the past. What happened between my father and your mother can't be changed. And regardless of what you say, she is your sister, at least your half-sister, and it's hard for me to believe you're as unfeeling as you pretend."

Mark bit at his lower lip so hard it began to bleed. He turned and marched back towards the cash register, slamming an open cabinet on the way. About halfway there he stopped and wheeled around to face Brian. "I don't give a crap one way or the other what you believe. She's an embarrassment to the family, and I want nothing to do with her."

Realizing he was fighting a losing battle Brian said, "I'm sorry to hear you say that, Mark. I was hoping you might have mellowed some over the years."

"Look at you," Mark said, the veins on his forehead near bursting. "You stand there with your self-righteous attitude in your cheap suit and K-Mart tie. Why don't you use some of that money my parents saw fit to waste on you to buy a decent suit?"

Brian's fists clenched. "That money's for Elaine's expenses!" he shouted. "I've never touched a penny of it for my personal use, and you know it!"

"You should never have gotten a dime. They must have been delirious when they made you Elaine's guardian."

Realizing he was one breath away from an assault charge, Brian took a step back and prepared to leave. "You really are a pathetic, bitter person, Mark."

"Get out of my store!" Mark yelled, pointing towards the door. "And don't come back."

Brian turned and stormed out of the store. Outside, he marched down the sidewalk towards his car attempting to curb his anger. About halfway down the street, he passed a dress boutique and then stopped in front of the World Flower Shop. Through the storefront window, he could see an array of brightly colored flowers in a variety of pots and vases. The sweet fragrance of the flowers radiated from the store and filled the air with the scent of spring. The delightful aroma seemed to calm him. He felt almost human again.

Feeling renewed, he walked to his car, listening to a flock of birds chirping in a nearby tree and the faint sound of a distant wind chime. He unlocked his car, climbed in, started the engine, and switched the radio on. The unmistakable voice of Smokey Robinson drifted through the speakers. Brian felt his face widen into a broad grin. Things were looking up.

(11)

Several miles from the antique store, Brian picked up his cell phone from the seat beside him and called Melissa White.

"Hi, Brian," Melissa said cheerily. "I was just getting ready."

"Good," Brian said. "I should be there in about fifteen minutes. I just need to make a quick stop at the market. Is there anything you're going to need?"

"Nope. I'm all set."

"Okay, I'll see you in a few."

When he pulled up in front of Melissa White's house, she was sitting on her suitcase on the front steps. When she saw Brian she waved, jumped to her feet, grabbed her suitcase and headed for the car.

She was a small boned woman of twenty-nine with mousy brown hair, a turned up nose, drooping shoulders, and a never-ending smile. Her below-the-knee sundress swayed as she ran towards the car.

Brian reached down below the seat, popped the trunk and jumped out of the car. He took Melissa's suitcase, put it in the trunk and opened the passenger side door.

"My, aren't we the gentleman," Melissa said, holding her dress down with one hand and slipping into the car seat. "I didn't think you guys existed anymore."

"Am I out of style?" Brian asked, smiling.

Melissa's thick lips and wide mouth fashioned an expansive smile while a pair of luminous brown eyes looked up at Brian with an innocence and purity he'd forgotten could exist. "Not as far as I'm concerned," she said. "I like it."

Brian closed the door, hurried around to the driver's side, climbed in and pulled away from the curb. Halfway down the street Brian asked, "So how does Chester feel about this?"

"Oh, he was pretty upset with me when I walked out the door," she said, adjusting the air-conditioning vent so it wasn't blowing on her face and pulling her dress down over her legs. "But he'll get over it."

Brian stopped at the corner, let a speeding Ford pick-up pass, and turned left. "I suppose he's not going to like being cooped up in the house for a week by himself?"

"He'll be okay." Melissa giggled. "I left plenty of food, cleaned out his litter box, and put his favorite ball in the middle of the living room, but I have no doubt something will be chewed beyond recognition by the time I get back. He does that sometimes just to let me know that he's the boss."

"I wish I could let you bring him with you, but you know how Elaine gets around animals. They just scare her to death. I don't really understand it. She must have had a bad experience when she was little."

"It's okay," Melissa said. "Chester will appreciate me more when I get back."

They fell into the kind of silence where everything that needs to be said has been said. Melissa looked out the window, humming softly.

Brian concentrated on the road, his mind periodically settling on the unique relationship he shared with the special young woman seated next to him. Melissa had been Elaine's nurse, confidant, and friend for over three years. She had taken the job shortly after Brian had received the news of Elaine's parents' untimely death while on a commuter flight to Vail, Colorado and found himself the executor of Elaine's trust fund. Melissa had been a godsend. She had the patience of a golden retriever, the sense of humor of Bill Cosby, and a loving nature about her that made Brian wonder why she didn't have a dozen guys hanging around trying to marry her. But Melissa seemed happy in her circumstances and never had an ill word for anyone. Brian was almost envious of her marvelous gift.

The humming stopped. Melissa shifted her position, faced Brian, and put her arm on the seatback. "So how does Elaine feel about you going away for a week? Is she okay with this?"

Brian raised his eyebrows, tilted his head to one side, and shrugged his shoulders. "I'm not exactly sure. She was very attentive when I explained it to her over the phone this morning, but I think she knows something is wrong. She got real talkative about her photography. Sometimes I think she's remarkably intuitive and then other times she reverts back to being a child. It's hard to tell what's going on in her mind."

"Well, I think she knows more of what's going on than people give her credit for," Melissa said. "She just doesn't know how to express it."

Brian nodded. "I think you're exactly right."

He pulled the Taurus into the parking lot of the Palm Apartments in south Scottsdale and took an empty space close to the building. Climbing out of the car, he removed the suitcase from the trunk and seized the grocery sack from the back seat. Melissa climbed out, and together they started across the parking lot towards the complex. A black Cadillac that had pulled into the parking lot behind them stopped and allowed them to pass. When they reached the complex, they strode down the covered walkway until they arrived at apartment number 127. Brian knocked, inserted his key, and opened the door.

The high pitched scream startled him as Elaine jumped to her feet, thundered across the room and thrust herself into Brian's arms. He dropped the suitcase but held firmly to the grocery sack. She squeezed him so tightly he felt his face begin to burn.

She was a plump young woman of twenty-eight, with short, curly black hair streaked with blonde highlights, a round face, and large brown eyes that seemed to sparkle. She wore bright red shorts and a sleeveless white blouse.

When she released her grip, she screamed again, grabbed Melissa by the arm and led her into the bedroom, rattling at high speed about her newest achievement.

Brian took the opportunity to take Melissa's suitcase into the second bedroom, plopped it on the bed, and came back into the living room. He wandered into the kitchen, opened the refrigerator, and peered inside; it was nearly empty.

After he had put away the groceries, he went back in the living room, sat down on a tan sofa, and set his feet on the coffee table he had refinished for Elaine shortly after her parents' death. There was a small TV sitting on a glass stand, a brown recliner by a window overlooking a grassy area near the pool, a small desk covered with papers and children's books, and every inch of the walls were covered with photographs kept in place with white thumbtacks.

A moment later Elaine and Melissa emerged from the bedroom holding hands and chattering away like long lost friends. Brian smiled. They genuinely enjoyed each other's company. It somehow made Brian feel better about leaving.

"Look, Brother Brian," Elaine said in her slow and deliberate way. "I got a new picture."

She held up a photo of a red maple leaf that took up the entire print. The clarity and color was breathtaking. Brian found himself mesmerized by the photo.

"It's fantastic," Brian said. "Where in the world did you find such a perfect red maple leaf around here?"

Elaine bounced up and down where she stood, clapped her hands with obvious joy. "Francis lets me help her at the greenhouse sometimes," she said. "She lets me take pictures. She's a real nice lady. Gives me Oreos and soda."

"Well, it's a beautiful photo, Elaine," Melissa said. "You're getting better all the time."

"I just like to take pictures," Elaine said. She plopped down next to Brian and put her arm around his shoulder. Craning her chubby neck towards Brian, she kissed him on the cheek and then giggled.

"We're going to have so much fun," Melissa said with genuine enthusiasm. "It'll be like a big, long slumber party."

Elaine clapped her hands and laughed, her eyes sparkling.

"Are you guys hungry?" Melissa asked suddenly.

"Yeah," Elaine cried, gleefully. "Hungry. Make sammiches."

Melissa chuckled. "How about peanut butter and jelly?"

Elaine nodded energetically. "Peanut butter and jelly sammiches. With Oreos and milk."

"You got it, kiddo," Melissa said and headed for the kitchen.

Elaine leaned close to Brian and whispered in his ear. "I can make sammiches myself but Melissa likes to do things for me, makes her happy."

Brian's chest felt heavy. The corners of his eyes began to fill with tears. He cleared his throat. "You're right, sweetie. It makes her feel needed, and everybody likes to feel needed."

Elaine snuggled up close and laid her head on Brian's chest. She grew quiet. Her expression turned solemn. Then, very softly she asked, "Why you goin' away?"

Brian stroked her soft hair gently. "I have something I need to do. But I'll only be gone for a few days. And Melissa will take good care of you."

"You'll come back?" Elaine asked, expectantly.

"Yes," Brian reassured her. "I'll come back."

Elaine brought her large, sincere eyes back up to him. "I like Melissa. She's my friend."

He swept Elaine's hair from her face and placed it behind her ear and gently caressed her cheek. At the same time he could hear Melissa humming in the kitchen. "She likes you, too, sweetie . . . very much."

Elaine snuggled closer, pressing her head into Brian's chest until it began to hurt.

"But you'll be back?" Elaine persisted.

"Of course, I will. And I'll tell you what; when I do, we'll spend the whole day together. We'll go to the art gallery, see a movie and I'll take you to lunch wherever you want to go."

"McDonalds?" Elaine shouted, bolting upright on the sofa.

"If that's what you want."

"I'll get a Happy Meal and a big Coke and an apple pie."

Elaine grabbed Brian's hand and squeezed it. "I love you," she said softly. "You're the bestest."

He wrapped his arm around her shoulder and pulled her close. "I love you too, sweetie."

(12)

The temperature gauge was slowly climbing as the engine of Jerry Travers' Cadillac labored to keep the air-conditioner cooling the cab. Travers looked at the gauge and then his watch. It had been more than two hours since Fogarty had gone into the apartment with the young woman.

"Geez, Fogarty," he said aloud. "What are you, some kind of Don Juan? I'm dying out here."

The rap on the window startled him. He instinctively reached for his weapon but drew up short when he saw the security guard standing outside the car. When he had lowered the window, he looked up and smiled.

"This area is for residents only, sir," the tall, dark-haired guard informed him. "You're going to have to move your vehicle."

"I'm waiting for a friend," Travers said.

"You've been out here for a good two hours, sir," the guard said. The look on his face was one of amused curiosity more than suspicion. He wore a pair of cut off Levis, red tennis shoes and a white sport shirt with PALM APARTMENTS SECURITY stitched over the left pocket. His skin was tanned a golden bronze and seemed to glisten in the sun. "I'm going to have to ask you to move your car to the visitors section in the back." He shrugged his shoulders. "Sorry."

Travers rolled his eyes. He pulled his wallet from his pocket and flashed his badge at the guard. "What's your name, son?"

The kid leaned down, put his hand on his brow to block the sun, and inspected the badge. "My name?"

Travers frowned. "Yeah, your name."

"Jimmy, sir. Jimmy Fortier."

"Well, Jimmy," Travers said in his best official voice. "This is police business, and I'm staying right here."

Jimmy's face brightened. "You on a stakeout?"

Travers nodded. "You could say that, and I need to stay right here so I can make sure I don't miss him if he leaves."

"Anything I can do to help?" Jimmy asked.

Travers considered the question; there were possibilities here. "You know who lives in apartment 127?"

"Sure. I know everyone in these apartments and most of what everybody does. But there's no way Elaine's involved with anything illegal."

"Elaine?" Travers asked.

"Yeah. Elaine Taberhaun. She's a real nice girl, but she's not all there." He squatted down on his haunches, placed his forearms across his thighs, and looked up at Travers with interest.

"What do you mean, 'not all there'?"

The guard glanced over his shoulder towards the apartments. "She's a mental case. You know, a retard."

Travers raised his eyebrows. "How long has she lived here?"

Jimmy scratched his head and gazed up towards the sky. He moved his lips in silent thought.

Travers waited, a trickle of perspiration rolling down his chest.

"Oh, about a year and a half, I guess," Jimmy said. "Give or take."

"Does she hold down a job somewhere?"

Jimmy lowered and shook his head. "No way, man. She's helpless."

Travers pursed his lips, rubbed his hand across his chin. This was getting interesting. "So, who pays her rent?"

"I don't know for sure. You'd have to ask Francine in the office. But there's a guy that does come by pretty regular.

Sometimes he stays for a few hours, sometimes takes her out. They seem pretty friendly. Is he the one you're watching?"

"Maybe. What's this guy look like?"

Jimmy ran his hand through his short-cropped brown hair and whistled through his teeth, then crinkled his nose as if in pain. "Medium build and height; curly dark hair, kind of long. Looks like a real loser to me." He latched on to the car door with both hands and lumbered to his feet. "He's not a drug dealer or something, is he?"

Travers bit his lip. This guy was something, but maybe he could prove useful. "I could use your help," Travers said.

Jimmy's perked up. "Oh, yeah? What can I do?"

Travers pulled a card from his pocket, wrote down his cell phone number, and handed it to the kid. "Keep an eye on Elaine's apartment for me. If anything unusual happens, no matter how small you might think it is at the time, give me a call. It might be something I can use."

"Sure thing," Jimmy said, taking the card and studying it.

"It's real important that you keep this quiet, Jimmy. I don't want this guy getting wind that I'm watching him."

"No problem," Jimmy said. "I won't say a word."

"Great. Now run along so we don't attract attention."

"Okay," Jimmy said. He turned to leave, stopped, twisted back around and said, "I always thought I'd make a good cop, you know."

"No kidding," Travers said.

After Jimmy had gone, Travers observed Fogarty emerge from the apartment unaccompanied, get into his car and drive away. For the next several hours, Travers tailed Fogarty to a variety of retail establishments: a grocery store, a sporting goods store, a gas station and a bookstore. A little after five, as the rush hour traffic began to intensify, Travers lost him when a tan Mercedes cut him off at an intersection and he caught a red light.

On his way back to the station, Travers called his partner, Marty Kirkland.

"Anything on Gabe Bethencourt?" Travers asked when Kirkland picked up the phone.

"Not really," Kirkland replied. "I tailed him to the cleaners, a bookstore in old town, a men's store, and then a night club where he picked up a real nice looking blonde. She followed him to his house in a sweet little red two-seater convertible.

"A little early for a night club, isn't it?" Travers asked.

"Apparently not. I think this guy could score anytime. Every place he's been, he seemed to have women hanging on him. You were right, the guy's a real Don Juan. Anyway, I'm sitting across the street right now. I'd really like to get out of here for the day, Jerry."

"Okay," Travers said and quickly changed lanes to avoid slowing down for a car preparing to make a right turn. "Let's call it a day. But I want you on Bethencourt's tail all day tomorrow. Sooner or later he's going to make a mistake, and when he does, I want to know it."

(13)

Brian slammed the trunk of his car and wiped the palms of his hands together. "Well," he said, stuffing his shirttail back into his jeans. "I think that's everything."

Christine stood with her arms folded and looked at Brian with a wrinkled brow. "It had better be. I don't think I've seen a car that full since we moved from the old rental house." She had on a sheer crimson blouse tucked into khaki shorts, white Nikes, and a pair of pink wire rimmed sunglasses. Her short blonde hair was stuffed under a wide-brimmed straw hat.

Brian paused, remembering the days when he and Christine were newlyweds. Those had been good times. They were young, madly in love and full of hopes and dreams for the future. And the first few years had been wonderful. But the day Brian Jr. emerged from an alley on his new bicycle and was struck and killed by a passing motorist, everything changed. Christine became distant, withdrawn, sometimes lashing out at him for no apparent reason. He had passed it off as her way of suffering, her way of releasing the anger she harbored from losing her only child. And Brian knew he was not without fault. He retreated to a different place, throwing himself into his work. He had accepted double shifts and made record arrests for seven months straight. Then he was promoted to detective, which required more time away from home.

Then, as if to test his marital resilience, fate took another twist. Marion Bantor was transferred into the precinct. She was not a beautiful woman by society's standards — frumpy was the word used around the stationhouse — but something about her intrigued Brian. He found himself thinking about her often. And Marion had made it clear she was interested. They had come close one time, when several officers had gone for drinks at the local bar. It had grown late. Brian didn't want to go home. He had talked with Marion until the bar closed. In the parking lot, as they stood by their vehicles, Marion told of her bitter divorce and how she had sworn off men and drowned herself in her work. The story sounded hauntingly familiar. They seemed to understand each other.

Then came the kiss. Brian wasn't sure exactly how it happened. One moment they were talking, and the next they were embracing. And not a mere peck on the lips either, but a long passionate kiss, the likes of which he hadn't experienced in a long time. Suddenly, for reasons he still could not understand, he pulled away, explaining he couldn't do this to Christine. But the memory and the desire lingered.

Then a few months later, Christine suggested they go away. That's when the old fire returned. They fell in love all over again. Christine had come home to him and he welcomed her with open arms.

"Hello," Christine was shouting, jerking him from his remembrance.

Brian focused in on her, feeling startled.

"Earth to Brian. Are you in there?"

Brian turned his palms upwards and shrugged his shoulders. "I was just thinking about when we were first married. Those were wonderful times."

Christine came close, touched him on the cheek and kissed him gently on the lips. "You're being sentimental. How sweet." She hugged him tightly, her perfume engulfing his senses, arousing him. When Christine released her embrace she asked, "So, we going fishing or what?"

"Let's do it," Brian said, excited by the prospect of a few days away from work, traffic, ringing phones, beepers, crime, and all the things that go along with living in a big city and wearing a badge.

The sun had just crested the horizon and turned the sky a soft orange. The air smelled of wet grass and sweet lavender, and the scent of Christine's perfume lingered on his collar. He breathed it in slowly. It caressed his nostrils the way a fine wine tempts the pallet.

They climbed into the car, and Brian fired the engine. As he backed out of the driveway, he could hear the phone ringing inside the house.

"Is that the phone?" Christine asked.

"Of course."

"We should get it."

"No. If we do, we won't leave."

"But it might be important."

" I'm sure it isn't," Brian said, feeling a little guilty for not answering but a bit satisfied with his mild rebellion.

He wheeled the car into the street, pulled the lever down into drive and stepped on the gas.

Traffic was light at that time of morning and Brian reached the freeway in near record time. The hum of the wheels against the pavement and the freshness of the morning were exhilarating. Brian felt free. No deadlines or commitments. No paperwork.

Christine began to drift off to sleep, as she always did when the whine of the highway took over. He followed the freeway until it intersected with Hwy 60 and turned east. Desert foliage slowly yielded to scrub oak, juniper and pinion pine. The air cooled. Clouds grew thicker and denser. The car engine labored on long, steep grades.

Shortly after the final paved turnoff, Christine groaned and opened her eyes. She looked around, half dazed and confused. "Where are we?"

"We just passed the Gamma System," Brian said, pleased with his quick wit. "We should be in Jupiter's orbit within an hour."

Christine rubbed a hand across her face and sighed. "You're a very strange man, you know that?" She rubbed her eyes and sat upright in the seat. "So how much longer, Captain Kirk?"

"We just took the last turnoff," Brian said glancing down at the odometer. "Another ten miles to the pull-out."

Christine gazed out the side window, her soft face reflected in the glass, her right thumb idly rubbing the upper button of her blouse. "I forgot how beautiful it is up here."

"It most certainly is."

Two lanes of blacktop stretched across an otherwise undisturbed landscape, turned and disappeared around the bend. Tall grass hugged the roadside while sprawling oaks and ponderosa pines reached high into a stormy sky. The Little Colorado River ran parallel to the road. The scent of fresh water and the roar of the rapids filled the air with sweet music. Beyond the rapids, the river meandered through a lush, green valley spotted with multi-colored wildflowers. A flock of mallards flew high above the clouds then disappeared between two towering pines.

Up ahead on Brian's left, a solitary fisherman emerged from an outcrop of thick brush and out onto the shoulder of the road. He had curly brown hair and from a distance could have been mistaken for Brian's twin. He carried a string of rainbow trout as he waddled along in a pair of baggy waders towards a blue and white Suburban. As Brian drove past, his heart skipped with recognition. He applied the brakes and slowed the car.

"Isn't that Pete?" Christine said, glancing back over her shoulder.

Brian nodded his head, a sense of excitement swelling inside him. "It sure is."

It was indeed Pete Williams, a boyhood friend and one-time rival for the affections of one Wilma O'Hara, a redheaded fireball and free spirited sixteen-year-old with the body and passion of a mature woman. She had left for New York shortly after high school graduation with dreams of bright lights and stardom. To Brian's knowledge, no one from Greer ever heard from her again.

Brian turned the car around, pulled up behind the Suburban and climbed out onto the gravel shoulder.

A massive smile crossed the face of Pete Williams as Brian approached. He raised his free hand and waved.

Brian waved back. "How you been, Pete?"

Pete cocked his elbow and stuck his hand out. "Man, it's good to see you, Brian."

Brian grasped Pete's hand firmly and shook it.

Christine strolled up behind them, arms swinging at her sides, her face aglow.

"Christine," Pete said, his eyes flashing up and down her body and settling on her face, "you're still as gorgeous as a spring morning in the mountains."

"Hi, Pete," Christine said, her face flushed. "Still the charmer, I see."

Pete hugged her. Christine wrapped her arms around his broad shoulders and patted his back.

"How are Angie and the kids?" Christine asked.

"They're doing great. But you guys just missed them. They're at Angie's mom's in Albuquerque for a few days, so I decided to take some time off work and do some fishing."

Brian looked at the string of trout. The smallest one seemed to be about eight inches and the largest over twelve. "You did well."

Pete shook his head. "Not really. They just stocked it yesterday. I caught my limit in less than an hour."

"Well," Brian said. "They look good enough to eat."

An old, rusty Ford pick-up came rattling down the road with exhaust smoke barreling out the tail pipe. Brian recognized the driver as Henry Wellington, the owner and sole employee of Wellington Lumber over near Summit Lake. Henry honked the horn and waved as he went past. They all returned the gesture.

"Hey," Pete said, holding up the string of trout. "I have an idea. You guys want to help me eat these?"

Brian looked at Christine who gave an approving nod.

"Sound's good," Brian said. "Your place or ours?"

"We better make it yours. My place is kind of a shambles right now, what with Angie at her mother's and all."

"Great," Brian said, placing his hand on Pete's shoulder. "You remember how to get there?"

"Of course I do, you jerk. I could walk there blindfolded."

Brian felt stupid. Pete had been to the house a hundred times while they were growing up. It was like asking the Pope if he knew the Nicene Creed by heart.

Brian glanced at his watch, looked up towards the sky. "How about four o'clock," he said. "It will give us time to get settled and clean up the place."

"Four o'clock it is," Pete said. He opened the back of the Suburban, put the fish into a blue and white cooler and climbed into the vehicle. As he fired up the engine, he called out the window, "I'll pick up some beer and a bottle of wine. Any requests?"

"White Zinfandel," Christine said. "Christian Brothers."

Pete waved, pulled out onto the road and drove away.

Christine and Brian climbed into the Taurus and continued down the highway, the smell of fish wafting from Brian's right hand. It was a familiar and oddly pleasing aroma that reminded him of his youth, a time when fishing, swimming and hiking had taken precedence over school and paper routes.

Ten minutes later Brian slowed the Taurus and began his turn down the narrow dirt road that would lead to his boyhood home.

"Strange," he said, noticing an orange ribbon tied to a tall ponderosa pine next to the road. "That big pine looks like it's tagged for cutting. There's no reason to cut a tree that close to the highway unless it's dead or diseased. And it looks perfectly healthy to me." He thought a moment longer. "Maybe they're going to widen the road. I'll ask someone in town tomorrow."

Pulling off the highway and onto the dirt road, Brian's car rattled and creaked as he found himself engulfed by a thick canopy of trees and tall brush. The road jarred and rattled the Taurus. The washboard effect of the road pulled the car in several different directions as Brian struggled to gain control. He slowed and clung to the high spots at the center of the road. "Riding the ridges" was what they had called it when he had first learned to drive. After several destroyed oil pans and broken axles, Brian became a master of the technique.

Once through the entrance, his eyes adjusted to the dim light. Out in front of them, thick grass engulfed the road. Dim shadows dipped in and out of the trees and the light of day struggled to reach the forest floor.

They continued down the road, tossed from side to side like a small boat in a stormy sea. Two mule deer darted across the road and disappeared into thick underbrush.

After the road made a sharp turn and came out of the trees, Brian stopped the car across from a large clearing. Tall grass swept the entire glade and swayed in the breeze like ocean waves. Wildflowers dotted the field. At the far edge of the clearing beyond a stream that wandered through the grass, was a small log cabin.

Christine cleared her throat and licked her lips. "It looks smaller than I remember."

Brian wiped his clammy hands on his pants and looked out across the glade. "It looks wonderful to me." He eased off the brake and continued down the road.

Raindrops began to splatter against the windshield from dark, ominous clouds overhead as a brisk wind whipped through the trees, creating an eerie howl that seemed to engulf the entire glade.

A hundred yards down the road Brian eased the Taurus over an embankment and down a rutted lane. The gravel drive that Brian and his father had once so carefully laid had been swallowed by time and mud. As they drew nearer the house, he could see the deterioration. Both front windows were broken along with one of the porch rails. Several chimney stones had broken loose and were scattered around the yard. There were numerous dry splits in the eight-inch logs that made up the cabin walls and the lacquer was cracked and peeling. Tall grass had almost swallowed the far wall. Clinging spider webs were everywhere.

Brian stopped in front of the cabin, turned off the motor and climbed out of the car. Christine followed.

"We definitely have our work cut out for us," Christine said, gazing around the area, her mouth hanging open.

Brian stood next to the truck, his hands on his hips. "It's pretty bad, isn't it?"

Christine produced her killer smile. "What do you say we spend the rest of the day cleaning up the place? Then tonight we celebrate the beginning of our vacation with your old friend, Pete. And tomorrow morning, if we're not too hung over, we'll see if we can beat Pete's one-hour record for catching his limit."

"Sounds like a good plan," Brian said, wrapping his arm around Christine's shoulder. Glancing up at the stormy sky he said, "But first things first."

Christine turned her head slowly and looked at him, her head tilted to the side like a quizzical canine.

Brian bent down and kissed her on the cheek. "When was the last time we made love in mountain grass under a stormy sky?"

Christine shook her head, closed one eye and looked up towards the heavens. "It's been a long time."

Grasping each other's hands, they strolled around the cabin and down to the creek. They found a soft grassy spot and made love under the canopy of an ancient oak, the gentle rustling sound of running water echoing off the sheer cliffs beyond the stream; rain dripping from the oak leaves and pelting their naked bodies with crystal clear water.

(14)

Marion Bantor's second floor apartment was located near Arizona State University in Tempe. She loved living near the university, loved the way it made her feel to be part of the atmosphere of higher learning. She had dropped out of college at nineteen after she and her high school sweetheart had married. Ron had been an overbearing, old fashioned man who believed his wife was meant to stay home, take care of the cooking and cleaning and provide him with a son. For several years they tried to have a child, even went as far as to try a fertility clinic, but nothing worked. When it became apparent they would spend their lives together childless, Ron grew distant and eventually became abusive. At first it had been a slap across the face, then a fist to the stomach. Marion had tried to convince herself it was the stress from his job as a stockbroker. His sales had plummeted and his clients were seeking counsel elsewhere. But the night he threw her against the bedroom wall and broke her arm was the night the marriage ended. Marion had moved out and filed for divorce the next day.

She went back to school, earned a degree in Justice Studies and enrolled in the police academy. She was hired by the Phoenix police force immediately after graduation.

Then, one bright summer day, she spotted a dorky looking guy with a mass of unruly brown curls, a wide, round nose and a crooked smile. It was Brian Fogarty. She had feelings for him instantly. But he was married, and of all things, faithful to his wife. Go figure.

She went into her tiny kitchen, made a ham sandwich, and went back out into the living room. The small one-bedroom apartment had been all she could afford at the time of her divorce, and it still served her well. She had everything she needed: a loveseat, chair and lamp in the living room; a two-seater table off the kitchen; a small bedroom with an adjoining bathroom; and, more importantly, her stereo, TV, and a complete collection of Nora Roberts novels.

She stretched out on the sofa, and gazed up at the ceiling. A tear formed in the corner of her eye as she tried to escape the lingering picture of the battered young woman lying in the bushes at El Dorado Park, her tear-stained blue eyes staring skyward. Marion knew her last few moments had been sheer terror. Although many of her colleagues, including her partner Nick Carey, had grown indifferent to the sights and smells of a murder scene, even going so far as to crack vulgar jokes about the victim, Marion had never grown used to the ugliness and finality of death.

She closed her eyes. As she slowly drifted off to sleep, she thought about Brian and the tears flowed freely once again.

* * * * *

Jake Leighton walked across the lobby of the Hilton Hotel in downtown Phoenix and stopped at the front desk.

"I'm in the mood for a steak," Jake told the clerk. "Do you have any recommendations?"

"Austin's Steakhouse in old town Scottsdale is my personal favorite," the slick headed clerk said. "They serve only corn-fed beef. Absolutely to die for."

After Jake acquired directions, he took the elevator down to the parking garage, climbed into his rented car, turned on the engine and switched the air-conditioning to high. Checking the map provided by his employer, he reexamined the route he had picked earlier and estimated the driving time at roughly six hours. It would be best to arrive shortly before dawn. This would give him the element of surprise and ensure the success of his mission.

He plugged in the latest Winston Marseilles CD and headed for Scottsdale; envisioning a thick, Filet Mignon, a salad with raspberry vinaigrette, a freshly baked loaf of pumpernickel and a '77 Pinot Noir. The next few hours would be his and his alone. He would dine slowly, savoring every morsel. It was going to be a long night. He would need his strength.

(15)

Brian was sitting in his father's old rocking chair on the front porch trying to rid his sinuses of the lingering aroma of pine-scented detergents and furniture polish. Rubbing his hand across the back of his aching neck, he sighed heavily.

Looking over the cabin had brought back a flood of emotion. At the far end, against the back wall, was a small utility kitchen with a sink and a black, cast iron stove, where he and his mother had spent many Sunday afternoons baking cookies, breads and pies; he could still hear the laughter. About two-thirds of the way down the inside wall, a door led to the master bedroom (or what passed for one), which held a double bed, a chest of drawers, and a rickety wooden rocking chair. The second bedroom, which he had shared with his brother, Tom, had been turned into a storage room: boxes, old bikes, various pieces of furniture and books were stacked from floor to ceiling. The hardwood floor had seen better days. It was badly scuffed, with a few of the boards warped and cracked. Despite the appearance, Brian felt as though he had truly come home again.

There had been a great deal of satisfaction after the work had been completed, with the cabin transformed from a dusty, cobweb infested shack to a clean, tidy home. With the inside clean and the outside picked up and straightened, the place looked close to the way it had when he was growing up, only smaller. He found it interesting how time had a way of making things that seemed so much larger than life in one's youth seem almost insignificant.

With the work finished, Brian sat back in the old rocker listening to it creak and groan. It brought back memories of the many evenings he and his father had spent on the porch discussing the day's events. His father had been a large, quiet man, with a subtle dignity that Brian had grown to admire. He had worked for the county as an electrical lineman for over twenty-seven years. He had been discussing retirement when the cancer struck. It took him quickly. Three months after the initial diagnosis, he was gone.

Shortly after his father's death, Brian's mother had boarded up the house, moved the family to Phoenix, and taken a job as an electrical assembler in a large manufacturing plant. Brian did not adjust quickly to city life. Never before had he seen so many cars and people in one place. The schools were crowded. The houses were crammed together like cord wood, all resembling each other. Shopping malls, houses, and apartment buildings seemed to pop up overnight, like a malicious virus engulfing the land. For Brian, life would never be the same again. And he would never lose his desire to return to the mountains and live the quiet, simple life.

Then he met Christine: a beautiful, vivacious creature who captivated him. She was a city girl through and through, with an intense desire to succeed. They fell in love, married and had Brian Jr. within a year after taking their vows. At Christine's suggestion, Brian enrolled in the police academy and found that it suited him. Christine took classes for her real estate license then took a job with Century 21. Two years later they bought a house and settled into domestic life. Brian often found himself wondering where the years had gone, and if there was a way he could slow things down so he could enjoy the life that was passing him by so quickly.

The rain had stopped and turned the afternoon cool. Dark clouds hovered overhead, with a hint of occasional blue sky peeking through the mass. The air smelled fresh and clean. There was a hint of autumn lingering in the breeze. It pushed over the south ridge behind the cabin, bending and winding its way through the trees and meadows that Brian knew so well. From the creek out behind the cabin, a gentle hush of rushing water hummed.

Brian found himself looking forward to the morning, when his real vacation would begin. At sunrise they would go fishing for trout in the Little Colorado. After lunch he would take Christine hiking. Not the intense kind of hike he and his father used to take that would leave Brian gasping for air, but a mild hike, maybe down to the old beaver pond where he used to swim as a child. He remembered fondly how the beavers would fuss and squawk then disappear into their den, reappearing the moment the intruders would leave.

Then, after dinner, he would build a fire and enjoy the mountain silence. It was funny how the quiet used to frighten him as a child, but now it seemed to give him a much sought after sense of peace.

In the distance Brian heard the familiar rumble of a vehicle coming down the narrow dirt road. He looked out across the clearing at where the road disappeared into the shadows of the trees. Sitting forward in the chair, he waited. Then he saw Pete Williams' Suburban emerge from the trees. It slowed, turned, rattled up the drive and stopped next to the Taurus. Easing out of the rickety old chair, he watched Pete climb out of the Suburban and wave. Brian waved back.

"Pete's here," he called out to Christine over his shoulder.

"Good," Christine said from inside the house. "I'm thirsty."

Pete reached across the seat and plucked a twelve-pack of Coors from the seat. He held it up in the air like a prize. "I bring refreshments and sustenance, my lord."

Brian lumbered down the steps, supporting himself with a firm grip on the handrail, feeling all of a hundred, and strolled over to Pete's vehicle. "Let me give you a hand."

Pete had the back door open and handed Brian the beer and a gallon jug of White Zinfandel.

Brian snorted as he inspected the massive jug of wine. "You think this will be enough?"

"It's party time, buddy. Don't be a pooper." Then he removed a clear, plastic container that held six cleaned and scaled trout. Lastly, he grabbed a grocery sack full of corn-on-the-cob and handed Brian the trout.

With the echo of the slamming car door still ringing in Brian's ears, Christine appeared at the door to the cabin. "You two going to stand out there in the drizzle like a couple of stupid turkeys or are we going to eat sometime today?"

Pete looked up at her admiringly. "I bear refreshments, my lady. The finest drink in all the land, prepared specially for thy delicate palate. And, I must bring to light, me lady, 'tis a pleasure to cast mine eyes upon thy loveliness this fine, if somewhat dreary, afternoon."

Brian shook his head. Still the same old Pete, he thought.

Christine rolled her eyes and said, "Good grief, you need to get out more, Pete. You've been watching too many late shows." She waved them in. "Now hurry up. If I have to put up with you two, I'll need wine . . . a lot of wine."

"To the castle, my lord," Pete said. "We've a feast to prepare for the queen."

As the two climbed the porch, Brian could feel his worries slipping away, the way sleep comes slowly after a hard day. There was sentimentality in the presence of an old and dear friend. The boy he had met during his first season of little league had grown into a fine, caring man with whom he had shared many dreams and aspirations and, yes, even a few secrets.

Once inside, they all bellied up to the counter in the small kitchen and began to prepare the feast. Brian cut up some vegetables for a salad, Christine shucked the corn and Pete breaded and fried the fish. When the meal had been prepared, they sat down at the table and dug in.

"Remember Harry Millstone?" Pete asked, a mouthful of half chewed fish shoved to the side of his mouth.

"It would be impossible to forget him," Brian said and took a long pull on a cold Coors.

Christine tipped back her glass and finished off her fifth glass of wine. She licked her lips, her eyes searching for Pete. When they found him, they lingered on him for a few moments, apparently trying to focus. "Who's Harry Fills . . . Bills . . . What's his name?"

"Harry Millstone," Pete said with obvious amusement. "He was the school bully in middle school. He gave Brian and me a lot of trouble for about three years. Until . . ." Pete let it hang, as if building suspense, his crooked teeth abundant in his large mouth.

"You're messing with me," Christine slurred. "Just tell the stupid story."

Brian nodded, the corner of his mouth raised, wrinkles at the sides of his eyes.

"First," Pete said loudly, "the lady needs more wine." He picked up the half empty jug of wine, reached across the table and filled Christine's glass.

Christine stared at him, then slowly at the glass. Her head jerked and she fixed her eyes back on Pete.

Brian took a sip of beer, wiped his mouth with a paper napkin, leaned back in his chair and folded his arms across his chest.

"Okay," Pete said. "But I think I better give you the short version." He took a sip of beer and smacked his lips. "Well, Harry Millstone was a big kid, probably six foot by the time he was twelve. Everyone was afraid of him simply because of his size. And Harry took full advantage of this fact. One day in January, just after the Christmas break, we were outside making a snowman."

"You and Brian?" Christine asked, her wine-induced slur barely recognizable as the English language.

Pete punched Brian lightly on the shoulder and smiled. "Yuppo. We were making a snowman. It was going to be the best snowman in Greer. Anyway, we had the thing almost finished and were searching for some small rocks to use for the eyes and nose when Harry comes along. And with one sweep of his big right arm, he knocks the head off our snowman. Then, as if to add insult to injury, he kicks the head and disintegrates it."

Christine slammed her hand on the table. "What a crappy thing to do."

Brian took a sip of his third beer. He was enjoying this immensely. The story became more elaborate every time he heard it.

"Anyway," Pete continued. "Brian got so mad that he ran and tackled Harry and knocked him clear off his feet. They fell in the snow with Brian on top. Well, Harry was so surprised by what happened, he just laid there, with his big black eyes staring up at Brian."

Christine looked over at Brian, the glaze on her eyes growing thicker with every passing minute. "Brian?"

"Yuppo. Mr. Control. So Harry's lying there, staring up at Brian. And Brian's got his hands around Harry's neck and he's squeezing so hard Harry's face is starting to turn purple."

"Didn't somebody do something?" Christine asked.

"No," Pete said and let out a long spurt of sputtering laughter. "We were all so taken back that Brian actually got mad that nobody knew what to do."

"It wasn't—" Brian started to say.

"So," Pete interrupted, pointing a long index finger at Brian. "Brian's got this rock in his hand that he was going to use for the snowman's nose. I didn't think it was big enough to do anything with, you know. But then Brian doubles up his fist with this rock in it, and smacks Harry right in the face." Pete threw his head back and spurted another round of almost hysterical laughter. "It was fantastic. The blood spurted from Harry's nose, and he started screaming. Everybody was hollering for

Brian to hit him again when Mr. Chambers, our history teacher, came outside and pulled Brian off him. There was a huge stink over it. Brian was expelled for three days. Harry, or anyone else for that matter, never messed with us again. It was a great day."

Brian sighed, gave Pete a disapproving glance and then looked at Christine. "That's not exactly how it happened."

"That's exactly how it happened," Pete said. He looked over at Christine. "So I'm telling you, darling, you got to watch out for the quiet ones. There's a fire festering down inside. And when it blows, you best be in another state."

Brian felt his face turning red and decided to change the subject. "So when did you say Angie and the kids would be home?"

"Yes, sir," Pete said, ignoring the question. "It was one heck of a day."

After dinner they sat in silence, each with their own private thoughts. Christine downed the last of her wine, a glazed look covering her eyes as if the occupant had vacated the premises. Brian nursed a warm beer, his fourth of the night, while Pete polished off the rest of the twelve-pack.

Christine's eyes were drooping. Her face seemed to sag. Tufts of blonde hair stood out in all directions. Her full bottom lip hung open and quivered. Her head fell forward and her chin slapped her chest. The pop of her neck sounded like a distant firecracker. She raised her head, shook it, and rubbed her hands across her face. "Well," she said, "I'm going to bed before I pass out here at the table."

Brian stood to help her.

She held up her hand and said, "No, no. I can do it." Struggling out of the chair, she stood upright, swaying on her feet. Regaining her balance, she staggered to the bedroom.

"My lady," Pete called out. "May I humbly request the use of your sofa this fine evening? Me thinks a night off for my steed would be appropriate under the circumstances."

Christine turned around and faced him. After a long pause she said, "Do you snore?"

Brian snickered. "Quite loudly, if memory serves."

"Regrettably, my lady," Pete said, holding his hand high into the air. "'Tis true."

"Well, tonight I probably wouldn't hear it anyway." She disappeared into the bedroom, switched on the light and closed the door. A moment later, there was a loud thump from the bedroom followed by a heartfelt, "Crap!"

Brian stood up from the table, went to the bedroom and opened the door. "Are you all right?"

"No!" Christine cried. "I just jammed my foot into the bedpost."

He watched her slip off her shoe and examine her foot. "You want some ice?" he asked.

"No, I'll be all right. I just need to sleep."

Closing the door, Brian turned to Pete and said, "It's going to be cold tonight. I'll get you some extra blankets." He walked to the closet, his footsteps sounding heavy on the old wooden floor, and removed two blankets and a pillow. Then he walked across the room and threw them on the sofa. "Better get some sleep. I have a feeling morning is going to arrive a little early tomorrow."

"Hey," Pete said, his dark eyes peering out of narrow slits. "Do you want to go fishing in the morning? I have my fly rod."

"That was my plan. But I believe we will be getting a later start than I had originally hoped."

"Hey, Brian," Pete said. He stood, staggered to the sofa and plopped down. The springs groaned with disapproval. He turned his gaze to Brian. "It's good to see you, buddy. I've missed you."

Brian smiled slightly, his head feeling the effects of a long day. He ran his hand across his face and looked at his friend. "We had some good times, didn't we?"

Pete lay back on the sofa and closed his eyes. "The best, my friend. The absolute best." A moment later his mouth dropped open and he began to snore.

Brian walked over and covered him up. Then went into the bedroom, took off his clothes, switched off the light and climbed into bed. Christine was already humming that rhythmic, gurgled breathing associated with alcohol induced sleep. He closed his eyes and breathed in the cool air. Good food and good friends, he thought as he felt himself drifting off. Now that's what its all about.

(16)

Jake Leighton leaned forward in the car seat and gazed past a wall of trees and brush searching for the marker. Thick foliage seemed to blend into one massive, complex system, like a finely woven basket. He eased the car to a crawl, edging along a single lane of deserted blacktop with his right tires scraping a loose gravel shoulder.

On the eastern horizon, the morning sky was a brilliant shade of blue, packed with gathering clouds that moved and transformed with the wind. The southwestern skyline had not yet received the morning and was filled with mounting thunderheads. The wind was bringing them ever closer. Lightning flashed in multi-veined splendor, illuminating the fading darkness.

Flicking on the overhead light, he retrieved the instructions he had received in the envelope from the restroom and once again read them carefully: 2.7 miles past mile marker 298 on the right side of the road, there will be a small, dirt road hidden among the trees. There will be an orange ribbon tied to one of the trees. Turn right and follow the road for 6.3 miles. The cabin will be across a large meadow, on your right.

He placed the note on the seat beside him and removed a photograph from the envelope. The man in the photo was a well-built man with a round jaw and curly brown hair. He studied it carefully, then put the picture in his pocket and continued to search for the marker.

The windows had begun to fog over so he rolled down the driver's side window for a better view. A moment later he spotted the orange marker, turned off the main highway and stopped. He looked up and down the main road. It was empty. He felt uneasy. Beyond the constant drone of the engine, there was a persistent, low-pitch hum that circled his head and grew increasingly intense. He could hear his heart pounding life through his veins. Then something rustled in the brush nearby, drew nearer, and moved on.

Off to his right, he caught a flash of light. The entire sky flickered out beyond the thunderheads, followed a moment later by rumbling thunder. Large raindrops began to pelt the car. The trees rocked with the wind.

He rolled up the window and edged the car forward. The road had become slippery from the ever-intensifying rain and grabbed at the tires, pulling the car in different directions. There were deep ruts carved in the road like a well-marked trail. His low-slung car bottomed out on the ridge that had formed between the ruts. He forced the tires up onto the ridges but the possessed steering wheel jerked and tugged as the car slid down the road. This kind of driving was foreign to him. He'd take city traffic over this any time.

As he continued down the road, keeping an eye on the odometer, he noticed large potholes filled with rainwater. At low crossings, running water carved deep channels through the soil, creating patches of foaming rapids that carried fallen leaves and branches downstream through the timber. The windshield wipers beat a steady rhythm as rain slapped against the glass. Several threads of lightning materialized overhead and flashed across the morning sky. The area lit up like daylight; a titanic clap of thunder followed. The rain persisted.

Creeping down the road for what seemed an hour, Jake came to a clearing that brushed the road. In the distance, he could see a small structure made blurry by the heavy rain. There were two vehicles parked out front. He frowned. "Somebody's in for a surprise," he said aloud.

As he applied the brakes, the car slid to a slow stop. Pulling his jacket over his head, he climbed out of the car. There was an autumn chill in the air. It stung at his face like tiny ant bites. The rain dripped off his parka hood in a steady stream.

He surveyed the area and noticed the main road turned north away from the cabin. A smaller trail careened off to the right and headed away from the cabin. There didn't seem to be a clear-cut path across the clearing. Then he saw it about twenty yards down the road on the shoulder; a break in the tall grass with two rotten, wooden rails about fifteen feet apart. Sloshing through the mud, he hurried down the road. As he came closer, he spotted a piece of carved wood lying among the grass near the drive. He picked it up and brushed away the mud. It read: FOGARTY'S HIDEAWAY. He dropped the sign, wiped the mud from his hands on the legs of his pants, and went back to the car. He eased the car down the road and turned into the drive. Tall grass bordered the roadway. He kept the car at a crawl. When he reached a safe distance, about a hundred yards, he stopped the car and turned off the engine.

As he gazed out through the rain towards the cabin, he almost laughed. It looked like something out of an old "B" western. The cabin was made of eight inch, pine logs. There were two foggy windows along the front, a tall, pitched roof, a stone chimney along the side, and a large deck along the front.

This is going to be too easy, he thought. He started towards the cabin, his right hand clutching his trusty Beretta.

* * * * *

When Pete Williams awakened, he stretched and immediately felt the pain. His muscles ached and his head felt like someone had been pounding on it with a hammer all night. He could feel the damp, morning chill on his face. Although he knew better, he glanced over towards the fireplace with the faint hope Brian had awakened early and was in the process of building a fire. No such luck. The room was quiet and empty.

He cursed under his breath. Then he remembered seeing a stack of dry firewood on the side of the house under a low-hung shelter as he came up the drive yesterday. He smiled as he envisioned a warm fire and a hot cup of coffee. When he threw back the covers, the chill air caused his muscles tensed and his entire body began to shake. He hurried towards the front door, wincing with each creak of the old wooden floor, the image of a roaring fire dancing in his head. When he opened the door, his heart skipped a beat and he stopped in the doorway. At the bottom of the steps was a large man in a hooded parka. The man was pointing a handgun directly at him. At the same time he opened his mouth to scream, he thought about Angie and the kids and how much he loved them.

(17)

Brian Fogarty awakened with a jolt and sat upright in bed.

Christine leaned up on one elbow, her disheveled blonde hair matted down on one side, the creases from the pillow formed into her face. She craned her head towards the door. Through her one open eye, she looked at the door then at Brian. "What was that?"

"Shhh," Brian mouthed the word, holding his palm up in the air. He knew the sound all too well. It was the unmistakable crack of a handgun, and it was close. That fact alone eliminated any out-of-season hunters, and it was too close to be youngsters popping off cans. Someone was in or near the house, and Brian had the feeling the owner of the weapon was not making a social call.

His heart pounded with the intensity of a long distance runner. He threw back the covers and stepped out of bed, oblivious to the morning chill. Making his way across the bedroom, ensuring each step was as silent as possible on the hardwood floor, he drew up next to the door and placed an ear against it. He could hear nothing but the wind outside the window. Grasping the cold, metal doorknob, he turned it slowly, felt the latch give, and cracked open the door. As he peered out into the main room of the cabin, he could see a large man with a thick, bulky parka leaning over Pete's twisted body; a pool of blood slowly widening around Pete's motionless head.

Brian eased the door closed and crept to the bedside table where he would normally keep his .32 revolver, but the table was

90

empty. He swore under his breath, realizing it was lying on the seat of the Taurus. Stupid. Stupid. Stupid. How could he have been so stupid? It was a rookie mistake. "Never let your weapon out of your sight," was what the instructors had drilled into his head at the academy, and until now, he had adhered to that philosophy.

His mind raced to find a solution. There was a rifle in the living room and knives in the kitchen, all of which were unobtainable under the circumstances. To try for them would be suicide. He could hear footsteps creeping across the hardwood floor, creaking and groaning with each slow and calculated step.

This isn't happening. It can't be. Taking me out is one thing, but not Christine. No way.

He thought about trying for the car and his .38, but it was too far. He'd be cut down before he reached the drive. The woods out behind the cabin would be the best bet. If he and Christine could make it across the clearing and into the safety of the woods, there were a hundred places they could hide. Brian knew every hill, stream and valley for a hundred mile radius. It would be their only chance for survival.

Anger replaced fear with the intensity of a leopard lunging on its prey. A voice from within urged him to rush the demon that had taken Pete's life and tear his heart out. His whole body shook with anger.

But he knew, now more than ever, he needed a level head. They had to get out of the cabin, and they had to do it now. He hurried to the window and eased it open. When the window crackled from lack of use, Brian winced. He whipped his head around and looked at the door, waiting for the man to rush the door and come crashing into the room. But he could hear nothing but the wind rattling some loose boards on the front porch and the rain hammering the ground and dripping from the roof into puddles outside the window.

Christine sat silently in the bed, covers pulled up to her neck, both eyes open wide and bulging.

Brian looked outside. He could see a clear path to the trees. They had to hurry. Motioning her to the window, he mouthed the words, "Come on."

Christine shook her head. Tears began to flow. The knuckles on her hands were turning white from her death grip on the blanket.

Brian stepped towards the bed, jerked the covers off her, latched onto her left arm and pulled her from the bed. She held her arms close to her body with her hands clamped together under her chin. Brian took her by the elbow and helped her out the window. She gasped when her bare feet hit the cold, wet grass and turned and looked at Brian.

Slow and cautious footsteps creaked across the floor, drew up next to the bedroom door and stopped.

As Brian put one leg out the window, the doorknob turned, then moved back and forth. Brian swung the other leg out.

The bedroom door crashed violently but held.

Brian leaped out the window and hit the ground rolling.

Christine screamed.

The door crashed open and slammed into the wall.

Brian did not stop to look. He grabbed Christine by the hand and screamed, "Run!" They raced for the safety of the trees with the rain pelting their faces. Each footstep rattled Brian's teeth and sent brown water fanning out across the ground.

From behind them, Brian heard a pop. A fraction of a second later, a bullet buzzed past them and struck a large pine where the clearing met the forest. Pieces of bark shattered and flew in every direction.

"We have to get to the trees," Brian shouted.

Christine was screaming, her face distorted, water streaming down her cheeks.

The trees were getting closer.

Christine gasped for air, each breath a labored wheeze. She began to slow down.

Another pop. This time the bullet slammed into a tall oak tree with a dull thud.

Christine tripped and went down, taking Brian with her. Brian ducked his shoulder and rolled into the fall, pulling Christine back to her feet with him. A moment later they reached the trees.

Christine stopped. Panting hard, her hands resting on her knees, she looked straight down at the ground while shaking her head.

"We can't stay here," Brian said, glancing back over his shoulder towards the cabin and seeing nothing but a swirling mist of rain. "We have to keep moving."

"No," Christine wheezed. "This isn't happening."

Brian grabbed her by the arm. Together they set out through the brush and into the forest towards the sound of the roaring river.

* * * * *

Jake Leighton leaned out the window, his gloved left hand clutching the window frame, his gun hand dangling down beside him, watching the man and woman disappear into the trees.

He scrunched his face and climbed back into the bedroom. Retracing his steps, he stopped and leaned down next to the dead man. Removing a photo from his pocket, he held it out in front of him and looked at it. Then looked at the dead man. "Shit," he blurted. He raced outside and around the side of the house, across the clearing and up to the edge of the forest where the man and woman had disappeared into the trees. They were gone. Peering out through the dense foliage, his eyes searched for movement. Hundreds of brown and yellow leaves swayed with the breeze and fluttered to the ground. He listened carefully, hoping to pick up the sound of his prey. Nothing. They were gone.

Turning on his heels, he hurried back across the clearing, past the cabin and out into the drive. He raised his weapon and put a bullet in the front tires of both Pete and Brian's vehicles and one through each radiator. Then he inspected both vehicles carefully, inside and out. On the seat of the Taurus, he found a fully loaded .38 revolver, which he stuffed into the front of his pants. In the Suburban, a 12-gauge shotgun lay across the back seat with a box of shells next to it. Jake's lucky day. He tucked the shotgun under his arm and stuffed the box of shells into the pocket of his parka.

Back inside the cabin, he looked around the primitively furnished room and spotted an unfinished bottle of wine sitting on a large spool they must have used for a table. "Ah," he said. "A little fruit of the vine. Just what the doctor ordered." He chuckled, poured himself a glass, moved the glass under his nose and took in the aroma and then tasted it. Through pursed lips and squinted eyes, directing his comment toward the dead man he said, "Your taste in wine leaves something to be desired, sir." Inspecting the bottle, he shook his head. It was a screw top. He should have known.

Then he shrugged his shoulders, raised his eyebrows, and cocked his head to one side. He picked up the bottle, poured a full glass and held it tightly in his hand. "Under the circumstances, one must learn to make concessions." He raised his glass towards the dead man. "To your journey, my good man." He tossed back the wine, grimaced, swallowed. "Give the devil my regards."

After grabbing an apple from the table, he walked outside onto the porch, adjusted his tie and looked up toward the stormy sky. From within a murky gray backdrop, churning black clouds rolled and heaved as the rain persisted. The tops of the trees swayed in the breeze. Lightning flashed in the distance, and a moment later a muffled rumbling sound filled the air.

He had hoped to finish the job and be back in Phoenix for dinner. The reservations at the Ritz Carlton were for two. According to the escort service, Ginger was a fiery redhead who was game for anything.

Frowning at the thought of missing out on Ginger's favors, he checked his watch. It was seven-thirty. He still had time. It all depended on his quarry. And how badly they wanted to stay alive.

"Well," he said, pulling his parka hood up on his head, "let the hunt begin." Stepping down from the porch, he snapped a fresh shotgun shell into the chamber and headed towards the woods.

(18)

"Are you all right?" Brian asked, laboring to catch his breath.

They had pulled up next to a shallow stream near a cluster of cattails. Brian squinted through the mist back down the path, looking for signs of pursuit. Reassured they were in no immediate danger, he turned to Christine and repeated the question. "Are you all right?"

Christine was leaning against a tall ponderosa, eyes closed, resting her head against the bark. Her chest heaved in and out. "No! I'm not all right."

"Come on," Brian said glancing down the path again. "We have to keep moving."

"I can't go another step. I have to catch my breath."

"We have to go," Brian persisted.

Christine opened one tear-filled eye and fixed it on him. "What about Pete?"

Pete had not been far from Brian's mind. The sight of his friend lying on the floor in a pool of blood sent a surge of anger through him that he could barely contain. Brian would see justice done; he'd make sure of that. But at the moment, the more pressing problem was finding shelter. The drenching rain combined with the brisk mountain air had chilled them both to the bone. Already he was shaking uncontrollably, and he could hear Christine's teeth chattering.

He turned to her and said, "We have to get you out of here. After we find some shelter and I've made sure you're safe, I'll go back and see about Pete."

Christine began to cry. She buried her face into cupped hands. Brian moved closer and put his arm around her. Then she buried her head in his chest and let go. Knowing nothing could ease the pain of the moment, he simply let her cry.

Brian began to feel antsy, though, like time was running out. He released his grasp on Christine, cupped his hands under her chin and lifted her face. "We have to get out of here, honey."

"Where are we going?" Christine asked, looking up at him through blurry eyes.

"Old Man Murphy's cabin is about five miles due west of here. We can get dry and figure out where to go from there."

Christine wiped a tear from her cheek with the back of her hand. "Will he be home?"

"I don't think so," Brian said. "He only used it during hunting season and the occasional fishing trip. But he must be . . . " He thought about it a moment. "Old," Brian finished. Mr. Murphy had been old and bald when Brian was a youth. For all he knew, Mr. Murphy had passed on and someone else now owned the cabin. Regardless, the Murphy place was their destination, no matter who the present owner might be.

She held out her hand and placed it on Brian's forearm. Feigning a smile she said, "Let's go."

His clothes wet and clinging, Brian shivered against the cool, autumn air and wished he had grabbed some clothes on the way out of the cabin.

Cursing himself for his lack of foresight, he led Christine through the trees toward the Little Colorado River, the cool air biting at his exposed skin. Glancing back over his shoulder as they trudged through the mud, Brian noticed the deep footprints they were leaving in the spongy ground. It would be an easy trail to follow.

Soon, Brian could hear the sound of running water. They made their way down a steep, wooded ravine until they came to the rain swollen banks of the Little Colorado. Brian glanced over his shoulder once again at their footprints.

"We have to cover our tracks," he said. "If we walk upstream through the water a ways, we should lose him."

Christine stared at him, her eyes wide and moist. "You think he'll follow us?"

"Probably not," Brian lied. "But I don't want to take the chance."

Brian helped her into the river. She grimaced as her feet touched the icy waters. A bitter chill worked its way through Brian's entire body as he followed her in. Every hair on his body seemed to be standing on end.

A clap of thunder boomed overhead, then another. The relentless downpour felt like tiny needles drilling into his skin. The wind whipped through his wet clothing and gnawed at his bare skin. His body shook. Time was running out. Hypothermia would soon rob him of his senses. They would have to hurry.

Half an hour later, freezing and exhausted, they came upon a fork in the river. The main tributary careened off to the left while a smaller offshoot meandered through reeds and tall grass until it formed a small pond surrounded by tall pines, thick brush and dozens of swaying cattails. They climbed over a mass of twigs and sticks that held the pond in place, then onto the dry bank, their clothing drenched and dripping. At the far side of the pond, there was a large mound of twigs and branches that formed a strange dome.

"What is that?" Christine asked, staring at the dome as they passed by.

"A beaver lodge," Brian replied.

"I didn't know we had beavers in Arizona."

"Lots more to Arizona than deserts and cactus."

"Right now the desert heat sounds pretty good," Christine said though chattering teeth. She had her arms across her chest and her hands tucked under her armpits.

The pond was filled with lily pads bobbing in the green, rippling water. A brown trout jumped out of the water in search of a meal as the rain pounded the surface of the pond. Brian remembered the many times he'd fished this pond as a youth and longed for happier times.

"Have to rest," Christine said, taking a seat on a large rock next to the trail under the cover of a large ponderosa branch.

Brian wedged his way under the branch and sat down beside her. His lungs labored for air. Despite his previous state, the uphill battle against the river's current had rejuvenated him. While the cold still cut at his wet and exposed skin, he had regained his senses and was thinking clearly.

The wind picked up and whistled through the treetops, their branches nodding back in perfect rhythm, leaves flying in the breeze like tiny kites. The rain continued with no sign of stopping.

Christine's whole body jerked. She went rigid, hugging her knees, shaking. "I'm so cold, Brian." Her voice was soft and pleading.

Brian stood and helped her to her feet. He wrapped his arms around her and moved his hands up and down her back vigorously, creating friction so as to warm her as best he could. "Come on," he said. "The Murphy place isn't much farther."

* * * * *

Jake Leighton stood by the edge of a fast moving, narrow river looking at the footprints that disappeared at the river's edge. He glanced in both directions, trying to decide which way his quarry would have gone. The deep footprints in the mud had been easy to follow, even for someone who had spent most of his life in the city, with his country visits limited to large paintings hanging on the walls of New York City art museums and the occasional trip to the theater or the movies, provided, of course, Hollywood had decided to make something worth watching.

As he surveyed the area, he frowned. There were no footprints on the opposite bank. They simply disappeared at the river's edge. There was only one possible solution: Fogarty must have walked in the water to cover his tracks. Jake smiled, recalling an old western movie where a similar tactic had been used. Perhaps Hollywood *did* have some redeeming qualities.

The river that had paralleled the road on the way in was flowing past him. This led him to believe that the road would be to his left, downstream; and by his estimation, approximately eight to ten miles. His first instinct was to head that direction, figuring Fogarty would head for the road to get help. But something told him this Fogarty character was different. He would be cunning in trying to elude the hunter. Besides, he was undoubtedly wet and cold and would be in need of shelter somewhere nearby. Someplace he could change into some dry clothes and warm up by a nice fire. The decision made, Jake turned on his heels and headed upstream.

* * * * *

Cold and exhausted, Brian and Christine were standing on the front porch of Old Man Murphy's dilapidated cabin. Nestled deep within the woods and almost invisible from the river, the place looked as deserted as an ancient tomb.

The tiny, one-bedroom cabin had been constructed of pine logs. There were two windows along the front, both muddy and fogged, and a single window along the back wall. It had a tin roof with a stone chimney, towering high above the peak.

The door gave way under the weight of Brian's shoulder. Christine followed him in. A damp, musty smell filled the room. Brian left the door open to clear it. The furnishings were sparse. Against the far wall was a dingy white sofa with a freestanding lamp at one end and a green, print chair in the corner. A wooden crate sat in front of the sofa. There was an old cable spool over by the kitchen counter with three small barrels placed around it. A large, pine armoire engulfed most of the north wall and stretched nearly to the ceiling, six feet from a massive stone fireplace covered with black soot from years of wood smoke.

"Can you make a fire?" Christine asked.

"Not a good idea."

She hesitated. "You really do think he's following us, don't you?"

"I don't know, probably not. But I don't want to take the chance."

Brian walked over to the pine armoire and looked inside. There were two tattered blankets, a brown pillow, and several articles of clothing, none of which, Brian thought, would fit.

Christine stood in the middle of the room, her body shaking violently with chill. "I have to get out of these wet clothes."

Brian reached inside the armoire and removed a pair of maroon sweatpants and an oversized, gray sweatshirt with a Ford emblem across the chest. He handed them to Christine and pointed towards the bedroom. Grasping the clothing tightly in her shivering hands, she disappeared through the bedroom door and closed it behind her.

Brian smiled. Modesty. That's new. He liked it.

While Christine changed, Brian went to the sink and turned on the faucet, but nothing came out. He found a plastic bucket under the kitchen sink and took it out front. From the porch, he scanned the area for signs of the hunter but he was nowhere in sight. Then he searched the sky for a break in the rain but found only low, black clouds. Shaking his head, he thought it was strange. This was an unusual rain. In Arizona, showers normally came in fierce, rapid and noisy, then cleared out just as fast. But this was a winter rain: cold, determined, with the promise of a harsh and bitter winter to follow. He took the bucket, sauntered down the steps, splashed through puddles of water and placed the bucket out in the open where it could gather the rain.

Inside the cabin, Brian could hear Christine moving about. He went back inside and found her in the kitchen. She had wrapped a brown towel around her head. The sweatshirt was at least two sizes too big, and she had an old black belt around her

101

waist to hold the sweatpants in place. Brian fought back a smile. Not her best look. But under the circumstances, it would have to do.

"Okay," Brian said, strolling over to the armoire. "It's my turn."

On the top shelf, under two worn and faded pairs of jeans, he found a Green Bay Packers sweatshirt and a pair of camouflage army pants. He took the clothes from the armoire, stripped and put on the dry clothing. They were a couple sizes too big, but they were dry and felt good against his chilled skin. If it were not for the ensuing madness awaiting him back at his own cabin, he would have almost felt human again.

Christine emerged from the kitchen holding a can of Pork-n-Beans. "This is all I could find to eat." She shook her head.

"Well, it will do. Open it up. I'll bring in the water."

"A can opener," she murmured, and went back into the kitchen.

When he came back in with the bucket, Christine had the can open. She held up a tiny piece of metal with a small hook on the end. "It's a can opener, like the military uses. I found it in the drawer along with two spoons and two forks. And there are a few dishes in the cupboard above the sink."

"Great. I'm glad I brought you along."

Christine's face went blank. Her eyes narrowed and her muscles tensed. "Well, I'm not!" She spit out the words violently. "I would just as soon be sitting at home with my feet up watching TV. This whole fiasco was your idea — remember. I only came up here because I felt . . . " She stopped. Her face softened. And she forced a smile. "I'm sorry. I'm cold and tired and frightened. You may be used to this kind of thing what with your job and all, but I'm not."

"This is not the normal course of my day either, Christine."

Christine turned and went into the kitchen, rummaged through the bottom cabinets and came up with an old, dented pot. She lit a match, switched on the stove, but nothing happened.

"There's no gas." The words were forceful, like she was fighting to remain calm, and Brian knew it.

"I'll check the tank." He went outside, plodded through the soggy ground to the side of the cabin where he found a large, cylindrical propane tank about a hundred feet from the house. Thumping the side of the tank with his knuckles, the tank sounded hollow. The needle on the gauge read empty. He shrugged his shoulders against the rain and headed back for the house.

Once inside, he grabbed a towel from the armoire and looked over at Christine. "Tank's empty. We'll have to eat them cold."

Christine scrunched her eyes, opened her mouth wide and let out a piercing scream. Brian cupped his hands over his ears and cringed.

"I can't take this," Christine said. She threw the can across the room. It slammed into the wall and fell to the floor. "I've been shot at, Brian. Do you understand that? Somebody tried to kill me. I'm cold. I'm tired. I'm hungry and I want to go home." Tears were streaming down her cheek, her body shaking with rage.

Brian went to comfort her. When he held out his hands to embrace her, she pushed him away and stomped off towards the bedroom. After she reached the door she turned and glared at him. "You get me out of here. Do you hear me? I don't care how. Just get me out of here." She slammed the door behind her.

(19)

Jake Leighton stopped in his tracks when he heard the shrill scream of a woman. For over a minute he stood quiet, listening. Then he hurried along the bank of the river until he stumbled onto two sets of deep footprints in the mud. They seemed to be coming out of the river. He had been right. As he followed the prints up a steep embankment, he could hear the faint sound of voices coming from over the ridge. He trudged up the hill, his lungs burning with each step. The voices grew louder. Or were they? He had heard how voices travel in the wilderness and guessed they were further than he thought. When he reached the top, he stopped and leaned over. His chest heaved in and out as he struggled to catch his breath.

Through squinted eyes, he searched the woods. Then he spotted it: a small cabin nearly invisible within a dense, patch of aspen trees. Positioning the shotgun at the ready — his hands numb from the cold — he eased towards the cabin. He hadn't noticed it before, but each step seemed to slosh as he walked across the saturated ground.

The voices had stopped. He could hear footsteps on the cabin's wooden floor. As he drew nearer the cabin, he looked around for signs of life, but there was no movement outside the cabin. He crept up to the side of the cabin, popped a shell into the shotgun chamber, and eased towards the front porch.

* * * * *

Brian stood on the front porch, eating beans from a fresh can he found in the kitchen. He took a sip of rainwater from a plastic cup and thought about his next move. His first instinct was to leave Christine at the cabin, retrace his tracks back to the house and check on Pete. If he met up with the stalker along the way, he might be able to surprise and capture the man. If not, he would surely encounter the man once he reached his cabin; unless, and this would be too much to hope for, the man had packed it in and headed for home.

A patch of blue sky appeared to the south and streaks of sunlight filtered through thick, dark clouds as the rain began to ease. He breathed in deeply, taking in the clean mountain air.

Just before he heard the metallic sound of a shotgun pumping a shell into the chamber, he caught the faint scent of Christian Dior's Fahrenheit. He recognized the scent because Christine had bought him some for Christmas one year.

His heart skipped as he spun and headed into the cabin. When he flung open the bedroom door, Christine sat up in bed, eyes wide.

"He's here, isn't he?" she whispered, as she jumped from the bed.

Brian nodded. He took Christine by the hand and hurried out into the main room. They paused in the middle of the living room, waiting, listening. Brian's eyes flashed from window to window, trying to ascertain where the man might be. But all he could see through the foggy glass were the distorted shadows of ponderosa pines swaying in the wind. A twig snapped outside. When Brian heard it, he sucked air into his lungs so fast it whistled. His head whipped in the direction of the sound. He watched the front door, waiting for it to fly open as the bedroom door had at his own cabin. His mouth hung open. White noise rang in his ears. The outside seemed to hiss. Despite his pounding heart, Brian heard a single pair of hard-soled shoes step onto the porch. Slowly, they thumped across the wooden porch heading for the front door. Brian tightened his grip on Christine's arm and hurried towards the rear of the cabin. When they reached the back door, Brian flung it open. Together they ran down the hill through the thick, wet grass.

* * * * *

Jake Leighton came through the front door with his shotgun at the ready. He focused in on the open back door and hurried towards it. Drawing up by the threshold, he cursed. In the distance, he could hear his quarry sloshing through the mud. He slammed his fist into the side of one of the kitchen cabinets. The thin paneling cracked and gave way under the force.

"I'm going to kill you very slowly, Fogarty. And then I'm going to show your girlfriend the time of her life."

He ran towards the woods.

* * * * *

"If we can beat him back to the cabin," Brian said as they ran along the waters edge, breathless and aching, "maybe my gun will still be there. If not, maybe he didn't find my spare behind the seat."

"But what if he did?"

"Then we'll hike out of here and get help."

A few minutes later they stopped to rest near the same rock as before, overlooking the lake and beaver lodge. Christine labored for breath, her face as red as the sun on a foggy morning.Brian turned and looked behind them. In the distance he could hear thunder; and through the thunder, footsteps moving swiftly across the soggy ground. Before he had a chance to warn Christine, Brian spotted the man coming though the trees, his gaze off to the left. He hadn't spotted them . . . yet.

Brian grabbed Christine by the hand, gesturing towards their pursuer and moved towards the pond.

Christine's eyes went wide. Her whole body trembled. She latched on to Brian's arm.

As quietly as possible, Brian and Christine eased down to the shore and stopped.

The man had worked his way down the embankment and was heading towards their position.

"I see him," Christine whispered. "He's getting closer."

Brian searched his surroundings. When his vision focused in on the beaver lodge an idea came to him. He wasn't sure it would work, but his options were growing thin. "Follow me," he said. "And stay quiet."

Taking Christine by the hand and crouching low, Brian led her into the freezing lake. Christine gasped when the frigid water reached her mid section. Her eyes and mouth were wide. Blue lips quivered above her chin.

When they were up to their necks, Brian could feel the water encircle him, compressing his chest like a Sumo wrestler squeezing the life out of him. The frigid water pricked at his body like millions of tiny needles. His lungs burned, each breath labored. His legs and arms felt like telephone poles. It took all the strength he could muster just to stay afloat. He swam as quietly as possible across the pond, keeping close to the reeds, listening to Christine's heavy, short breaths behind him.

Back over his shoulder, Brian could see the man had stopped by the edge of the pond and was carefully scanning the area for movement. For the first time, through the reeds, Brian got a close look at him. He was a husky man, in his late thirties with dark hair, an oval face and small round eyes. But something about him said city. Something in his face said he had led a soft life. Brian could only hope he was right. If the man were indeed city, Brian could use this to his advantage. Only time would tell.

Suddenly a duck that had been startled by the intrusion squawked and flew from its hiding place among the reeds.

Christine let out a gurgled cry.

The man on the bank spun around, raised his rifle and peered through the reeds towards Brian and Christine's position.

They remained as still as possible while treading water.

The man eased along the bank, crouched, shotgun out in front of him, peering into the reeds. He seemed to be looking right at them. A sudden burst of laughter broke the mountain silence followed by a deep, resonating voice. "Hey, Fogarty, how's the water?"

At that moment, Brian felt as if his heart would burst through his chest. Each wheezing breath sounded like an alarm, betraying their position.

The man on the bank glanced around the area and then sat down on a nearby rock. "About now," he said, his soft voice a mere whisper but clearly audible in the thin mountain air, "your body must be feeling numb and shaking uncontrollably. Probably going into hypothermia. A crackling warm fire would be nice about now, wouldn't it? Come on out, Fogarty. I have blankets in the car. Maybe we can work something out."

Thunder rumbled in the distance. The wind moaned in the treetops.

"I'm so cold, Brian," Christine whispered.

"Me, too. Let's keep moving." He jerked his head to their left towards the far bank near the beaver pond. "Keep close to the reeds."

"I can see the whole lake from here," the man said. "There's no escape. If you come out, I know we can work something out. Rumor has it you have some money stashed away. You beat the going price on your head, and I'll walk away."

The rain pounded the surface of the water like shotgun blasts.

Brian and Christine kept moving.

"What do you say, Fogarty? Come on out and let's talk. I know we can make a deal."

Brian could no longer feel his legs. They had to get out of the water soon or die. He knew it and so did the stalker.

"What's he talking about?" Christine said.

Brian held his finger to his lips.

The stalker stood up and gazed out towards them, then leaped to his feet and ran along the bank. He was coming right at them and Brian knew time was up.

His idea seemed extreme, a slim chance at best. He had tried it once before in his youth on a dare. The quarters had been cramped but dry. Saying a silent prayer, he looked at Christine and said, "Take a deep breath and follow me."

Brian sucked in as much air as his lungs could hold and ducked under the water. After the initial shock to his eyes, he realized he could see for a good fifteen or twenty feet. Small pieces of moss floated with the currents like tiny leprechauns. Several curious trout swam around him and nipped at his legs. One large fish he didn't recognize scurried away, its tail whipping furiously as if waving goodbye. Below him, long strands of weeds seemed to be reaching up to greet them. Up ahead, he spotted what he hoped was the entrance to the beaver den.

Glancing back to check on Christine, Brian saw that her cheeks were bulging, her eyes pleading. He waved her towards him and then pointed towards the beaver lodge. Christine shook her head as a rapid fire of bubbles emerged from her nose and mouth. Brian grabbed her by the wrist and pulled her another few feet until they were directly under the beaver lodge. Then he latched onto her waist and pushed her under the mangle of twigs just below the surface of the water and followed her in.

A moment later they burst through the surface and into the small confines of the beaver lodge. In perfect unison, Brian and Christine sucked in the dank air. As Brian looked around the cramped quarters, he realized it would not hold them both. Helping Christine out of the water and onto a bed of twigs and dried leaves, it became painstakingly clear what he would have to do.

"Stay here," Brian whispered, with his face close to hers.

"What! You can't leave me here!"

Brian put a finger to his lips and cocked his head to one side, listening for movement outside the lodge. He could still hear the wind and the rain pelting the surface of the pond, and Christine's chattering teeth, but nothing else. Placing his hand on her face, he pulled her close. "We have no choice. I know you're cold but at least you're out of the water."

"But you . . . "

"Listen to me. I'm going to try to lead him away from here. Do you think you can find your way back to Murphy's cabin?"

Christine nodded, her whole body shaking violently.

"Okay. Give me about ten minutes and then head back to Murphy's. Keep moving. Don't stop for anything. It will help keep you warm. When you get there, stay there. After I lose him, I'll come get you."

Christine had balled herself into a fetal position, her arms wrapped around her shoulders. "But what if he comes back?"

Brian shook his head. "I don't think he will. He's after me. And I intend on taking him in the opposite direction." He thought a moment. "But if I don't show up by nightfall, there's an old smokehouse out beyond the outhouse where you can hide 'til morning. Then keep the sun on your right and walk north until you reach the main highway. It's about six or seven miles. You can flag a car from there. Go to the police station in Greer and ask for Eddie Condolora. He's an old friend. Tell him what's happened. He'll take care of it from there."

Christine opened her mouth to say something, then stopped. She nodded.

Brian leaned forward and kissed her on the cheek. "I love you." Taking a deep breath, he dropped down into the water.

(20)

Once again Brian felt the water close in around him. Deep within his ears, an agonizing low hum seemed almost unbearable. His forehead and temples pounded. He swam towards the north shore, keeping to the reeds and cattails, his arms and legs like fifty-pound weights at his side.

His oxygen nearly exhausted, he surfaced, eased his head out of the water, and sucked in the cold damp air. Realizing his eyes were blurry from the icy water, he tried to focus on the shoreline to find the stalker. But all he could make out for sure was a gray stormy sky, and what seemed like a million cattails. Twisting his body away from the reeds, he faced the opposite shore. There he spotted a large, twisted pine tree hanging out over the water. Taking another deep breath, he submerged and made for the irregular tree.

Several times he felt as though his body wanted to shut down. Arms and legs moaned and ached with each stroke. A thumping heart seemed sluggish. Lungs burned. Still he pressed on. He thought about Christine, and his father and mother, and Brian Junior and the day he died. Doubt clouded his mind with every stroke of his weighted arms. Just when he thought he could go no further, the mossy bottom gave way to sand. Looking up, he could see the odd shaped tree hanging out over the water. With utmost caution, he eased his head out of the water and gasped for air. Then he lumbered out of the water, cleared the reeds, and dropped to his knees on solid ground. The outside air seemed colder than the water. His entire body tensed and began to shake. Holding his hands out in front of him he saw they were blue. He knew he didn't have long.

Back over his shoulder, he could see the stalker about two hundred yards off to the west near the beaver lodge. Keeping low to the ground, he crawled across the bank until he reached a thick batch of scrub oak and collapsed. *You can do this*, he told himself. *You have to do this. Your life and Christine's life depends on it.*

Still shivering, he removed all his clothing except his underwear and then put back on his shoes. Suddenly he could see his mother standing before him. She was beautiful, young and had an orange glow around her. Brian smiled. It was good to see her again. He had missed her. She smiled at him and motioned him to come to her. He stood and moved towards her. Then he shook his aching head. *You're losing it, Brian*, he thought. *Concentrate.*

A shot rang out. The bullet grazed a nearby pine tree, sending bark flying through the air and pelting the side of his face.

Brian snapped out of it and stared at the stalker running straight for him. Within the depths of his mind something popped. A fire began to burn. His body felt electrified. All his senses seemed to come alive. He clenched his fists, sneered at the stalker and screamed, "Come and get me!" He spun around and dashed into the woods.

Brian could hear the stalker's pounding feet behind him as he ran. As he dashed in and out of thick aspen groves, changing directions frequently like a deer fleeing a pack of hungry wolves, life-giving warmth began to pulse through his veins. The numbness in his fingers soon gave way to a stinging tingle.

When he was sure he had led the stalker far enough away from the lake to give Christine a chance to escape, he turned north towards his cabin. His legs were weak and his heart felt as though it would explode, but he couldn't stop. He pushed himself on, one step at a time.

After what seemed an eternity, he stopped to rest near a huge, fallen oak tree, his chest pounding furiously. Each breath burned his lungs as if he were breathing acid fumes. He thought about Christine. Had she managed to find her way back to the cabin? Was she warm and dry now?

Then off to his right he heard something, slow careful steps sloshing in the soggy earth. Brian stood motionless, trying to blend into the brush. His eyes darted from tree to tree, searching. He caught a glimpse of movement and focused in on the silhouette of the stalker against a misty backdrop, blending with the dew like paint on a canvas. He was coming straight for him.

Brian dropped down behind the fallen tree and searched the area for an escape route.

The stalker inched his way through the thick undergrowth, his path coming ever closer to Brian, the barrel of the shotgun panning the area.

Brian remained still behind the tree, his heart pounding, and his mind racing. He looked for an escape route; none existed. Then he spotted the huge root system sprouting from the base of the fallen tree. He eased along the tree trunk, the soggy earth squishing beneath his hands and knees, until he reached the sprawling mass of tangled roots. The end had mostly rotted away and it smelled sour. Chips of rotten wood spilled out like lava. He began to remove some of the rotten bark from inside the tree trunk. His hands burned with cold. Every scoop of putrid bark tore at his fingers like glass. His tongue hung from a dry mouth. Each breath was short and labored as he struggled to remain in control.

When the hole was large enough, Brian climbed into the root ball and pulled the rotten chips in after him. The smell caused him to gag, then vomit. He wiped his chin with the back of his hand. Behind him, deep within the hollow tree, he could hear the sound of tiny claws scurrying across the bark.

Brian could hear the stalker moving closer, each deliberate step slogging through the muddy clay. Then he stopped. His breathing sounded close.

The smell of Fahrenheit penetrated Brian's nostrils and made him gag once again. Then he heard a long, deep sigh, a groan, a striking match, and the smell of cigarette smoke.

Brian's heart pounded within his chest. His lungs began to make a strange flapping sound like something had broken loose. Certain his heavy breathing would give him away, he cupped his hands over his mouth and tried to stifle it. His body shook with cold. What seemed like hours passed. The pungent odor of cigarette smoke filled the air. Struggling to remain silent, he tightened his hands over his mouth. He felt his stomach churning.

Then, in a soft low voice, Brian heard stalker say, "I don't know where you are, Fogarty. But I can smell your fear . . . and I like it." He breathed in deeply and sighed. "Well, my friend. You're only postponing the inevitable."

The log shifted as the stalker groaned to his feet. Brian listened to the man's labored footsteps tromping off through the mud to the south until they faded into the silence of the forest. Still he waited, taking in the hush until he couldn't stand it any longer. Then he pushed the bark away from his body, climbed out of the log, and wiped the decaying bark and vomit from his legs and chest. From behind him he heard something stir within the hollow tree. As he spun around to face it, a red squirrel shot out of the hollow log, dashed across the mud and fallen pine needles, leaped onto the trunk of a towering ponderosa pine, and scurried up the tree until it reached a hefty branch. Spinning around, it looked in Brian's direction, it's nose twitching and it's tail flicking. Brian breathed a sigh of relief. Of all the things that could have been within the tree, a squirrel would have been his first choice.

Brushing the remainder of the bark off his legs, his body numb and full of anger, he no longer noticed the cold. His thoughts were on Christine. She had to be his main priority.

If all had gone well, she would be waiting at the cabin. He had to go to her.

Taking in his surroundings, he found himself encircled by dense forest. Hundreds of ponderosa pines, junipers and scrub oak rose from the muddy soil like grass. Along with thousands of discarded pine needles, a bed of soggy yellow leaves blanketed the ground. Above the trees, dark clouds hovered and shifted within a gray, murky sky.

His body weak and exhausted, Brian felt lightheaded. Everything appeared out of focus. The trees seemed to be swaying, distorting. He blinked his eyes and shook his head. But nothing helped. Taking in his surroundings, nothing looked familiar. But it had to. He knew this country better than anyone. Or at least he thought he had. A sudden sense of helplessness came over him. He was frightened, more so than he could remember. What if he couldn't find his way back? What if he wandered through the forest until hypothermia devoured him? What would happen to Christine? No. He had to think, put the pain out of his mind. Concentrate. Blinking angrily to clear his vision, he peered through the trees searching for a familiar landmark. Then he heard it — a distant roar rising from the earth. His heart skipped a beat. He recognized that sound. It was the river. He lumbered towards the sound, each step collecting more mud and causing the next one to be that much harder. He stopped, tapped his shoes against a tree truck, watching the mud plop to the ground, and then moved on. When he came to the top of a long knoll, he looked out over the valley below. For a brief moment his vision cleared. And in the distance, he could see the Little Colorado meandering through the trees. For the first time that day, he felt his cheeks rise in what must have been a laughable grin. He knew his position and exactly how to get back to the cabin . . . and Christine.

(21)

Brian arrived back at Old Man Murphy's cabin to find it empty. Christine was nowhere in sight. He grabbed some dry clothing from the armoire, put them on and then searched the house. The wet clothes Christine had been wearing were scattered across the bedroom floor. Recalling his words at the beaver lodge about hiding in the smokehouse, he went outside, walked directly to the smokehouse and opened the door.

A piercing scream came out of the darkness. Then a figure holding a shovel rushed towards him. Instinctively, Brian sidestepped and pushed the figure to the ground. Outside the smokehouse in the light of day, Brian saw Christine wheel around and swing the shovel in his direction, her eyes wide with terror. Brian ducked and lunged for her. He ripped the shovel away and tossed it into the grass.

"Christine!" he screamed.

But she didn't seem to hear him. Her face distorted, eyes wide and shining, she doubled up her fist and swung at him. He blocked it and it glanced off his arm. He lunged forward and grabbed her in a bear hug. She screamed wildly and struggled to free herself. Her teeth clacked like a rabid dog as she tried to bite Brian's hands and arms.

"Honey, it's me! Stop! It's all right. You're safe."

Suddenly she went limp and began to sob. She buried her face in cupped hands. Brian released his grip and she buckled to

116

the ground. It was all he could do not to join her. This whole thing was like something out of a B horror movie. The only thing missing was a chain saw and a hockey mask.

"Come on, honey," Brian said as he lifted her off the ground. "We have to get out of here."

As they headed north towards the highway, the afternoon sun was high in the sky with only a few lingering clouds as evidence of the earlier storm. A slight breeze whistled through the trees. Birds chirped. A squirrel clicked off to his left while a flock of geese flying in a perfect "V" formation, squawked overhead and then disappeared beyond the towering trees.

"We'll be all right," Brian said.

Christine walked in silence, her head down, her arms folded across her chest.

"Are you okay?" Brian asked softly.

No response.

The sun had moved a long way across the sky when Brian and Christine reached the highway. Traffic was light. A Lexus and a white, Chevrolet station wagon passed them by before they were able to flag down a rattling old, Ford pickup. Brian walked up to the door. The driver was an old man with a wrinkled face and a lopsided gray felt hat with dark sweat stains at the rim. He wore a tattered red flannel shirt tucked into a pair of faded blue coveralls. A two-day growth of gray stubble covered his face. Country music twanged from the radio.

"Car break down?" the man asked, revealing a mouth full of brown and broken teeth.

"It's a long story," Brian said. "Are you going into Greer?" He had to raise his voice to be heard over the music and the clatter of the aging engine.

The old man leaned over and popped open a squeaky passenger side door and said, "Sure enough. Climb in."

As they bounced down the highway, Christine turned to Brian and whispered, "The whole truck smells like manure."

Brian felt his mouth crimp tight. He shook his head gently, as not to draw attention. Christine let out a heavy sigh and turned back to watch the highway.

Ten minutes later they were passing the road that led to Brian's cabin. "Let me out here," Brian said.

The old man pressed his large foot on the brake and began to slow the truck.

Christine jerked her head and stared at him. She placed a hand on his thigh and squeezed. "What are you doing?"

Brian didn't answer. He turned to the man and said, "Eddie Condolora's still the sheriff around here, isn't he?"

The old man smiled. "Yup. Voted for him twice."

"Then do me a favor. Take my wife to Sheriff Condolora. He'll see that she's taken care of. Tell him that Officer Brian Fogarty of the Scottsdale Police Department is in pursuit of a murder suspect. Tell him I'm at my cabin. He knows where it is. Have him bring reinforcements A.S.A.P." Brian paused, watched the truck slip off the asphalt onto the gravel shoulder and then added, "Tell the Sheriff the man is armed and dangerous."

"Why don't you come into town with us and see the sheriff yourself," the old man said. "Maybe he and his men could come out and help you."

"There's no time," Brian explained. "If we wait too long, he's liable to get away and I can't chance that."

"Brian," Christine said. "What are you doing?"

Brian could have said any number of things. He could have told her he was doing his job, that he was protecting her and their future together. Or that he wanted to rid society of a dangerous criminal. But deep inside, he wanted one thing. He wanted revenge. He wanted to kill the man that had murdered his friend. Watch the life slowly fade from his face until the grasp of death was upon him.

"You don't happen to have a gun, do you?" Brian asked.

The old man glanced back at an empty gun rack over the rear window. "Nope, I usually do what with huntin' season comin' up and all, but not today. My son's got 'em. He's gonna clean 'em up and then sight 'em in for me." He shrugged and feigned a smile. "Sorry."

"That's okay," Brian said. But he didn't mean it. What he needed was a gun. How was he supposed to face the killer with his bare hands? It was madness, and Brian knew it. He would have to use every backcountry trick he could recall to come out of this alive. For a brief moment he faltered. Maybe it would be wise to go into town and report the murder to Sheriff Condolora. Wise or not, that was not what Brian intended to do. He would go after the guy, and when he found him, he would kill him.

The truck came to rest on the gravel shoulder. Brian latched onto the door handle and opened the door. He turned back to the old man. "Just make sure my wife is looked after and I'll be in your debt."

Christine stared straight ahead and released her grip on Brian's thigh.

The old man smiled. "It's my pleasure young man. It's been a long time since I've had this much excitement."

Brian leaned across the seat, put a hand on Christine's chin and turned her face towards him. He looked into her watering eyes. "I'll be okay." Cupping his hands around her cheeks, he pulled her face to his. When their lips touched, Brian felt the gentle softness of her moist lips caress his. Her eyes were closed but a single teardrop ran down her cheek and touched Brian's face. The whole thing made him more secure that he was doing the right thing. He let go of her, climbed out of the truck, and closed the door.

Standing on the side of the road, listening to the old truck's rattling engine grind up to speed, he watched the truck pull away and disappear around the curb. He turned and headed down the road at a slow trot, the mud sloshing beneath his feet. If the stalker tried to leave, he would have to come down this road. There was no other way. If he did, Brian would see him, and somehow stop him. And if he didn't, they would meet up at the cabin and finish it.

The trot turned into a jog. He kept up a steady pace, his legs pounding a constant rhythm against the earth. A strange sensation came over him, like he was outside his body watching the action from above. Hunger and lack of water were playing havoc on his system. Or maybe it was runners' euphoria. He'd heard of that before, a kind of high long distance runners experience after several miles of constant running.

Somewhere between pain and ecstasy, he found himself at a bend in the road. Across the clearing he could see the cabin. There were three cars in the drive: Brian's Taurus, Pete's Suburban and a black Cadillac.

Brian stopped. With his hands on his knees, sucking in the thin air, he surveyed the situation. There were no signs of the stalker. Perhaps he was still in the woods looking for his prey. Or better yet, maybe he was lost. Maybe he was wandering around aimlessly, frightened, cold and hungry, tired and bewildered. Brian laughed. It would serve the bastard right.

Cautiously, he made his way towards the cabin, keeping to the tree line and out of sight. *Now who's stalking who?* Brian thought.

(22)

Jake Leighton sat at the kitchen table of Brian Fogarty's cabin sipping cheap wine and eating cheese and crackers he'd found in a paper sack on the kitchen counter. Exhausted, he closed his eyes and sighed. His body ached. Anger churned within him. He would never have believed it would prove so difficult to kill one stupid cop. Including the man lying on the floor in front of him, he had thirty hits to his credit. And none, not even the F.B.I. agent assigned to hunt him down years ago, had been as evasive as this guy. But Fogarty's luck couldn't last forever. Jake would have to be patient. When the time was right, he would finish it and collect his money. Then he would call it quits, retire to some place warm and live out his days drinking fine wine, eating pineapple and making love to dark skinned, passionate women. He smiled. "I could think of worse things," he mused.

Shortly after he had lost Brian's trail, Jake had headed back to the cabin, following the river until he found his own tracks leading up the embankment towards the cabin. The decision seemed sound: go to the cabin, get warm, find something to eat and wait, but for no more than an hour. If Fogarty were not back within the hour, it would be too dangerous for Jake to stay. He would have to head back to Phoenix and go underground for a couple weeks and regroup. The contractor would not be pleased, but then one had to make allowances in this business. He would finish the job. He'd never failed before. And he wasn't about to let one lucky cop ruin a perfect record.

He glanced at his watch. It had been well over an hour. Cursing under his breath, he stood, grabbed his glass of wine and headed for the door. After all, he had a date . . . and he didn't want to be late.

* * * * *

Brian silently edged his way through the tall grass towards his car in the hope of finding his spare gun behind the seat. If he were lucky, the stalker would not have found it.

When he pulled up behind the car, he stopped and craned his neck over the trunk. From his vantage point, he could see the front of the cabin and a strangely shaped object holding open the door. Then his heart skipped. He had suspected his friend had been killed, but when he recognized the object holding open the door as Pete's lifeless body, Brian's heart sank. Then, as if someone had thrown a switch, his stomach churned with wild fury. Sadness turned to anger, anger to rage. With all his strength, he tried to remain focused. Now was not the time for foolishness. He had to proceed slowly, with calculated efficiency. The first order was to check on the gun. Then, if he was lucky and the gun was there, he would be on equal ground. He envisioned himself putting a bullet through the stalker's brain.

Twisting his head and glancing back down the road, he looked for any sign of reinforcements, but the road was as still and quiet as his friend lying on the cabin floor.

Cautiously, he eased around the side of the car and drew up next to the door. As he reached for the door handle, the stalker emerged from the cabin holding a glass of wine. Brian ducked down behind the car and froze, as still as a rabbit avoiding a hunter. He squinted his eyes and listened carefully. Breaking glass. A cough. Hard soled shoes on wooden porch steps, then the pounding of heavy footsteps coming across the gravel driveway, directly towards him. Brian crouched down like a runner taking his mark. Ears ringing and temples pounding, he concentrated, listening to his racing heart and the growing sound of approaching footsteps.

Suddenly the stalker's large frame crossed in front of the car. Brian screamed and lunged. The stalker spun on his heels, his eyes wide. He reached for his gun with the kind of speed that comes from experience. As his hand touched the gun, their bodies collided. For a moment they were airborne, grunting, wrestling for the gun. Then they plummeted to the soggy ground, mud flying through the air. Brian ducked, rolled and sprang to his feet. The stalker rose from the mud, his gun in hand. Brian froze, his heart pounding. The stalker wheeled around. Brian rushed forward and grabbed for the gun. They struggled for control. Jake brought his free hand around and laid it across Brian's face. For a brief moment, Brian thought his eye would explode. His face burned. His ears rang. He tightened his grip on the gun. The stalker screamed, straining to relinquish Brian's death grip. But Brian held tight. The stalker thrust his head towards Brian's, but Brian took the brunt of it with his shoulder. Then he twisted the stalker's wrist and brought the gun hand down across his knee. The gun came loose, spun though the air and tumbled into the mud. Brian threw a punch. Blocked. Brian kicked towards the stalker's knee and missed. He lost his balance. A fierce right caught him in the ribs. Brian doubled over and grabbed his stomach. His breath gone, he felt dazed. Then a sharp blow came down across the back of his neck and sent him crashing to the ground. He struggled to catch his breath. His whole body felt as though it were on fire. Light turned to darkness then back to light. Time seemed to slow. Swirling figures danced within the shadows behind his eyes. His ears rang fiercely. He heard laughter and footsteps, then something that sounded like thunder hugging the ground.

Slowly, his vision cleared. Shadows began to take shape. Ten feet away, he could see the stalker bending, his hand reaching for the gun half buried in the mud. Brian screamed, adrenalin pumping through his veins. Ignoring the pain, Brian charged.

As the stalker turned, gun in hand, Brian slammed into him. The gun went off. The stalker gasped. They tumbled to the ground, each with their hands in a death grip on the weapon. With a twist of his wrist, Brian wrenched the gun away from the stalker. He swung it around and caught the stalker across the forehead; blood instantly flowed from an inch long gash. Brian jumped to his feet. A moment later, he had his knee mashed in the stalker's chest and the gun barrel pressed against his forehead.

The stalker's eyes were wide.

Brian's entire body shook with rage. His head pounded with the intensity of a hurricane. He felt his finger pressing against the trigger. Something inside urged him on. "Kill him," the voice screamed. He clenched his teeth, pulled harder on the trigger. The hammer began to move. The gun shook violently.

Then he could hear Marion's voice: "No! You're a cop, not a murderer." Brian blinked, shook his head, and released his grip on the trigger. He realized he'd come within a second of becoming just like the stalker. The awareness raised the hackles on his neck.

The stalker's wide-eyed expression eased. The corners of his mouth rose into a defiant grin. "Don't have it in you, do you, Fogarty?" He shook his head. "You won't live to regret it."

"Who hired you?" Brian bellowed.

The stalker began to laugh. It was a deep guttural laugh that carried through the woods like a moan in the dark.

Brian grabbed him by the collar and pulled him close. "I want to know who hired you or I swear . . . "

He stopped. From behind him, he heard the same low thunder that had caught his attention earlier. But as it drew nearer, it no longer sounded like thunder, it sounded like the rattle of a worn out front end. When he turned to investigate, he could see a Jeep Wrangler rattling down the drive followed closely by a red and white ambulance. A moment later the vehicles stopped and a young, uniformed officer climbed out of the jeep with his gun drawn and rushed to Brian's side. Behind the officer, two men in white uniforms jumped from the ambulance and rushed to the back of the vehicle.

Brian clenched his teeth and lowered his face until it was inches from the stalkers. "You're going away for a very long time."

The stalker shook his head. "It will never come to that."

With his fist still grasping the man's shirt, Brian flipped him over onto his stomach and pulled his hands behind his back. "You're under arrest," he began. "You have the right to remain silent . . . "

(23)

The small town of Saint Johns, Arizona was located roughly forty miles north of Greer and housed the area's only medical facility. The old building also doubled for the town meeting hall, county polling place, and on the first Saturday of every month, a ballroom for senior dances. Built in the 1920s of gray brick and mud, the structure looked like it belonged in an old Civil War movie. There were two carved, oak doors under a large arch rising high into the night air; an American flag, illuminated by a single spotlight, flapped noisily in the cool, evening breeze.

Brian sat in an uncomfortable chair in the hospital lobby sipping coffee and eating a stale doughnut he'd pilfered from the nurses' station. Christine was seated next to him, motionless, staring out a pair of floor-to-ceiling windows at a grouping of aspen trees, their leaves twisting and dancing in the breeze. Her hands were wrapped around a white hospital blanket; her mouth parted, periodically moving in silent conversation.

Brian was worried. He had seen posttraumatic stress before. It could pass within days or it might require years of therapy and last a lifetime. Sadness fell over him like an early morning fog. She had begged him numerous times to leave the force and go to work for Bob McKeever; but he loved being a policeman. It was all he'd ever wanted to do. Asking him to resign was like asking him to remove an appendage. It had been as much a part of him as his mind and body. But looking at her now, her blonde hair disheveled, her face sagging, her eyes dull and lifeless, his heart sank. Although his tenacity and stubbornness had served him well as a police officer, it occurred to him now that it had caused irrefutable damage to his marriage. His bottom lip quivered.

As a nurse passed by and flashed Brian a reassuring smile, the decision became clear. As soon as he finished things up here, he would take Christine home, drive to the station and turn in his resignation; and this time he would insist the captain accept it. He let out a deep sigh, reached out his hand and placed it on top of Christine's hand. Her hand was cold and unresponsive. The decision to resign may have come too late.

Off to his right, Brian heard the automatic double doors open. The sound of thunder and wind followed. Brian looked towards the door. When he spotted Sheriff Eddie Condolora waddling into the lobby, he couldn't help but grin.

The sheriff was a giant of a man. He stood six feet six, with broad shoulders and an expansive stomach that suggested years of overindulgence. His thighs were thick and bulky and shook when he walked. He wore his thinning gray hair in a buzz cut, and his face was weathered and lined. Looking around the room, he spotted Brian and Christine sitting against the far wall. He nodded his head, ran a hand across his pants leg, and waddled over.

Brian used the arms of the chair to lift himself to his feet. He reached out his hand. "Been a long time, Eddie. How you been?" Eddie's huge hand engulfed Brian's and tightened.

Despite the joy of seeing his old friend, Brian felt awkward. His friend had changed. And not just a little. He was roughly a hundred pounds heavier and seemed to have grown jowls since Brian had seen him last. His face seemed hardened; and his eyes, somehow sadder. Brian released his grip and glanced down at Eddie's massive stomach.

Eddie took note of Brian's interest and looked down at his stomach. "Well," he said, his hand rubbing his belly like he had just finished a meal. "Aside from getting fat on Millie's good cooking, I'm doing fine."

Brian nodded, waved a hand through the air. "Yeah, as I remember, Millie puts on a nice spread."

Eddie smiled, still rubbing his stomach. "That she does."

Brian turned and motioned towards Christine sitting slumped over in the chair staring straight ahead. "This is my wife, Christine."

Eddie took a step towards her and held out his hand. "Very nice to meet you."

Christine stared straight ahead and said nothing.

Eddie dropped his hand to his side, the lines on his face deepened. He raised his bushy eyebrows and looked at Brian inquisitively.

Brian felt ill at ease. The introduction had not gone well. But given the unusual circumstances, Christine's reaction was understandable. He glanced down the hall, feeling irritable that it was taking so long for someone to get around to seeing Christine, and spotted two doctors chatting and laughing in the hall. His first instinct was to storm down the hall, grab one of them by the collar and demand that he check on Christine's condition immediately. Instead, he put an arm around Eddie's shoulder and ushered him across the hall. They stopped next to a potted palm tree in desperate need of watering. "She's not handling it well, Eddie. I could use your help getting someone . . . "

Eddie held up a hand and pursed his lips. "I'll take care of it." He walked over to the nurses' station and talked to a robust nurse with bright red hair.

A moment later, the nurse came over with a wheelchair and stopped in front of Christine. In a soft, caring voice she said, "Come with me, dear. We'll get you cleaned up and have a doctor take a look at you."

Christine's unblinking eyes stared straight ahead. The nurse took Christine's arm and lifted her from the chair. When she was seated in the wheelchair and the leg rests were in place, the nurse pushed the chair down the hall and disappeared around a corner.

Eddie shuffled from foot to foot, put his hand to his mouth and coughed. Then he motioned to a pair of uncomfortable looking chairs in the waiting room. They walked into the room and sat down. A deep groan emanated from Eddie as he eased himself into the chair.

"She'll be all right," Eddie said, folding his hands and placing them on his stomach. "She's in shock right now. Nurse Brown is a fine, caring woman. She'll make sure Christine is taken good care of." He paused, glanced around the empty room. Then yelled at a passing nurse out in the hall, "Janie, how about getting us a couple cups of coffee?"

The nurse stopped, put her hands on her hips and bellowed, "Does this look like a restaurant, Eddie?"

He flashed her a big smile. "Come on, Janie. Give a fat man a break, would you?"

"Fat man, my fanny," she said. "You want some coffee you get off your fat you-know-what and get it yourself. The exercise will do you good." With that, she stormed off down the hall, mumbling.

Eddie looked at Brian with large pleading eyes.

Brian sighed. "Where's the coffee machine? I'll get it. I can't stand to see a grown man whine."

"I knew there was a reason I always liked you," Eddie said as he raised a large finger and pointed down the hall. "On the left, just past the nurses' station."

As Brian went for the coffee, he remembered when he and Eddie had first met. It was during the homecoming game his freshman year in high school. Eddie was a senior and played right guard on the varsity football squad. His outstanding performance had attracted the attention of several college scouts. After graduation, Eddie moved to Tempe and attended A.S.U. on a football scholarship. Unfortunately for Eddie, he blew out his knee in the first game of the season and lost his scholarship.

Penniless and unemployed, he returned to Greer and took a job at the hardware store. A year later, he ran for county sheriff and had held the office ever since.

In the years that followed their initial meeting, Brian and Eddie's friendship deepened. They played on city softball teams, attended football games, hiked and hunted together. One night, at Eddie's insistence, Brian decided to ride along with Eddie on one of his shifts. As the night progressed, Brian found himself enjoying it. There was a thrill to it that he did not understand at the time. Perhaps it was the danger. Perhaps the respect the badge commanded. Or maybe it was the power. Whatever the reason, thanks to Eddie Condolora, Brian had found his calling.

After high school, Brian had moved to Phoenix and attended the police academy. During his schooling, he met and fell in love with Christine. After graduation, Eddie contacted Brian and offered him a position with the county sheriff's department. Reluctantly, Brian turned it down, stating he'd fallen in love with a beautiful woman in Phoenix and she was unwilling to leave the big city. Several odd jobs later, Brian was hired by the Scottsdale police force. He and Eddie had kept in touch over the years through letters, Christmas cards and phone calls.

When Brian came back, he handed Eddie a cup of coffee and sat down.

Eddie looked at the coffee, raised his eyebrows and said, "No cream?"

Brian wrapped his hands around the warm Styrofoam cup, breathed in the warm aroma, and eased back in his chair. "Don't push your luck, Eddie."

Eddie looked at the coffee, back to Brian and then the coffee again. He took a sip, winced and said, "So what happened out there? Billy was a little vague on the details."

Brian took a large pull on the coffee. The liquid warmed his chest and stomach. He considered the question. "Well," he began. "I've been feeling a little fried lately. I decided to take some time off. The cabin sounded like the perfect place to relax.

On the way up yesterday, I ran into Pete by the river. He had a bunch of trout and we all decided to help him eat it. He came over last night." Brian felt his throat closing up. He took another sip of coffee. Clearing his throat he continued. "We had a real nice dinner and spent most of the night reminiscing. Pete crashed on the couch and Christine and I went to bed. I woke up in the morning to a gunshot. When I peeked through the bedroom door, I saw Pete on the floor with this guy kneeling over him. I knew Pete was dead. There was blood everywhere."

Brian took a sip of coffee and frowned. He pointed to Eddie's hands. "Aren't you going to write any of this down?"

Eddie shook his head, raised a large finger to his temple and said, "Photographic memory."

A burst of air sputtered through Brian's lips. "Right."

Out in the hall, Brian observed a thin man in a flimsy hospital gown pushing a wheeled chrome rod down the corridor. Small plastic tubes ran from his right arm into a clear bottle attached to the rod. In his right hand, he carried a large bag containing a yellow liquid. When he reached the end, he turned around slowly and started back the way he came.

"Go on," Eddie said.

Brian sipped his coffee. It felt good on his throat. "Then we went out the window. The guy shot at us as we ran for the woods. We worked our way down to the river and then to Old Man Murphy's cabin." Brian paused. "He still alive?"

"Old Man Murphy?" Eddie asked.

"Yeah."

Eddie pursed his lips and shook his head. "No. He passed on about six years ago. Heart attack."

"Anyway," Brian continued. "We changed clothes at the cabin. I figured I'd either double back to see about Pete or we'd head for the highway. But we didn't have time. The guy showed up at Old Man Murphy's and we lit out through the woods. He cornered us near that old beaver pond."

"Collie's Pond?" Eddie said.

"Yeah. We were cornered, no place to go. I couldn't think of anything else to do so I hid Christine inside the beaver lodge while I led him away."

Eddie snorted. "Amazing."

"It worked, too. I led him away and Christine got back to Old Man Murphy's cabin. When I lost him, I doubled back and found her. Then we headed for the highway."

Eddie sat forward. "This is where I get a little confused. You hitched a ride in Red Billing's old pickup. But you got out and went after the guy. Why is that?"

Brian shook his head. That was a good question. "I thought if I didn't stop him, he'd get away. I didn't think I had time to go into town, get you, and get back out there before he got away."

Eddie put his index finger across his lips and squinted his eyes. "Curious," he said.

"Look," Brian said. "All I know for sure is that someone wants me dead. And as much as I hate to admit it, I don't have a clue as to who it is." He paused, looked into Eddie's bright eyes.

Eddie took another sip of coffee. "I had the ambulance driver take the guy's prints on the way to the hospital. I sent them out over the wire just before I came over here. We should hear something soon."

"Good," Brian said. "It always helps to put a name with a face. And once we find out who he is, we have a place to start looking for the person that hired him."

Brian sipped his coffee, cleared his throat. "What about Pete?"

Eddie shook his head.

Brian took another sip of coffee. It bit at the back of his throat as he choked back the acid churning in his stomach.

"We've already notified Angie at her mother's house in Albuquerque," Eddie said. "She's going to drive back tomorrow."

"I'll stay until she gets back and make sure she's okay."

"You need to take care of your little lady," Eddie said. "Angie has lots of friends here. She'll be fine." He set his empty coffee cup on an end table next to the chair and stood up. He cleared his throat. "So how's the big city treating you? You really like it down there in all the traffic and smog?"

Brian shook his head. "Not at all, Eddie. I miss the mountains and friendly, familiar faces. But Christine likes the city. She has a good job. She's in real estate. Does pretty well. She really seems to thrive on the challenge." He didn't want to say more. The topic was an old one, and a sore one.

"Well," Eddie said as he turned to leave. "If you ever change your mind about working for us, you know where I am." He chuckled. "I'm getting too fat for this job. Somebody's going to have to take over for me in the not-too-distant future. And while my deputy, Billy Waller, would be the obvious successor, I just don't think he's up to the job."

Brian frowned, recalling the officer that had shown up at the cabin and taken Jake Leighton into custody. "Oh, I don't know, he seemed competent enough to me out at the cabin."

"He does all right," Eddie said. "But he lacks experience. He's only been on the job for eighteen months." He paused, obviously searching for the right words. "I guess what concerns me most is his decision making. He doesn't always make sound choices."

Brian looked around, a thin line creasing his forehead. "Didn't you station him outside Leighton's room?"

"He'll be fine. If you're worried about Leighton slipping out of here, don't. I told Billy to guard that door with his life. I told the hospital staff to keep Leighton restrained and to use caution when approaching. And I had them put him on the second floor in the back. There's no way he could get out of this hospital unless he jumps out the window . . . and the fall would probably kill him, or at least break a leg."

"I hope you're right," Brian said. "I've had about all this guy I can handle for one lifetime."

There was a sudden rumble and Eddie rubbed his stomach. "Hey, I'm hungry." He put a huge arm around Brian. "Come on. I'm buyin'."

"I don't think I should leave while Christine's . . ."

"Oh, don't be silly. She'll be fine. We'll be back long before they're done with her."

Eddie hollered over to Nurse Brown, "We'll be at the diner, Martha, if anybody needs us."

"You sure Billy's got a handle on things?" Brian asked. "I'd sure hate to . . ."

"Oh, I don't think you'll have to worry about Jake Leighton anymore. He's in my territory now."

While they ate, Brian went over his story again. Eddie filled out his report and set it aside. With the official business out of the way, they began to discuss old times and Brian found himself enjoying Eddie's company the way he had so many years ago. Eddie was a fun-loving but serious guy with a heart as big as his stomach. Throughout the course of the meal, several people from Brian's past stopped by the table and inquired into his activities and seemed glad to see him.

Christine was sitting in the hospital lobby reading a magazine when Brian and Eddie walked through the main entrance. Nurse Brown sat beside her.

"So how's my girl?" Brian asked, placing a hand on Christine's shoulder.

Christine looked up; her eyes were a little brighter.

"She's been through a lot," Martha said, patting Christine's leg. "But she's going to be just fine."

Christine looked at Eddie. "You must be Eddie Condolora?"

Eddie stepped forward and held out his hand. "Yes, ma'am. That would be me."

Christine took his hand and shook it. "Christine Fogarty. Very nice to meet you."

"I'm glad you're feeling better," Eddie said, retracting his hand. "I know Brian's been very worried."

She forced a smile and looked up a Brian with big droopy eyes.

"Well," Brian said, turning to Eddie. "Unless you need me for anything else, I think I'll take Christine home now."

"I think we have everything under control. You head back to Phoenix and have your captain call me. We'll work out the details as to how to handle jurisdiction."

Brian sighed. One portion of the puzzle was solved. The guy was in custody and no longer a danger. Now he could set his sights on who hired the guy . . . and why. That would probably prove to be a greater challenge.

He helped Christine to her feet, thanked Eddie and Nurse Brown and walked out of the hospital.

On the road out of town, Brian observed the sun sinking into the western sky. Transparent clouds encircled an orange, flickering ball. Beams of yellow light stretched towards the sky, dissecting the sparse cloud cover.

After picking up their belongings at the cabin, Brian drove down the highway listening to the constant drone of tires against blacktop and Christine's rhythmic breathing as she slept. He, too, was exhausted. Sleep would be a welcome companion when they arrived home. His eyes burned as he struggled to remain awake. He cracked the window and let the cool air caress his face.

As he drove, a nagging feeling kept seeping into his consciousness and screaming for recognition. It lingered in the shadows as he struggled to bring it into focus. It was the answer. He knew it. All he had to do was concentrate. But he was too tired. Thoughts darted through his mind in fragments, confusing and frustrating him. Perhaps after some sleep, he would think about it some more and the answer would present itself. He would have to wait and see.

(24)

Jake Leighton awakened to a semi-dark room. The smells of antiseptic and sickness filled the air. A TV blared somewhere in the distance. Through the window he could see a sky painted in soft mauve with streaks of yellow darting among the ever-changing cloud formations. Multi-colored trees swayed with the wind while gold, rust and yellow leaves swirled in the breeze.

The door to the room was open slightly, a thin line of bright light shown through the crack and stretched across the floor. Inaudible voices mumbled in the hall. Soft-soled shoes squeaked up and down the corridor outside the door. In the distance, he could hear a woman laughing.

His head was bandaged. An IV bottle stood next to the bed with a tube leading down into his arm. The room seemed chilly despite the stack of blankets piled on top of him. When he moved his head it felt as though it would explode. He clamped his eyes shut and rubbed his forehead.

Ignoring the pain, he glanced around the room. His clothes were nowhere in sight. That figured. He eased back the blankets and sat up. Pain shot down his back and shoulders. He muffled a groan. This was not going to be easy.

Once the pain had dulled, he removed the needle from his arm, placed a piece of tissue paper over the hole, and clamped it tight with his arm. He placed both feet on the cold tile floor and felt his body tighten. He moved cautiously across the floor, pacing like an expectant father, until he regained a certain steadiness in his legs. He would need all his strength if he were to get out of there.

Creeping close to the door, he peered out though the crack. Only a short expanse of hallway was visible from his vantage point, but all seemed quiet, except for a constant drone of voices from down the hall. Then Jake saw the tip of a polished black boot.

He hobbled back across the floor to the window and checked the latch. It was open. Then he peered outside. He could see the street below and realized he was at least on the second story. The tops of buildings were silver with numerous vents, each building with it's own large, metal heat pump. He lifted the window carefully and peered out onto a narrow ledge, occupied by several pigeons and covered with droppings. The ledge ran across the length of the building but seemed to dead end about twenty feet from the last window on his left. He swung his head around and could see that the ledge stopped on the other side of his own window. A thin, drainpipe ran down the side of the building into a grated drain at the edge of the parking lot. This was not going to work. He'd kill himself on the flimsy pipe; and with nothing to grasp, the ledge was too narrow to make it to the next room.

Then he heard footsteps and voices just outside the door. He closed the window, hurried to the bed and crawled in, the pain in his shoulder and back making each step a new experience in pain. Just as he pulled the cover up to his chin, the door swung open. Light filled the room with the flick of a switch.

"Good evening," the nurse said. She was a young woman, tall with a broad smile. Her hair was the color of honey and was pulled back with a green bow. As she drew near, Jake could see her eyes were a startling green. Her nametag read: ASHLEY REEVES.

A uniformed officer loomed in the doorway, his dark figure silhouetted against the bright hallway. Although he could not make out the man's facial features, Jake had no doubt his every move was being scrutinized.

Nurse Reeves placed a tray of food on the portable table, rolled it close to the bed, and unfolded the silverware from a green, cloth napkin. Then she walked to the far side of the bed and poured some water from a plastic pitcher into a tan plastic cup.

"Dinner time already," Jake said, smiling. "My how time flies when you're having fun."

Ashley Reeve's smile vanished. She fidgeted nervously and bit her lower lip. Then she frowned and said, "You removed your IV. You shouldn't have done that."

The guard stepped into the room and the door swung closed behind him.

Jake grabbed Nurse Reeves around the neck with his good arm and pulled her to him, clamping his hand across her mouth. Pain shot through his arm like a jolt of electricity. For a moment he felt himself begin to lose consciousness, dark patches danced into view, mixing with flashes of white light. He shook it off, struggling to remain alert. Then with his good hand free, he snatched up the table knife from the tray and pressed it to the woman's neck.

The guard stopped, his surprised features now clear from the overhead lights. He held up both hands, palms showing. "Take it easy, pal. No one needs to get hurt." At the same time, his right hand eased down towards a revolver on his side.

"I wouldn't if I were you," Jake said, his usual soft voice barely audible over Nurse Reeves muffled sobbing. "This knife is not very sharp, but given enough force, it will slice her throat quite nicely." He smiled, nodded, and pursed his lips. "It's your decision."

"Okay, okay," the guard said, pulling his hands away from his weapon. "You'll never make it out of here. Don't make matters worse."

"Standard line, officer. I would have expected more under the circumstances."

The officer shrugged. "What do we do now?"

"First thing you do is unbuckle your gun belt, drop it to the floor and slide it over to me with your foot."

The guard shook his head. "I can't do that."

Jake pressed the knife hard into Nurse Reeve's skin. She gasped. The serrated blades began to flow red. Jake glared at the officer, a deep crease across his forehead. "I've got nothing to lose here."

Nurse Reeve's body stiffened. She continued to sob beneath Jake's huge hand. He pulled her closer and pressed the knife harder. Blood began to flow more freely. "I don't want to hurt you darlin'," Jake said. "Everything rides on our friend's next move."

Nurse Reeves flashed the officer a pleading expression. Jake smiled. That was exactly what he needed.

"Okay," the officer said. "Just don't hurt her." He eased both hands down and unbuckled his belt. With one hand, he lowered it to the floor.

"Now," Jake said. "Kick it over to me."

The guard did as he was told. The gun belt came to rest near Jake's left foot. With the nurse still tight in his grasp, leaned over, dropped the knife to the floor and snatched the revolver from it's holster.

Inside, Jake was glowing. The sense of power was stimulating. He noticed Nurse Reeve's hair against the side of his face. It felt soft and silky and smelled sweet. Her body was firm and well conditioned. Her sobbing and hot breath against his hand aroused him. Under different circumstances, he might be inclined to take advantage of the situation. But, unfortunately, now was not the time.

Jake leaned close to her ear. "Now, Ashley." He kept his voice calm and reassuring, the way a father would talk to a child. "Listen very carefully to me. If you don't want to leave this hospital in a bag, do exactly as I say. Do you understand?"

Nurse Reeves nodded, her wide green eyes shimmering with tears.

"I'm going to take my hand off your mouth now. If you scream, it will be the last thing you ever do. You understand?"

Ashley Reeves nodded. Perspiration ran down her face and trickled through Jake's fingers.

"Now what?" the cop asked. His tone said he was not pleased.

"Now you take your handcuffs, toss them on the bed and strip."

"What?" The guard's pale face was lined and distorted.

A sadistic grin crossed Jake's face. He scratched the side of his face with the gun barrel. Then he ran his tongue down the barrel like a kid licking a frozen treat. "Do it," Jake said firmly.

"You're insane," the guard said. He unfastened his handcuffs, placed them on the bed and disrobed down to a pair of red and blue striped boxers and a crew neck T-shirt."

Jake muffled a laugh. "Not much for fashion, are we?"

"Screw you," the guard said.

Jake shook his head and made a clicking sound through his teeth. "Now, now, officer. Is that anyway to talk in front of a lady?"

With Ashley Reeves in tow, Jake eased over to the window and opened it. Cold air engulfed him. He waved his gun towards the officer and then pointed to the windowsill. "You first."

The guard marched to the window, flashed Jake an evil glance, and started to climb through.

Just as he ducked his head to go under the raised glass frame, Jake brought the gun down across the back of his head. The officer's knees buckled but he stayed erect. Then he turned and looked at Jake.

"That's for being young and stupid," Jake said.

With his hand pressed against his head, the officer climbed through the window.

Jake put his mouth to Ashley's ear, her scent tantalizing him. "Your turn, darlin'. And don't forget what I told you. Not a sound. Or you'll force me to do something I really don't want to do. I would hate to mess up that pretty face." He held the gun to her temple, jerked his head towards the open window. Her body shaking, Ashley Reeves climbed through the window and onto the ledge.

Jake went to the bed, picked up the handcuffs and passed them through the window to the officer. "Clamp one end around your wrist, then reach around the drain pipe and clamp the other end around Ashley's wrist."

Reluctantly, the officer complied.

Jake pulled on the officer's uniform. It was a little large but it would have to do.

"I really wish I could be here to see the sheriff's face when he hears of this," Jake said. "I don't think you'll ever live this down, big fella." Jake began to laugh. "Now I wouldn't make too much racket for at least a little while. I'd hate to have to shoot my way out of here. A lot of people would get hurt. And I know you two wouldn't want that on your conscience, now would you?"

He smiled and closed the window. He holstered the revolver, pulled on the ball cap with the Deputy Sheriff emblem, swung open the door and stepped into the hall.

As natural as rain, Jake walked down the corridor, down the stairs to the main floor, through the lobby and out the front doors. He scanned the parking lot for a suitable car; but the best he could find was a green Chevy blazer in the far lot. He broke the window, cracked the plastic plate on the steering column, stuck the screwdriver he found on the officer's key ring into the small vertical slot and fired up the engine. *If you're going to steal a car*, he thought, *a Chevrolet was always your best bet.* He climbed in and drove off down the highway as naturally as if he were heading off to work. But as he drove, he thought about Brian. This was far from over.

* * * * *

Sheriff Eddie Condolora stood six inches from Deputy Billy Waller's face. Blue veins bulged on his red forehead. "What the hell happened, Billy? Didn't I tell you to watch him? And wasn't he supposed to be restrained? Why wasn't he? And whose bright idea was it to give the guy a knife with his meal? And you gave him your gun. Damn it, Billy, you never give up your gun. Never."

"I didn't think . . ."

"That's just it, Billy. You don't think."

Sheriff Condolora spun around and looked out the window. "I can't believe this." Then he spun back around and faced Billy, seething. "I want your badge and gun, Billy. You're going to get yourself or somebody else killed, and I won't have that on my conscience."

"But Uncle Ed, Mom will . . ."

"I'll deal with your mom, Billy. I want your badge and gun. Right now."

(25)

Shortly after midnight, Brian pulled the car into his driveway and turned off the engine. He found the garage door opener on the dash, pushed the button and listened to the door rattle and squawk its way open.

Christine stirred, opened her eyes and looked around. "Are we home?"

"Yup. Home sweet home."

Christine stretched and yawned. She opened the door and climbed out of the car. "Let's unload in the morning, okay? I don't feel like it tonight." Running her hand through her hair, she yawned again, slammed the door, and shuffled off towards the house.

Brian sat with his wrists draped across the steering wheel and watched Christine amble though the garage and enter the house through the side door. He sighed heavily and thought about unloading the car. It was the last thing he wanted to do after the long drive. But the thought of facing it in the morning held less appeal. So he climbed out of the car, unpacked the gear — including the two flat tires the Greer Tire Center had replaced after the car had been towed in from the cabin — and put everything away. Inside, he put the groceries that hadn't spoiled into the refrigerator and the dry goods in the cabinet, and grabbed a cold Coors.

Sitting in the familiar surroundings of his kitchen, listening to the refrigerator buzz and the clock above the stove hum, the events of the past two days seemed distant and blurry. But the cuts and bruises on his aching body brought the reality crashing home. In the morning he would check on Elaine and then head for the station to see if anything had developed in his absence; and, more importantly, if they had discovered the identity of his assailant. He would also begin the arduous task of tracking down the person who had hired someone to kill him, and trying to find out why. As he thought about his resignation, he decided to postpone it for a few days to give himself time to investigate.

The next morning he awakened refreshed. He made a pot of coffee, drank two cups and downed an English muffin. With Christine and Eric still sleeping, Brian jotted a note and left it on the kitchen table. The note read:

> Honey,
> Doing some errands. Back
> in a few hours. Thought I
> would take you to Red Lobster
> for lunch if you feel
> up to it. Have a great day.
> Love you. Brian.

Elaine's apartment was a short seven-minute drive from the house. Brian pulled into the parking lot and took an open spot under the shade of a rusty metal awning. As he climbed out of the car and headed for the buildings, he spotted two young boys playing basketball in a makeshift court at the far end of the parking lot. He smiled, remembering happier times.

He entered the apartment and was greeted with the kind of energetic enthusiasm that only Elaine seemed to be able to muster. After she let out an ear-numbing scream, she leaped from the sofa and into Brian's arms; he felt his back compact with the strain.

"You back," Elaine said. "I missed you."

"I missed you, too, sweetie." He patted her gently on the back and felt her grip relax.

Elaine wiggled out of his grasp, took two steps back and patted her hand at the side of her head. "You like my new hair? It's a no muss, no fuss hairstyle. Melissa gave me a perm."

Brian took a step back, folded his arms across his chest, and inspected her perm. His first thought was that she looked a little like a five foot tall Orphan Annie, but the sparkle in her eyes made her as lovely as any girl he'd ever seen. "It's very pretty. I like it very much."

Melissa came out of the bedroom, her smile as radiant as the brightest summer sky. She walked across the room and plopped down on the sofa; Elaine joined her and tucked her feet under her bottom.

"You're back early," Melissa said, pulling her knees up to her chest and placing her chin on her knees. "I thought you weren't coming back for another couple of days?"

Not wishing to burden either of them with the details, Brian shrugged. "We changed our minds. So what's been happening around here?"

"We've been having fun," Melissa said.

"Yeah," Elaine said. "We going to the park." She clapped her hands together and rocked back and forth on the sofa.

"That sounds good," Brian said, enjoying Elaine's enthusiasm. "I think I might join you. A quiet stroll through the park might be nice."

Elaine jumped up and wrapped her arms around Brian's neck. "Yeah. You coming to the park with us. I'll get my hat." With that, she ran out of the room and bounded down the hall.

Melissa was shaking her head and smiling. Her big sparkling eyes settled on Brian. "You did it now."

"What?" Brian asked. "What did I do?"

"You can't get out of it now. You've committed yourself."

Brian put his hands on his hips and cocked his head to one side. "Would you stop toying with me and tell me what you're talking about?"

"Amusement park, Brian. It's Saturday. We are going to the amusement park at Encanto."

"Oh no." Brian dropped his hands to his side. "I made plans to take Christine to lunch. And after that, I have a busy day planned."

Melissa raised her eyebrows and shook her head. "I don't envy you right now." She placed a hand over her mouth and stifled a grin.

Brian thought she was enjoying this far too much, but she did look awfully adorable doing it.

Elaine came back into the room wearing a pair of white shorts, a Hawaiian shirt and a blue, wide brim hat. "I'm ready. I want to ride the roller coaster first. I like that one the best. Then I'm going to buy the biggest cotton candy they have."

Brian looked at his watch. It was nine-thirty. The likelihood of driving across town, spending time at the park and making it back in time to have lunch with Christine, was not very good. He had to make a choice. As he stared into Elaine's glowing eyes, there seemed to be only one choice, he could only hope Christine would understand.

"Well," Elaine said. "What are we waiting for? We're burning daylight."

Brian laughed and gave Melissa his best look of disapproval. "You two have been watching old John Wayne movies, haven't you?"

Elaine raised a fist in the air and said, "The Duke rules." She marched over to Melissa and gave her a high five, then turned back to Brian. "Let's go."

"I have to make a quick phone call before we leave," Brian said.

"Okay," Melissa said, as she rocked herself off the couch. "I'll get my things and we'll be ready to go."

Elaine jumped up and down in place.

Brian got his home answering machine and left a message that he wouldn't be able to make their lunch date and suggested they make it dinner instead. When he hung up, Elaine and Melissa were standing by the front door waiting for him.

Elaine clapped her hands. "Lets go."

As they walked across the parking lot and headed for the car, Brian spotted the same black Cadillac that had followed him into the complex two days earlier. It was parked several spaces down beside a white pick-up with a camper shell. He frowned and pretended to examine the sky.

After they reached the car and everyone had piled in, Brian pulled out of the parking space and drove slowly past the Cadillac. Someone was seated in the driver's seat holding a newspaper at face level. If it hadn't been for his passengers, Brian would have stopped, marched up to the driver and confronted him . . . or her. However, given the circumstances, he opted for a mental note of the license number and planned on calling it in later. As he pulled out of the parking lot, he checked his rearview mirror for the Caddy; it remained parked.

Traffic was unusually heavy for a Saturday so Brian opted for the surface streets instead of the freeway. As he drove through the dilapidated buildings of central Phoenix with Elaine and Melissa chatting about their favorite carnival rides, Brian tossed around an array of scenarios that made his mind swim. It seemed probable the black Cadillac and the attempt on his life would be connected. When the time was right, he would run the plate and pay a visit to the owner.

Or maybe there was no relationship at all. Perhaps it was something altogether different. Maybe the person wasn't following Brian at all, but keeping an eye on Melissa. She had hinted at a failed relationship that had turned violent. Perhaps her former partner was stalking her. Or maybe the interest lay with Elaine. But who would be watching her? And why?

All these questions rambling around in his mind made him feel a little dizzy as he pulled into the massive expanse of black-top serving as the parking lot for Encanto Park. Brian shook them off and parked. They climbed out of the car and headed for a small corner of the park where the amusement rides were awaiting their arrival.

(26)

Brian pulled into the parking lot of Elaine's apartment complex and took a spot next to an old Ford. The site was comprised of eight, two-story stucco buildings sprawled across five acres of south Scottsdale real estate. Across from the rental office, near the center of the complex, was a greenbelt area consisting of a community pool, a shuffleboard area, several picnic tables with soot-encrusted barbeques, and a laundromat with six washers and six dryers. Potholes dotted the asphalt parking lot like gopher holes. Oleander bushes and date palms lined the parking area and the adjacent street. When Brian released the seat belt and popped open the car door, he could hear the raised voices of children coming from the pool area. He surveyed the lot for the Caddy, but it was nowhere in sight.

Breathing a sigh of relief, he awakened the girls who had slept the entire ride home, gathered their prizes and treasures, including a large, stuffed pink koala bear Elaine had won by tossing a basketball through a small hoop five times in a row, and climbed out into the midday heat.

Still dazed from sleep, the girls walked across the parking lot in silence with Brian close behind. Once inside, Brian turned to Melissa. "Would you mind staying for a couple more days? I'm going to be rather busy for the next few days and I don't want Elaine to be alone."

Melissa put a hand over her mouth, yawned and shrugged her shoulders. "Sure. I was planning on being here for the whole week anyway. Besides, I promised Elaine I would take her to the zoo tomorrow. She wants to take some pictures of the animals."

"That sounds great. I really appreciate it."

After hugging the girls and saying goodbye, Brian headed for the station and found himself stopped in heavy traffic wondering whom the captain had assigned to the case. He hoped it would be Marion Bantor. She was not only his friend and colleague, she was the best detective in the precinct, and she would be willing to work with Brian and keep him informed of any developments.

Brian had no doubt that Eddie Condolora had contacted the station with the information on his attacker and had filed a report as to the events at the cabin. And if Marion had indeed been assigned the case, she would have pounced on it like a mongoose on a python.

With traffic stopped and nothing to do but wait, Brian picked up his cell phone and called dispatch. After he gave his name and badge number, he asked the woman to run the license number of the black Caddy.

"One moment, please," the woman said in a nasal voice and the line went quiet.

Traffic crept forward about a hundred yards then stopped again. A man in a black Lexus was mouthing silent blurbs behind closed windows. The car in front of him was emitting a bone rattling base sound that shook the windows of Brian's worn out Taurus. Brian shook his head. It was not good to be back in the city.

"The car is registered to a Jerry Travers," the woman said when she came back on the line.

"Do you have an address?" Brian asked. He rolled the name around trying to place it. Somewhere in the recesses of his mind, the name Jerry Travers was ringing a faint bell.

The dispatcher gave him an address in an upscale neighborhood in north Scottsdale. Brian wrote it down in a small spiral notebook he kept in his shirt pocket, thanked the woman and signed off.

It had taken forty-five minutes to make the usual twenty-minute drive to the station. He parked in the underground lot, took the stairs to the second floor and went to Marion's desk. Unfortunately, the only person he found was Nick Carey sitting at his adjoining desk glancing though the latest issue of HUSTLER. He had on an orange shirt and matching tie loosened at the collar and black dress slacks. His face was smooth and shiny. The tip of his tongue protruded from the corner of his mouth. As Brian approached, Nick stuffed the magazine in his bottom drawer, wrinkled his nose, and looked at Brian through narrowed eyes.

"What are you doing here?" Nick asked.

Of all the people Brian knew, he cared for Nick Carey the least. The arrogance of the man was far more reaching than mere confidence. It seemed ingrained in him. His presence made Brian uncomfortable.

"I'm fine, Nick," Brian said. "Thanks for asking."

Nick Carey pursed his lips, leaned back in his chair and folded his arms on his chest. "Don't be a smart ass. I asked you what you're doing here?"

"I'm looking for Detective Bantor." Brian looked at her desk and noticed a half empty glass of iced tea. "Is she around?"

"She's taking a break. And if you're wondering if we got assigned the case, the answer is yes; but not without some protest on my part. We're homicide detectives, not babysitters."

Brian fought back the urge to smile. If he knew Marion, the moment she heard what had happened, she would have marched into the captain's office and demanded the case. From somewhere deep inside, in a place he kept pushed back and hidden from the rest of the world, the thought of Marion coming to his rescue pleased him. It was almost a counter culture reaction, but being politically correct had never been one of his great concerns.

Nick unfolded his arms, sat forward in his chair and placed his elbows on the top of the desk. He looked up at Brian with pure contempt. "If you didn't have your head buried up the captain's butt, you wouldn't be getting the V.I.P. treatment."

Brian shook his head. "You are a classless and vulgar man, Nick. I think one day someone will have to teach you some manners."

Nick leaped to his feet. His chair tumbled over backwards sending a loud crash through the station. He stuck his chest and chin out in Brian's direction. "You think you're the one to do it?"

"I think it will come to that, but not here and not now. But the time will come."

Nick stood glaring at Brian, veins bulging from his forehead like waterlogged worms. "Anytime, Fogarty. Anytime."

Brian could recall his dislike for Nick Carey the first time he laid eyes on him. It had been three years earlier when Marion's old partner, Billy O'Hara, took early retirement due to departmental cutbacks. Nick had transferred in from Missing Persons with a serious chip on his shoulder and immediately set his sights on Marion. When his advances were thwarted and he learned her interest was focused elsewhere, he turned his anger on what he must have considered the competition.

There are few secrets in a squad room. It's likened to a small town; everybody knows everybody's business. And if an officer isn't informed of the particulars the moment he or she transfers in, the dirt filters in slowly in bits and pieces until the whole puzzle fits together and they have something to discuss over morning coffee. It's what makes a good cop; they simply hate secrets.

It was common knowledge throughout the precinct that Marion held Brian in the highest regard—anyone who called himself a detective could see it in the way Marion reacted when Brian came into the room. And it hadn't gone unnoticed by Brian either. At first it made him uneasy. Later, when he and Christine lost Brian Junior and started looking for someone to blame, Marion's attentions seemed somehow soothing in a time when he needed someone. He would have been lying if he denied the thought of sleeping with Marion had never crossed his mind, because it had, on several occasions. But he pushed those thoughts back into the recesses of his mind and continued his dealings with Marion in a professional manner. Still, from time to time, he found himself glancing her way in the hope of catching the light just right across her light brown hair.

Brian heard footsteps coming up behind him. When he turned around, he found himself face to face with Marion Bantor. She wore a dark blue, pinstriped suit, a white blouse and black pumps. Her face was devoid of make-up and her fine brown hair moved with the breeze from the overhead fans.

"So," Marion said, removing her jacket and placing it on the back of her desk chair. "Are you two playing nice?"

The sarcasm in her voice did not go unnoticed. Brian felt a little ashamed, like a little boy caught pilfering a piece of cake before dinner.

"I'm going to get some coffee," Nick said. He walked away, storming past the other detectives in the room, his shoulders never wavering or yielding.

After Nick was out of earshot, Brian turned to Marion shaking his head. "How do you put up with that jerk?"

Marion sat down at her desk, cocked her head to one side. "He's a good cop, but I'll admit he can be a bit trying."

The conversation sounded familiar. They had discussed Nick Carey at great length more than once. Brian did not feel like going though it again. He decided to jump right to business. "You found out anything new?"

"Well, hello to you, too," Marion said. She leaned back in her chair, folded her arms across her chest, and pushed out her lower lip.

"Sorry." Brian sighed. "It's been a tough week."

Marion nodded her head, took a quick sip of iced tea. "I know. After the captain received the call from Sheriff Condolora, the news shot around the squad room like the flu. It must have been awful. Is Christine all right?"

The comment took Brian by surprise. Was Marion actually concerned for Christine's welfare? Or was she simply being polite? Perhaps she was genuinely upset. And why wouldn't she be? Any compassionate human being would have to sympathize with what he and Christine had been through. Brian shook his head. He felt confused. Then he noticed her watching him and feigned a smile.

Marion's brow wrinkled. "You don't have to look so shocked." She gazed around the room and then leaned towards Brian. "Just because I'm extremely fond of her husband doesn't mean I want any harm to come to her."

Brian was speechless. What was he supposed to say to that? He opted for silence. *Better to remain silent and be thought a fool, than to open your mouth and remove all doubt,* someone once said.

"Sorry. Sometimes I just do things for shock value," Marion confessed. "It's a weakness." She leaned back in her chair, her teeth gleaming in the soft glow of the fluorescent lights.

Brian shook his head. "You're never boring, Marion. I'll give you that."

As Marion's face turned a soft pink, she cleared her throat and picked up a file from the desk. "So, how is Christine handling things?"

Brian shrugged his shoulders, scratched the palm of his hand, and sat down on the edge of Marion's desk. "She's still in shock, but I think she'll be okay. I'm going to suggest she take the rest of the week off to rest."

"If I know you, you'll probably spoil her rotten."

Brian felt his face flush and decided to change the subject. "Have you seen Gabe around? I tried his house this morning from home but there was no answer. I wanted to talk to him."

"I heard he called in sick," Marion said, grabbing the computer mouse and clicking on the icon marked E-Mail. "But my guess is he picked up some wild girl last night and is so exhausted he can't get out of bed."

Brian laughed. "You have a good grasp for Gabe's weaknesses."

Still looking at the computer screen Marion said, "I'm a cop. It pays to be observant."

They both laughed.

From somewhere behind him, Brian heard the muffled voices of people talking behind closed doors. Someone picked up a telephone after the second ring. Footsteps pounded down the hall, maybe three people. The overhead lights buzzed. Through the window he could see the sun reflecting off the sidewalk and creating a rainbow of colors on the glass.

He fixed his eyes on Marion and noticed her small ears and the way her nose turned up at the end. Clearing his throat he said, "I understand you and Nick are in charge of the case."

Marion closed the e-mail and swiveled in her chair until she faced him. "I told you . . . news travels fast."

"Nick told me before you came in. I don't think he's overly pleased about it." The fact Nick Carey was not pleased about being assigned to the case somehow made it all the sweeter.

"He'll get over it."

Brian folded his hands across his lap. "So how did you end up with the case?"

"I asked for it." She inspected a loose thread on her sleeve and frowned.

Brian smiled and said nothing, but he was glad she did.

"I strongly urged the captain to let me handle it," Marion continued, as she opened the top drawer of her desk and removed a small pair of scissors. "I explained to him that he needed the best he had on this one and . . . " Her expansive grin widened and she held up her free hand. "Well, what could he say?"

Brian nodded his head as the corners of his mouth turned up. "At least Leighton is in custody. Before I left, Eddie told me he ran the guy's prints. Have you heard anything yet?

She clipped the loose thread, threw it in the wastebasket, returned the scissors to the drawer and closed it. "Yeah. His name is Jonathan Leighton. He goes by Jake. His address is in Manhattan, New York."

Brian pursed his lips. "Manhattan, huh? He must be good at what he does."

The phone on Marion's desk rang and she picked up the receiver. "Detective Bantor."

Brian watched Marion's face turn from a soft tan to pure white. He could feel his insides begin to churn. Whatever it was, it was not good.

Marion picked up a file from her desk and fumbled through it. She cleared her throat. "Okay. Thanks for calling, Captain."

After she had hung up the phone, she looked at Brian with a deep crease across her forehead. She looked almost . . . frightened.

"Something's wrong," Brian said. "What is it?"

"Something happened last night that complicates matters."

"Spit it out, Marion. What happened?"

She threw the file on the table. "Jake Leighton escaped from the hospital in Greer."

Brian felt his heart skip. His fist clenched tight and pressed against the side of his leg.

"Apparently, he overpowered a nurse and a deputy, got the deputy's gun and uniform, and walked right out the front door."

There was a long silence. A phone rang in the far corner of the room. Someone coughed. Brian felt nauseous.

"Oh, no," he said, his mind flashing to Christine. "I have to go."

Marion held up her hand as if reading Brian's mind. "That was the captain on the phone. Before he called me, he sent an officer over to your house to check on Christine. He's with her now. She's fine."

"Good." Brian sighed, relieved and thankful for the captain's quick and prudent action. His mind snapped back to business. "Now we need to issue an A.P.B. and find the S.O.B."

"Done. The captain's on top of it. If Leighton comes back to Phoenix, we'll have him within twenty-four hours, Brian. The whole city is looking for him. The captain is on the phone now calling all the other precincts to apply some pressure."

"That sounds like the captain."

"Yes, it does." Marion paused. She rubbed her finger across her lips and stared out into space.

Brian squinted, cocked his head to one side. "There's more, isn't there?"

Without looking at him Marion said, "The captain wants you to go home and stay there. He doesn't want you involved with the case. Says you're too close."

"Forget it. There's no way I'm staying out of this, Marion."

"I'm telling you what the captain said, Brian. That's all."

Brian eased back, released his clenched fist, and shook it down at his side to return the circulation. The last thing he wanted to do right now was alienate Marion. She would be his only friendly contact.

"The scuttlebutt around the squad room," Marion said, "is that the captain's heading for a breakdown." She paused, looked around the room. "He's drinking again."

Brian felt his head jerk back and his eyes widen. "Oh I can't believe that. He's been dry for what now . . . a year?"

"Give or take," Marion said. "I'm just telling you what I heard."

Brian shook his head. "Well I hope you're wrong."

"So do I."

They were quiet a moment. Brian thought of the ramifications for the captain if what he had just heard were true. He might be asked to resign, with or without his pension, depending on the board of inquiry's findings. Or he might be forced to step down and take a demotion. Maybe enter a voluntary detoxification center. Any one of the scenarios would cause a great deal of embarrassment to both the captain and the department. No matter how it played out, if the captain was drinking again, it was a no win situation.

Brian shook his head to clear his thoughts. "Leighton has to have a local residence of some kind: be it hotel, motel, house or condo. We need to find out where it is."

Marion blinked, came back from wherever her thoughts had taken her. "I don't imagine he'd be stupid enough to use his real name. He'd use an alias. But I'll get working on it right away."

They were quiet a moment. Feet shuffled through the squad room. Phones rang. Muffled conversations hung in the air. A nearby water cooler gurgled.

"I assume Eddie sent you the mug shots he took in Greer?" Brian asked a moment later.

Marion nodded. "According to the captain they went out on the wire a half hour ago."

"Good." Brian felt his fist tighten again and his foot pressing into the carpet. "I want this SOB behind bars, and I want to know who hired him. And when I find out, I'll take him down so fast it will seem like the aftermath of a tornado."

Brian realized his anger was getting the best of him. It was not something he enjoyed showing to the world. He forced a smile. "So who do you have in mind for the team?"

Marion leaned back in her chair and folded her hands in her lap. "I'll coordinate the operations here at the station; and I'll have Nick, Sam Newton and Bill Masters head up the groundwork."

Brian pursed his lips. Newton and Masters were good men, but the sound of Nick Carey's name sent an immediate jolt of annoyance wavering through his body.

"I know what you're thinking," Marion said, her palm raised awkwardly at her side.

"Sam and Bill are good men but . . ."

"Brian, Nick's a good cop."

"He's a jerk. I don't like the way he hovers around people. Have you ever looked into his eyes? There's something there that bothers me, but I can't quite put my finger on it. If I were you, I'd go straight to the captain and insist on a different partner."

A slow grin crossed Marion's face that gradually turned to an all out smile and broadened from ear to ear. Marion was beaming. "Why, Brian Fogarty, if I didn't know better, I'd say there was a touch of jealousy there."

"Don't be ridiculous," Brian scolded, feeling warmth flow to his face. "I just don't like the guy, that's all. He's odd."

Marion snorted. "Lots of people are odd, Brian."

"I just don't trust him, okay? Now let's drop it."

Brian felt uneasy. They had entered uncharted territory. So many emotions had engulfed him over the last few days he wasn't sure *what* he was feeling. In the midst of all the chaos, was he falling for Marion? While it was true she was more like him than Christine would ever be, in tune with his world and what goes along with it, Christine was his wife; Marion was not. And this was an undeniable fact he had best not forget.

"Brian," Marion said in a reassuring tone. "I can't believe that Jake Leighton would show up on your doorstep. He has to know we're on to him and would have every cop in the city looking for him. If he's as smart as we think he is, he will lay low. Maybe slip away quietly and disappear for a while."

"No," Brian said. "I don't think that's what he'll do. I think he'll come looking for me. Because of me, he can't ever show his face again. Every police force from Los Angeles to Boston is going to have his picture plastered on their bulletin boards. No, his career and his life as he knows it are over. And he's going to blame me. He's going to take this very personally. He's going to hunt me down and try to kill me. And this time it won't be simply for the money, but for revenge. He won't give up until he either succeeds or we find him and stop him."

"If that's true," Marion said. "Then he's more dangerous now than before."

"Exactly my point."

"We'll just have to find him first." Marion leaned forward and placed a hand on Brian's knee. "And we will, Brian. I'll ask the captain for more officers, overtime, stakeouts, whatever it takes."

Brian smiled at her, placed his hand on top of hers and patted it. "You're a good person, Marion."

Marion grinned. "It's about time you noticed."

(27)

Brian had no sooner climbed into his car and started the engine when his cell phone rang. It was Marion.

"Marion," Brian teased. "Long time no see."

"Listen, Records just dropped off a list of your past arrests. There might be something here. Can you come back to the station or do you want me to give it to you over the phone?"

Considering his recent confrontation with Nick, the last thing Brian wanted to do was go back to Marion's desk. He opted for a neutral site. "How about meeting me in the cafeteria? I'll buy you a cup of coffee."

"No way," Marion said. "You could plaster bricks with that stuff. Why don't we do something fast and easy . . . like Denny's? We could grab something to eat and go over the names."

"Denny's sounds fine but I'll just go for the coffee. I have dinner plans and don't want to spoil my appetite."

"I'll see you in ten minutes."

Brian hung up then dialed home. When the answering machine picked up, he left a short message that he would be home in an hour.

Fifteen minutes later, Marion and Brian were seated in a corner booth in the non-smoking section of Denny's. At the far end of the restaurant, two elderly men, wearing western shirts and ball caps, were seated at a long counter sipping coffee, smoking cigarettes and talking to a white haired waitress with bright red lipstick. Across the room, two youngsters clad in blue jeans and tie-dye T-shirts were seated on the same side of a large booth holding hands; both had streaks of orange running through their dark brown hair. A thin, wispy looking waitress methodically worked her way around the room filling salt and pepper shakers, ketchup bottles and sugar packets. The sound of rattling dishes and silverware filtered in from the kitchen along with the unmistakable aroma of charred meat.

"I don't know why they call this the non-smoking section," Marion said. "The smoking area is right on the other side of this half-wall without a partition or fans or anything. Besides, the whole place reeks of cigarettes."

Brian picked up his fork, inspected the tongs, and then wiped them with his napkin. "This was your idea, remember?"

"Yeah, yeah," Marion said. She laid a hand across the back of the booth and drummed her fingers on the vinyl.

"You want to go someplace else?"

"No. I'm short on time. This will be fine."

"Excuse me," Brian said to the waitress with a handful of sugar packets. "We'd like to order now."

"Ethel!" the young woman bellowed in the direction of the kitchen. "Table three's in a hurry!"

Brian and Marion exchanged an embarrassed glance just as a busty brunette with a round face and big lips emerged from the kitchen and sauntered over to the table. She pulled a pencil and order pad from inside her apron pouch and said, "What can I get you?"

"The B.L.T. good?" Marion asked.

The waitress shrugged. "Good as anything else."

After some deliberation, Marion went with the B.L.T. and an iced tea. Brian asked for coffee, black.

The waitress scribbled it on the pad and turned and walked away.

Marion removed a file from her briefcase and pulled several sheets of paper from the file. "The only names that seem remotely possible—and I emphasize remotely—are three recent parolees from Florence."

Brian slipped a notebook and pen from his pocket and placed them on the table. "Let me have the names."

The waitress came back with the drinks, plopped them on the table, turned around and hurried off toward the kitchen.

Marion squeezed some lemon into her tea, stirred it slowly as she leafed through the pages with her free hand and then emptied half the glass in one breath. She wiped her mouth with her napkin, stopped on the third page and looked up at Brian. "Does the name Jason Duffler ring a bell?"

Brian thought a moment, trying to put a face with the name. "Oh, yeah. He was a young kid, about twenty or twenty-one, very polite. I busted him for bringing in several pounds of pot from Mexico. Mexican dirt weed they used to call it. He had it stashed in a house just a couple blocks from city hall. Acted surprised when we arrested him, kept saying 'yes, sir' and 'no, sir' like he'd been brought up in a good family. But I never saw either of his parents at the trial. If memory serves, he got two to six for possession to sell."

Marion didn't look up from the paper. "Says here he served two and a half years of his sentence and was released about six weeks ago . . . give or take. Looks like his parole officer is Merle Rancor."

Brian wrote it all down. "Next."

"Next we have a young woman named Betty Applegate. She did a year and a half on a two to five for possession of drugs for sale and prostitution."

"I remember her, too. She was one of those girls you can't help but feel sorry for, a really rough childhood. Her mother had turned on to drugs early and became pregnant. The father left for parts unknown and then Betty's mom took up with a truck driver who moonlighted stealing cars for a south side chop shop to cover his hundred-dollar-a-day cocaine habit. The mother had Betty at County Hospital two weeks shy of her fourteenth birthday. Betty became a ward of the state after her mother went to prison for stabbing the boyfriend to death with a carving knife."

"Why did she kill him?" Marion asked.

Brian paused, cleared his throat. "She caught the boyfriend in bed with Betty. She was eleven at the time."

Marion clicked her tongue as a deep line formed on her brow. "I'd have given her a medal," she said, and continued to flip through the pages. After a moment she stopped, her lips moved slightly as she read. "What do you know? Rancor is her parole officer as well."

"Good," Brian said. "It will save time. Next."

Marion smiled. "If I didn't know better, I'd swear you were enjoying this."

"I wouldn't say I'm enjoying it. But I feel better if I'm doing something. All this hanging around waiting for Leighton to make the next move is a total mind game. It's driving me nuts. I need to be proactive."

Marion nodded. "I know what you mean." She perused a few more pages.

The waitress came back with the B.L.T., waited for Marion to clear a spot, and set the plate down. She stood back, one hand on her hip and looked at Brian. "You sure you don't want anything, honey? I could have the cook whip you up something special."

Brian felt his face flush. "I'm fine, thank you."

The waitress turned around, and with a deliberate sway to her hips, sashayed away.

Marion watched the show and shook her head. "She's working for her tip."

Brian held his hand to his mouth and rubbed it across his chin. "That woman's going to hurt herself."

"A chiropractor's dream," Marion agreed.

They were quiet while Marion ate. Brian observed her delicate and ladylike manners as she dabbed at the corners of her mouth after each bite of her sandwich. An uncomfortable feeling fell over him when he realized he was sitting alone in a booth with Marion Bantor. To the casual observer, it would look like they were an item. And what if someone from the precinct happened on the scene? It could easily start the rumors all over again. But at the moment, Brian was beyond caring. Marion was the only person he felt comfortable dealing with at the department. At least Marion was trying to help and for that he was thankful.

The restaurant began to fill up as early diners filtered in from the late afternoon heat. Dozens of separate conversations intermingled; the result was something of a low, constant whirr. From the kitchen, a bell clanged and someone said, "Order up." The frail looking waitress now scurried about placing paper napkins and silverware on the tables.

Brian downed the last of his coffee and motioned to the waitress for a refill. She ambled over, filled his cup, smiled and winked, turned and strolled over to a table of newcomers. Brian tasted the fresh coffee; it was hot but had been on the burner too long and had turned bitter.

"Okay," Marion said, dabbing her hands with a napkin and pushing her plate aside. "The last guy on the list is Frank Westbrook."

Brian drew a blank and looked to Marion for help. "I don't recall him."

Marion flipped to the next page. "Says here he was sentenced thirty to life for possession and murder."

"Now I remember," Brian said with cold recollection. "It was a long time ago, shortly after I made detective. My old partner Clint Roth and I had been tailing a mule from Bernie Martin's—"

"I remember Martin," Marion interrupted. "He was a big drug lord when I first moved here from Jersey. Somebody fired a bullet into his brain right through the front window of his Paradise Valley home as he was reading the morning paper." She shook her head. "I don't think anybody was ever arrested on that one."

Brian pushed his coffee away and leaned back in the seat. "I don't think anyone put a lot of effort into it."

Marion nodded in agreement.

"So anyway," Brian continued. "We'd been watching Bernie for a few weeks and then we got the break we were waiting for. We tailed him across town and into a south side alley. So we parked the car and took after him on foot. We found his car parked by a dumpster next to a steel blue door. We were all set to wait it out when Gabe noticed a small, narrow window about six feet off to the side of the door. We worked our way to the window and peered inside just in time to watch the buy take place. We pulled our revolvers and were about to go in and make the bust when we heard a ruckus from inside the building. When we got inside, Westbrook was standing over a guy with his head bashed in, holding a baseball bat. We arrested him on the spot. Westbrook told us later the guy tried to short him a hundred bucks."

Marion pursed her lips and scowled. "I don't care how long I do this job, people never cease to amaze me. A hundred lousy bucks."

They were quiet while the room bustled around them. Brian wrote in his notebook.

"I really appreciate your help, Marion. This gives me some-place to start."

Marion leaned forward and placed her folded hands on the table. "You know this is not officially your case and the captain ordered you to stay out of it."

Brian folded his arms across his chest and nodded. "That's what I hear. But I never heard it from the captain."

Marion smiled. "A technicality. But I was asked to convey the message and I have done so. My obligation to the captain has been fulfilled."

"I know. So it would probably be best if I didn't tell you what I intend to do with my day tomorrow?"

"Probably not." Marion twirled her thumbs and stared at Brian. "But keep me informed anyway. We'll keep this between the two of us. Less trouble that way. And I'll keep digging. Something will present itself. It always does."

* * * * *

When Brian arrived home he found Christine in the master bathroom primping in front of the mirror. She appeared to be her old self. Her hair and make-up were perfect and she was wearing a long black dress with a diamond necklace and matching earrings. She flashed Brian a smile that made his heart flutter.

He stood in the doorway with his hands in his front pockets, leaning against the doorframe, watching her apply mascara. "You look great," he said.

"Why, thank you, sir," Christine said in her best mock southern accent. "I do believe I'm famished. Shall we dine?"

"I take it we're going someplace other than Red Lobster."

"Oh, I think I've roughed it enough for one week. I believe something a little more elegant is in order tonight."

She had finished with the mascara and was now working a subtle melon colored lip-gloss onto her lips.

"Where did you have in mind?" Brian noticed the curve of her waist and the shapely form of her bottom and thought about skipping dinner altogether and going straight for the dessert.

"We have reservations for two at The Other Place."

"Oh," Brian said, nodding his approval. "That is nice. I guess this means you're not upset with me anymore."

"Old news," Christine said, waving her hand through the air.

"Then I guess I'd better change."

Christine capped off the lip-gloss, twisted her head to the side and looked him up and down. "I do believe that would be appropriate, sir."

Brian leaned forward, kissed her on the cheek and let his hand drift to her bottom. He could feel the silk panties under her dress. Dessert was sounding better all the time.

"After dinner," Christine said, as she pushed his hand away and walked past him into the bedroom, "I thought we might stop by the Hilton. I heard they have a great swing band playing there this weekend."

Brian entered the bathroom, removed his clothes, threw them into a small hamper under the window and turned on the shower. "Sounds great. I hope they play some mellow tunes so we can slow dance."

Christine produced a low, sexy, almost amused laugh that stopped Brian where he stood. She came to the bathroom door and stood in the doorway staring at Brian in his nakedness. "Oh, we're going to slow dance tonight, darling, but it won't be on the dance floor."

Brian felt his eyebrows raise and his mouth tighten. "We could skip right to the slow dance as far as I'm concerned."

Christine shook her head. "All good things to those who wait." She blew him a kiss and closed the door.

(28)

When Brian awakened the next morning he was surprised to find Christine already up and dressed and sitting at the kitchen table with Eric. She was hunched over a bowl of Cheerios dabbing at the floating Os, a full cup of steaming coffee at her left hand. She had on a melon colored suit with matching blouse and shoes. Her fine, blonde hair had been fixed in a hurry, with one side pressed closer to the scalp than the other.

"Good morning, killer," Christine said when Brian shuffled into the room.

Brian felt his face flush and headed for the coffee.

Eric smiled and returned to the large bowl of Cheerios he cradled in front of him. He wore a pair of gray, cut-off sweat pants and a yellow tank top. His tan, hairy legs were stretched out under the table and crossed at the ankles.

Brian removed a brown mug from the cupboard, poured himself a cup of coffee and sat down at the table opposite Eric. He leaned over the mug, breathed in the aroma and turned to Christine. "You're up early."

Christine nodded and took the last bite of cereal. "I thought I'd go into work and see if they survived my absence. It'll probably take me a week to get things back in order."

Eric lifted the bowl from the table, tipped back his head, and drained the residue from the bottom. He smacked his lips and glanced at the clock above the stove. "Gotta go," he said, getting out of the chair. "Big doin's today."

Brian jerked his head back and felt his eyes widen as he watched Eric drop the bowl into the sink. "What do *you* have going on?"

Eric spun around and leaned against the counter. "Got a job."

Brian felt his mouth drop and shifted his position in the chair. "A job?"

Christine turned and glared at Brian through tightly clenched eyes.

Eric produced a close-lipped grin and folded his arms across his chest. "You don't have to look so surprised."

The news of Eric's new employment should have brought great elation to Brian, but it didn't. He knew Eric too well. The kid was as repulsed by an honest day's work as a cat was by water. Attempting to conceal his skepticism, Brian put on his best friendly face. "That's great. What kind of job did you get?"

"I took a position with a marketing firm downtown," Eric said, throwing back his shoulders and lifting up his chin.

Brian frowned and narrowed one eye. "Doing what?"

"Marketing. What else?"

Brian nodded. "That's great."

"Well. Gotta rush. Don't want to be late on my first day." He hurried out of the room and down the hall to his room.

"Isn't it great?" Christine asked, still watching Brian carefully. "They're starting him at thirty-thousand a year, with unlimited potential for advancement."

"What's the name of the company?" Brian asked, and took a large gulp of coffee.

"Masterson and something Investments. And you don't have to be so suspicious. It's a job. He has to start somewhere." She stood and took her dishes to the sink and began loading the dishwasher.

Brian sat quietly at the table sipping his coffee and running the day's itinerary through his mind.

When Christine had finished with the dishes, she came back to the table, bent down and kissed Brian on the cheek. "Thanks for last night. I had a wonderful time."

Brian smiled and looked up at her. "It was my pleasure, believe me. You never cease to amaze me."

"'Keep 'em guessing,' my mother used to say. Keeps them coming back for more."

"More would be nice. I especially like that thing with the . . ."

"Shhh," Christine said, laying her hand across the back of Brian's head. "You're embarrassing me. Besides, I have to go."

Brian pushed his chair away from the table, stood and gave her a firm hug. He put his lips to her ear and whispered, "I'll miss you."

"Of course, you will," she said and pulled away.

Brian watched with admiration as she gathered up her purse and briefcase, threw him a goodbye kiss and walked out the door. He stood for a moment with his head tilted back, breathing in her lingering scent, listening to the whine of the clock above the stove and the purr of the engine as Christine pulled the car out of the drive.

A few minutes later, as Brian poured the last of the coffee into his cup, he heard Eric pound down the hall, cross the living room, and storm out the front door. Something inside told him Eric was blindly speeding towards an unfinished bridge with no thought of slowing down. Brian felt like a caged and gagged observer, unable to stop the inevitable.

When he had finished his coffee, he headed for the bedroom, dressed, strapped on his shoulder holster and was in the car and on his way in less than twenty minutes. He marveled at his efficiency around the home. If only he could handle his job as well.

His first stop was Merle Rancor's office. He waited in the parole officer's tiny lobby until the receptionist, a very tall and pleasant looking young woman, showed him into Rancor's boiler room of an office.

Merle Rancor was perched behind a beige metal desk. It was the kind the government probably purchased by the gross from cut-rate wholesalers. Rancor was a bull of a man, with a huge, round head that flowed into his chest eliminating any resemblance to a neck. He had a massive stomach, disproportionately short arms that strained to reach the forms piled high on his desk, and short, stubby fingers that held a silver pen in one hand and a cheese danish in the other. He wore his clay colored hair over his ears; Brian suspected it was to hide their size.

"Yeah," Rancor said through a mouth full of danish. "What can I do for you?"

Brian introduced himself and produced his badge. "I'm investigating an attempted murder. You have three recent parolees who might be able to help me."

Rancor looked up from his stack of forms and motioned to a small chair in front of his desk. "Oh, yeah? Who?"

"Let's start with Jason Duffler."

Rancor wheezed. Brian assumed it was his way of laughing, but he couldn't be sure.

"Jason Duffler is a mouse," Rancor said, as he wiped a hunk of danish from the corner of his mouth with a white, paper napkin. "He's a nice kid. He was in for drugs, nothing violent. There's no way this kid would be involved with anything like that." He waved his hand dismissively. "Who else?"

"Frank Westbrook," Brian said.

"Now Frank is a totally different matter. How the parole board let that guy out is beyond me. He even gives *me* the creeps, and that ain't easy to do. You want to talk to him, be my guest." He shuffled through another pile on the credenza behind him and handed Brian a file. "Who's next?"

"A woman named Betty Applegate."

"Man," Rancor said. "You got anyone you want to talk to other than the people under my care?"

"No." Brian raised one eyebrow. "Rather coincidental, isn't it?"

Rancor looked up from his papers and stared at Brian. "If you're going to try and make something out of that, forget it. I ain't got a dishonest bone in my body." He wheezed again. His face turned red. "Well, maybe one or two. But I ain't got nothin' to do with no attempted murder, detective. I guarantee. I got six years to retirement. Then I'm moving to California to live with my daughter and her family. They got a swimming pool and a slide and two of the sweetest kids there ever was. I wouldn't mess that up for nothing." He tore off a hunk of danish and stuffed it into his mouth.

Brian smiled. He could spot sincerity when he saw it. Rancor may have been a little disheveled, but he seemed okay.

"I appreciate your cooperation, Mr. Rancor." Brian eased back in the uncomfortable chair, heard it groan under his weight, and crossed his legs.

Rancor waved a hand. "Call me Merle," he said. He chomped and smacked away at the danish, holding his finger in the air as if pointing to the ceiling, and watching Brian with big, sorrowful eyes. After swallowing several times, he washed it all down with a can of Mountain Dew he produced from somewhere under the desk. He wiped his mouth and said, "Sorry about that. I didn't get breakfast this morning."

"No need to apologize. Now what about Ms. Applegate?"

"Oh, yeah . . . Betty." Rancor swept the crumbs off his desk with one hand and into the other and tossing them into his mouth. "She may be a little messed up, but I doubt she'd be any more involved in a murder plot than Jason."

"What do you mean messed up? Has she given you any indication that she's not living up to her parole agreement?" Rancor leaned back in his chair. "Let's just say I've been doing this job long enough to know something ain't right when I see it." He placed his hand to his mouth and stifled a belch. "I don't have no real evidence, mind you, but I think she might be up to her old tricks. No pun intended. I been trying to find a way to catch her in the act so I can send her back inside."

"Maybe she doesn't need to go back inside," Brian said. "Maybe she needs someone to help her."

Rancor inspected the paper bakery sack and appeared disappointed to find it empty. He wiped his finger across the bottom of the package and then licked his finger. "Maybe, but I ain't Dear Abby. I got problems of my own. I got over two hundred and fifty parolees under my watch and more coming in every day. I'm only one guy, what can I do?"

"One more thing," Brian said as he stood to leave. "If you could see your way clear to go ahead and let me have the other two files, or copies of them, I would really appreciate it. I'm sure Jason didn't have anything to do with this, but maybe he's heard something on the street that could point me in the right direction. I learned a long time ago to cover all my bases and somewhere in the mess you find your answer."

Rancor shrugged his shoulders and waved a hand. "Sure. No skin off my neck." He shuffled through the papers and handed Brian the files. "Do me a favor. There's a copy machine out in the reception area. Copy the files yourself and give the originals back to my secretary. I got a bad leg. It's hard for me to get up and down."

Brian nodded, imagining what the leg hidden behind the desk might look like and glancing at the empty danish package. "I'm sure it is."

(29)

Jason Duffler lived in an apartment on the west side of Phoenix behind a discount dry cleaner. The complex consisted of eight, single story, slump block apartments on either side of a narrow, asphalt drive. To the south, a chain link fence separated the parking area from a vacant lot littered with discarded wood and batches of brown tumbleweeds. Duffler's unit was on the end. It had a small rock yard and a short walkway leading up to the front door. Dozens of weeds grew out of the sidewalk, emitting a pungent, sour odor.

Brian rapped on the door several times. No answer. He was about ready to give up when he heard a soft voice behind him.

"You looking for Jason?"

When Brian turned around, he found himself staring into the deep-set eyes of a frail man with white hair, a mass of age spots on his forehead, and skin sucked so tight to his bones it almost looked painful.

Brian approached the man, produced his badge and held it out in front of him. The old man narrowed his eyes at the badge and frowned.

"That's a Scottsdale badge," the man said. He clamped his left eye shut and looked up at Brian with the other. "Not Phoenix."

"Yes, sir," Brian said. "That's correct." He slapped the bill-fold shut and stuck it in his back pocket. At this point he decided a small white lie might help ease the situation. "But I'm

173

working in conjunction with the Phoenix Police Force on an ongoing investigation."

The man seemed to consider this. He shifted his weight to one leg, brought a shaky hand up to his chin and worked his fingers across his gray stubble. "Jason in some kind of trouble?"

"No, sir, not at all. I just thought he might be able to help me."

Placing his arms across his chest, the man shifted his weight to the other leg and said, "Help you with what?"

Brian felt a bead of sweat trickle down his back and became aware of his growing impatience. "I'm not at liberty to say, sir. Do you know where Mr. Duffler might be?"

The man stood silent, working his right thumb across his left wrist, studying Brian. After a few moments of contemplation, he took a deep breath and released it. "I imagine he's at work like most young people." His lower lip quivered as he watched Brian through one watery eye. The other eye was clamped tight against the sun beating down on the side of his face. "You say you're a detective?"

"Yes sir," Brian said, somewhat surprised by the pride he still felt for his profession.

"Then you're not a very good one, are you?" He slapped a hand on his knee and laughed; his toothless mouth wide and silent.

Brian frowned. "What makes you say that?"

"If you were a good detective, you would a figured Jason's whereabouts out for yourself and not have to rely on an old man to tell you where the boy is."

Brian smiled. He couldn't help himself. "You're right, sir. I should have figured that out for myself. It's been a long week. You wouldn't happen to know where Jason works, would you?"

"You know Saunder's Cement Company over on 75th and Olive?" the man asked.

"I've been by it a few times in the past."

"Jason drives a mixer for them. Try over there. He's probably out on the road right now but they might be able to tell you when he'll be back. If not, he leaves here around five-thirty in the morning. You could catch him then, if that isn't too early for you."

"Thank you, sir. You've been most helpful."

(30)

The Saunder's Cement Company was a sprawling mass of trucks, piles of dirt and odd looking buildings covered with a film of dry paste that looked as permanent as an overcast winter sky.

Brian parked his car next to the office and went inside. The desk attendant—a gruff man with a hardhat and a two-day growth of black beard—told Brian that Jason had come back early with transmission problems and was busy out back going over the following day's delivery schedule.

Brian thanked the man and went out back. He found Jason sitting at a picnic table, chomping on a wad of gum and shuffling a mound of yellow delivery manifests. He was a slight young man with tufts of brown curls sticking out from under a blue baseball cap. A long, narrow nose seemed to accentuate his close and deep-set eyes. He wore a sweat stained T-shirt with a local food chain's logo above the left pocket, a pair of faded blue jeans with a rip at the right knee, and a pair of black tennis shoes.

"Hello, Jason," Brian said.

When Jason raised his head, he peered at Brian through squinted eyes that suddenly grew wide.

Brian stopped across from the boy, placed his foot on the bench, and cupped his hands around his knee. "How you been, Jason?"

Fixing his sights back on the papers, Jason asked, "What do you want, detective? I haven't done anything wrong."

"I know. I just wanted to see how you were doing."

A slight grin crossed Jason's face. He gathered up the yellow manifests and tapped them on the table. Then he shoved them into a clipboard and let the clasp slam shut. Tipping his hat back on his head he looked up at Brian with obvious amusement. "Yeah, right. And I'm up for the Presidency. Why are you really here? I haven't done anything, so it must be something else. What is it?"

Brian brought his leg down, pulled out the bench, and sat down opposite Jason. "You hear from any of your old contacts, Jason?"

Jason shook his head, pushed the clipboard aside. "Now you know I'm not allowed to do that. If I do, they can put me back in. And I'll tell you something, detective, that's the last thing I want."

"I'm glad to hear that. Merle Rancor set you up with this job?"

"How do you know Mr. Rancor?"

"I did a little checking."

Jason stood up, walked around the wooden table and over to a cold drink machine against the wall. He fumbled through his front pocket, counted out the correct change, and dropped the coins one by one into the machine. They jingled as they went down the slot. After punching one of the buttons, the machine produced a low, rumbling sound and a can of soda pop thundered down the shoot and came to rest in the black plastic tray. Jason picked up the can of Pepsi, popped the top and took a long pull. He wiped his mouth with the sleeve of his t-shirt and turned to Brian. "Rancor's okay, for a parole officer."

Brian nodded in agreement. It was pretty much his estimate of the man as well.

"Why are you here?" Jason said retaking his seat.

Brian decided to come clean. "A guy named Jake Leighton is trying to kill me. He's a professional, and I'm trying to find out who hired him and why."

Another long pull off the Pepsi produced a scrunched face followed by the longest and loudest belch Brian had ever heard. Jason giggled. "And you think *I* know something about it?" Instantly, Brian regretted his candor. He was wasting his time on Jason Duffler. It was obvious the kid had no knowledge of any of this. Brian stood up. "I thought maybe you'd heard something, Jason. That's all."

"Man, I don't know nothin' about no professional hit," Jason said, running his palms across the sides of the can. His eyes narrowed as he looked up at Brian. His foot tapped under the table. "I'm clean, detective. Mr. Rancor got me this job and I'm gonna make the best of it. I'm gonna save some money and go back to school so I can do something with my life. I'm never going back to the way I was, detective. I swear."

The kid was either the best actor Brian had ever come across or the most sincere. Brian decided on the latter. He removed his billfold from his back pocket, took out one of his cards, and handed it to Jason. "You need anything, you call me."

Jason looked at the card, studied it, and placed it in his shirt pocket. He fixed his eyes back on Brian. "Thanks, detective, but if it's all the same to you, I think I'll limit my police contact to the movies. Less trouble that way."

Brian laughed. "I think you're going to be just fine."

(31)

Betty Applegate's apartment was off 68th Street north of McDowell in what was referred to around the precinct as Apartment Row. Brian parked the Taurus on the street, walked across a small patch of dead grass past a swimming pool with water the color of lime green Kool Aid, and knocked on the door of Apartment D. The door opened revealing a stout young woman in her late twenties with short brown hair and an oversized man's t-shirt draped over her expansive shoulders. A Marlboro dangled from the woman's thick, painted lips and one eye was clamped closed, presumably to escape the sting of smoke. There was a black and blue bruise across her right cheek. Except for the bruise and a shorter haircut, she looked just as she had the day of her trial. The look of recognition crossed her face almost immediately upon seeing Brian at her door.

"What do *you* want?" she asked. Her raspy voice suggested serious consideration should be given to breaking the cigarette habit before she found herself talking through a hole in her throat.

"Hi Betty," Brian said, the unpleasant odor of cigarettes attacking his senses. "I see you remember me."

"Of course, I remember you. How could I forget?" She placed a hand on her hip and glared at Brian. "Why are you here?"

"May I come in please, Betty? I would like to ask you some questions."

"About what?"

Brian heard a door open behind him and turned to investigate. A large man with a shaved head holding a can of Bud emerged from the apartment across the tract. "Everything okay, Betty?" he called out. "You need some help?"

"Maybe we could talk inside," Brian suggested.

"It's all right, Tom," Betty announced. "He's an old acquaintance."

"Okay," he said, easing his hefty load down on the cement stoop in front of his door. "But if you need me, you call me, you hear?"

"Thanks, Tom."

"Please," Brian insisted. "I'd rather talk without an audience."

Betty stepped aside and motioned him in.

Inside, he felt a flood of surprise engulf him. The furnishings were new, and, he imagined, fairly expensive. A white sofa and loveseat were nestled in the corner with two crystal lamps sitting on a pair of glass and brass end tables; a matching square coffee table sat in front of the sofa. There was a Bose stereo system in the corner next to a 36" Sony TV. Several paintings of various themes adorned the walls and plants of every size and shape were scattered about the room in no apparent order.

Betty closed the door behind him and stood swaying from side to side puffing on the cigarette that never left her mouth.

"What do you want to know?" she asked as the cigarette bounced up and down and sent fragments of ash spewing in all directions.

"Just a little information, Betty. Relax."

She leaned against the door, her arms dangling at her sides. "Look, I go to my parole officer every week just like I'm supposed to and I got a job at the market as a cashier. I'm living up to my parole." She strolled across the room, puffing and then blowing smoke through her nose, and leaned her forearm on the TV. "Why don't you tell me what you want? Then I can tell you I don't know nothing and I'll be rid of you."

Brian smiled, decided no invitation to sit was forthcoming, and took a seat on the sofa. Crossing his legs, he laid his right arm across the back of the sofa and looked around the room again. "From the look of things, I'd say you still have an ear to the street. If that's true, I was wondering if you'd heard anything that might involve me?"

"You?" Her eyes narrowed suspiciously. "Why would I hear anything about you?"

"I seem to have made someone very angry. And—"

Betty burst out laughing, ashes dropped to the floor. There was a crackling sound within her lungs as she began to cough. She removed the cigarette from her mouth and crushed it out in a white, porcelain ashtray on a small table by the TV. Then she grabbed a tissue from the same table, coughed up something and spit it into the tissue. When her coughing fit ceased, she looked up at Brian. "I can't imagine who could be mad at you, detective."

Brian pursed his lips, uncrossed his legs and stretched them out in front of him. "You ever heard of a man named Jake Leighton?"

She ambled over to the loveseat and sat down on the arm. "Nope. Never heard of him."

"He's about six-two, two hundred twenty pounds, round face, stark white hair."

It was subtle, but it was there. A raise of an eyebrow, a crease in the forehead, a twitch of the mouth—they were all things Brian looked for when questioning a suspect. And the slight movement of Betty's hand along with the widening of her eyes at the mention of the Leighton's hair betrayed her. Brian felt a twinge of excitement. This was the first moment he felt as though he might actually be gaining some ground. But it was also a time for caution. He'd learned long ago playing your trump card too early could cost you the game.

He glanced around the room. "They must be paying cashiers well these days. You have some nice things here."

"Don't read more into it than there is, detective. I had most of this stuff before I got sent up. It's been in storage. Besides, living in a nine by six cell with a woman who took up half the room has given me an appreciation for my own space. How I fill that space is my business."

He decided to play a high card, hoping she would play her ace. "I could use some cooperation here, Betty. Finding this man is very important to me. And if you've had contact with him, you could be in danger."

She lifted one shoulder and wrinkled her nose. "I told you I don't know him."

"I know that's what you said. But you're a lousy liar. You were bad at it when you tried to talk your way out of the prostitution rap, and you're still bad at it. When did you last see him?"

Betty leaped to her feet and pointed towards the door. "Get out! I got nothing more to say to you."

Brian lifted his arm off the back and patted the seat beside him. "Sit down, Betty."

"I said get out." She walked to the door and grabbed the knob.

The time had come to play hardball, time to raise the stakes, and Brian was ready. "I'm sure Mr. Rancor would be interested to know how you make your living, Betty; and I'm not talking about your daytime job. And I'm sure the parole board would be interested as well." He waited.

Betty's hand released the doorknob. She walked over to the cocktail table, retrieved a cigarette and a Bic lighter and touched flame to tobacco. Smoke rose towards the ceiling in a blue gray haze. She stuck the cigarette in her mouth, folded her arms, inhaled deeply and blew the smoke out her nose. She began pacing around the room, eyeing Brian with every turn.

Watching her pacing and puffing on her cigarette gave Brian a feeling of satisfaction. He was getting to her. That was good. If he proceeded cautiously, didn't overplay his hand, he might come out of this thing on top. "The next move is yours, Betty. I advise you to consider it carefully."

She walked to the far corner of the room, picked up another pack of Marlboros, lit one off the other, snuffed out the butt in a crystal ashtray, and leaned up against the wall as a cloud of smoke engulfed her. "I can't go back to prison. It almost killed me."

"You don't have to."

She took another drag, inhaled, and blew the smoke towards the ceiling. "What do you want to know?"

Brian felt his heart skip. He had to fight back the urge to rapid-fire questions, to show his excitement. But that was not the way to handle it. He had to at least appear calm. "Tell me how and where you met him, and when you last saw him."

"I got a call from my . . ." She let the words trail away, took another drag and exhaled through her nose.

Brian smiled. "I told you before, you're were a lousy liar. What's your pimp's name?"

"I can't tell you that," Betty scolded. She ran her fingers through her short-cropped hair. "He'd kill me."

"He won't know where I got the information."

She hesitated, sucked on her cigarette and fanned away the smoke. "You don't know him."

"Try me."

Betty took another drag. The ash on her cigarette must have been an inch long. It glowed a bright orange in the dim light of the apartment. She went to the far corner of the room and leaned against the wall, her eyes lowered. "His name's Jackie. I never knew his last name."

"Where can I find him?"

"I don't know where he lives, but he stops by here every morning sometime before noon. And he hangs out at a bar called The Pub."

The Pub was a dive little hole in the wall on the south side frequented by dealers and prostitutes and anyone looking to find either of the aforementioned. Rumor had it the only reason the place stayed open was due to some healthy payoffs to state and local officials. Ongoing investigations had turned up nothing more than some minor health infractions, probably put in place to keep the owner in line and shelling out his monthly payments.

"I know the place," Brian said

"That's where I met the guy you're looking for," Betty continued. "He bought me expensive drinks, opened doors for me and treated me like a lady. He was pretty good looking too. Like you said, he had all this thick white hair and real pretty blue eyes." She paused. The lines on her face crinkled. Her gaze never left the floor. "Then I brought him home." She took another drag and coughed. "Afterwards, he got really weird. So I asked him to pay up and leave. That's when he got mean. He called me a whore and started knocking me around. I picked up a vase and tried to hit him with it, but he slapped me and must have knocked me out because the next thing I remember is waking up in the morning and the guy was gone."

"Did you go to the hospital?" Brian asked, leaning forward on the sofa.

"No. They have to report stuff like this and I don't need no trouble with the law." She puffed on her cigarette and tapped her hand against her hip. "No offense. Besides, if Rancor found out about any of this, I'd be on my way back inside before I could spit."

Grateful for the information—and feeling somewhat guilty for pressing so hard—Brian asked, "Are you all right? If you need medical attention I can arrange it, no questions asked."

She shrugged and waved her hand through the air. "No, I'll live. It's not so bad anymore. The swelling's gone way down and I can see clearly out of my eye again."

"Is there anything else you can tell me?"

"No." She shook her head. "That's everything I remember."

Reaching into his shirt pocket, Brian pulled out a business card and placed it on the table. "If you think of anything else, please call me."

For the first time since she started her confession, she looked up at Brian. Her eyes were filled with tears. She sniffed and rubbed the back of her hand across her nose. "What'd this guy do anyway?"

"We just need to ask him some questions."

Betty sniffed again, coughed, and then spit into the tissue. "Now who's a lousy liar?"

Focusing in on the cigarette dangling from her lips Brian said, "Those things are going to kill you, you know."

She shrugged, sniffed and wiped her nose. "There's worst ways to go."

"I suppose."

Betty shuffled from foot to foot, puffing and blowing smoke through her nose. "You gonna tell Rancor what's going on?"

Brian studied her. She put on a good front, played the tough street kid to the hilt. But when it came down to it, she was just another lost child in need of help. Sadly, the situation was not a new one.

Picking up his card from the table, Brian pulled a pen from his pocket and wrote a name and number on the back. "Call this lady, Betty. Her name's Phyllis Bihar. She's with social services, and she can help."

Snuffing out her cigarette in the crystal ashtray, Betty folded her arms across her chest and pushed her hip to one side. "I'll think about it."

(32)

Brian pulled up in front of The Pub and parked. He climbed out of the car and headed for the door. On the opposite side of the bar, an old warehouse stood deserted; windows broken, paint chipped and peeling, graffiti spewed across the walls in black and red spray paint, and weeds swallowing the abandoned railroad tracks running past the building.

As he walked through the open door, he felt accosted by the smell of beer and cigarettes and that indefinable odor that permeates every bar from Boston to Los Angeles. When his eyes adjusted to the light, he noticed the bar was like a thousand other dives across the city. There were small metal tables in no apparent order, a row of booths against the far wall, and a pair of pool tables illuminated by low-hung rectangular lamps advertising the beer of choice. A long wooden bar, complete with foot rails, stretched the length of the room. Cheaply framed western paintings, large mirrors and beer advertisements hung on the walls.

"We're not open yet," a man behind the bar called out, working a bar towel across the counter top. "I just opened the door to air out the place."

A good idea, Brian thought. He walked over to the bar and sat down on a stool in front of the bartender.

"What are you . . . deaf?" the bartender complained. He stopped polishing. "I said we ain't open."

"I don't want a drink," Brian confessed, folding his hands on the bar. "I want some information."

The bartender stood upright and looked at Brian thought-fully. He was in his late forties, with thinning gray hair, a round body and an oval face sporting a thick mustache and goatee. His eyes seemed dull and glazed. A toothpick hung from the side of his thin lips and bobbed up and down as he spoke. "You a cop?"

Brian reached in his back pocket, produced his badge, and showed it to him. "Name's Fogarty."

The bartender threw his towel on a stainless steel sink below the counter, grabbed a nearby glass, and jammed in onto a long, round brush protruding from a sink filled with steaming water. "I ain't too crazy about cops." He pulled the glass from the brush, plunged it in another sink and then set it on a black dish drainer.

"Why's that?"

"Got no use for 'em, that's all."

Behind the man was a multi-level shelf filled with various liquors. Below it was an antique cash register with a beer-splattered nameplate on top that read: HENRY ROGERS.

"You Henry?" Brian.

The man paused; his hands emerged in the water. His eyebrows rose and the lines between his eyes deepened. "How'd you know my name?"

Brian pointed to the nameplate and smiled.

Henry rolled his eyes and resumed washing. "Why are you bothering me? I done nothin' wrong."

"Look, I only came in here to ask you a few questions about one of your regulars."

"I don't know nothin' about no guy." He dried his hands on a fresh towel and flipped it over his left shoulder.

Brian strained to remain calm. "What guy?"

"What do you mean, what guy?"

"You said you didn't know anything about a guy. I didn't even give you a name or description."

Henry stepped back, leaned against the back counter and chomped on his toothpick. "I don't know nothin' about nothin'."

Lumbering to his feet, Brian leaned over the counter and stared straight into the frightened man's eyes. "Look, other than the guy I'm looking for, I don't give a crap what goes on in here. That's not my concern right now. I'm only interested in one man. But if you insist on making my job difficult, I will return the favor." Brian eased off, holding his anger in check, and sat back down on the barstool.

"You threatening me?" Henry asked, grabbing his towel from his shoulder and wiping his dry hands.

"Oh no, sir. It would be illegal for an officer of the law to threaten a taxpayer. After all, you pay my salary, right?"

Henry was silent. He rolled his tongue around inside his mouth. It made his cheeks bulge in and out like a frightened mouse. His toothpick fell to the floor. "Man, you cops are all alike."

"It's the training."

Henry glared at Brian and flared his nostrils.

The wind picked up outside and a tree limb raked the outside of the building. A few yellow leaves blew through the open door and swirled around the floor.

"What do you want to know?" Henry asked, folding his arms across his chest.

"I'm looking for a fellow named Jackie."

Henry shuffled from side to side. His eyes darted around the room as if searching for the cavalry. "I suppose it wouldn't do any good to tell you I don't know nobody named Jackie?"

"Nope."

From across the bar came a heavy sigh. Henry unfolded his arms and slapped them down at his side. "You said if I cooperate, you'd leave me alone?"

Brian nodded. "Total isolation."

"And nobody has to know where you heard it?"

"Not a soul."

Henry turned and grabbed a bottle of Cutty Sark from the shelf, poured himself a generous snifter, and downed the contents in one practiced motion. He placed the glass on the counter, wiped his mouth with the back of his hand and looked Brian in the eyes. "Jackie runs a small operation, only a half dozen girls, but he's always talking about expanding. As a matter of fact, he just got a new one a few months ago, some chick right out of the slammer. Anyway, Jackie sends some business my way, if you catch my drift, for letting his girls meet the guys here."

"Does he come in every night?"

"Most nights. Keeps pretty good tabs on his ladies. Doesn't want anything to happen to his bread and butter."

"If Jackie's small time like you say, why are you so worried about telling me what you know? Has he ever threatened you in any way."

Henry laughed, turned his palms up at his sides. "Jackie? No way. I'd crush the little piss ant with my thumb. But he's got connections. I don't know who, and that's the honest truth. But he always acts like he knows people, people that could cause you a great deal of pain if you crossed him. So I don't ask no questions. Keeps me in pocket change and out of trouble, so I figure what's the harm."

"The harm is that prostitution is illegal."

Henry produced a wry chuckle. He poured another scotch and tossed it down his throat and clenched his eyes shut. When he opened them he asked, "What are you, the Pope?"

Brian reached in his shirt pocket and removed the photo of Jake Leighton he had received from Marion earlier and laid it on the counter. "Do you recognize this man?"

The recognition wasn't as subtle as Betty's twitch of the finger, but it wasn't thunderous either. Henry simply opened one eye wide while the other squinted at the photo.

"When was he last in here?" Brian asked.

Henry wiped a bead of scotch from the corner of his mouth. "Never seen him before."

The stool squawked on the wooden floor as Brian pushed it away from the bar and stood up. "I'm very sorry to hear that.

I truly am. I hate to see any hard-working man lose what he's worked so hard for."

"When you came in you said you were only interested in one man."

Brian lowered his eyes, ran a hand across the back of his neck. "Well, I wasn't exactly honest with you on that count, Henry."

Taking a step forward, Henry leaned his palm on the counter. "Why are you hassling me?"

Pushing the stood aside, Brian brought his face to within inches of Henry's foul smelling mug. "Tell me what you know, and, like I said before, nobody's going to know where I got the information."

"You're not going to go away are you?"

"Annoying, isn't it?"

Backing away, Henry snatched a fresh bar towel from under the bar and started wiping down the countertop. "You're going to put me out of business one way or the other, aren't you?"

"Talk to me" Brian persisted.

After a moment of deliberation, Henry sighed. "I never seen the guy until a couple nights ago. Came in, picked up one of Jackie's girls, and left. I ain't seen him since."

Brian reached across the counter and nabbed a handful of peanuts. He tossed them around in his hand and popped a few in his mouth. "Now, why were you so afraid to tell me that?"

(33)

Jake Leighton wiped his fingerprints from the stolen car in the back parking lot of a northwest Phoenix Safeway Market. Feeling secure he'd left no trace, he walked across the street to a Waffle House restaurant, ordered a short stack with boysenberry syrup and called a cab from the payphone in the waiting room. When he had finished breakfast, he went outside to wait, but the cab had already arrived. He climbed in, gave the driver his destination, sat back and closed his eyes.

Forty-five minutes later, he was walking through the baking sun towards his downtown Phoenix hotel. He felt like a fool in his straw hat, mirrored sunglasses, orange and green striped shorts, Arizona Cardinals t-shirt, black socks and white Nikes. But the outfit suited his needs and, with a little luck, would allow him access to his hotel so he could pick up his belongings and find safer surroundings. If the police had been competent at all, they would have discovered his lodgings by now and were waiting. His best hope would be to slip in and out quietly, lay low for a few days and then finish the job.

As he strolled along the busy sidewalk, he noticed up ahead but across the street, two men were sitting in a tan sedan with the windows up and the motor running.

About a hundred feet in front of him, he noticed another dark car parked next to a withering tree that protruded from a grate in the sidewalk. Two men leaned against the car smoking cigarettes, attempting to stay within the small amount of shade the little tree provided.

As he approached the men, they turned and looked at him. Jake produced a killer smile; and in his best southern drawl he said, "Ya'll know where the capitol building is?"

The two men looked at each other and smiled. The man with no necktie and receding hairline looked over his shoulder and pointed in the direction of a copper-topped domed building sticking up above the downtown buildings. "You see that building that looks like a football helmet?"

Jake nodded his head.

"That's the capitol building. It's about a ten minute walk from here."

Jake tipped his hat. "Thank you kindly. I do believe I'll jog on over there after I freshen up." Jake turned and walked away.

"Have a nice day," the balding man called out.

A moment later, Jake walked through the double doors of the hotel lobby; the sudden change from one hundred plus degrees to seventy made his body tense and the hairs on his neck stiffen. He stood for a moment in the doorway letting his body adjust.

The lobby before him was an expansive display of outright decadence, and Jake loved it. Dark green carpet with white and gold borders stretched across the room and drew up next to a long reception counter. An attractive uniformed woman with bright red lipstick stood behind the counter conversing with an older couple wearing matching shorts and shirts.

With utmost care, Jake proceeded through the lobby towards the copper colored elevators. Off to his left he noticed three men milling about. Maybe it was their unmistakable off-the-rack suits or the way they scoped in on every person with unusual interest that gave them away. But whatever the reason, Jake knew they were cops and they were waiting for him.

To his right, two elderly women were standing at the check-in counter loudly expressing their dissatisfaction over their proposed accommodations; the woman with the red lipstick was trying to remain calm.

Jake hustled by them, drew up next to the elevators, and pushed the up button. Urgency came over him and he felt a sudden need to push the button again but refrained. With utmost care, he glanced over his shoulder.

At the same time a young bellhop was herding the cackling women through the lobby towards the elevators, one of the men broke away from his companions and hurried over to the reception desk. He had a strange look about him, like his eyes were about to pop out of their sockets. After he managed to acquire the desk clerk's attention, he gestured towards Jake with a twist of his head.

When the elevator bell rang and the doors opened, two men and a woman emerged. Jake immediately plunged in and pushed the fourth floor button. As he waited what seemed an eternity for the door to close, he weighed his options. Obviously, he had been made. He would have to move quickly.

Outside the door he could hear a group of women approaching. He pushed the fourth floor button again. When the door started to close, the bellhop called out, "Hold that door."

Jake let the door close in their faces and breathed a sigh of relief. When the doors opened again, he stepped out into an empty hallway, his right hand gripping the handle of his Beretta. He marched down the hall and pulled up in front of room number 412. Slipping his card into the lock, he pulled his gun from under his shirt, turned the knob, and entered the room. It was dark and empty. He sped about the room with utmost precision, gathering his belongings and making sure he left no trace. When he stepped back into the empty hall, he turned left away from the elevators, walked to the far end of the hall and knocked on the door of room 401.

A meek voice came from inside, "Who is it?"

"It's the manager, sir. I need to speak with you. We have a slight problem."

A moment later an elderly man in a blue bathrobe opened the door and said, "What kind of problem?"

Jake smiled. "This will only take a minute, sir." He stepped inside.

(34)

"Hi, Marion," Brian said when Marion picked up the line. "I've been thinking. Why would someone be after me and not Gabe if it involved someone we were investigating or had busted within the past few years?"

There was a lull as Marion obviously considered this. A moment later she said, "Either it goes back a few years or it's not related to the job at all."

"That's what I'm thinking. Do me a favor. Go way back. Maybe as far back as when I first came on board."

"That's not going to be easy," Marion contended. "A lot of that stuff was never put in the computers. I'm not sure I can find it."

"I wouldn't ask you if it wasn't important. And I'd do it myself if I could get access. But since it's not my case . . ."

"I understand. I'll do my best."

"Thanks, Marion. I can't thank you enough for all your help."

There was a momentary silence. Brian felt uneasy. "What is it?" he said a moment later.

"I'm really sorry, Brian." There was a croak in her voice. Brian's heart sank. He wished he could figure out a way to make things easier on her. But he hadn't a clue how, which seemed to be his life story lately.

"You have nothing to be sorry about. You're doing the best you can. We'll figure out what's going on and we'll put Jake

Leighton behind bars. We know what he looks like. We know where he is staying, and unless I miss my guess, you've got the hotel staked out waiting for the S.O.B." He paused, trying to find the words. "It'll be fine. You're a good cop. Between the two of us, we'll figure it out."

"You're right," Marion said after clearing her throat. "I should be more professional and not let my feelings . . ." She let it trail away.

"Like I said, you're a good cop; a lot better than most." *Perhaps another place, another time,* he thought. "Thanks again, Marion. I owe you one."

"When this is all over, I'll find a way to make you pay."

Brian felt his face flush.

Marion had no sooner hung up the phone with Brian and picked up her purse to leave when the phone rang. She cursed under her breath. It had been a long day, and her stomach had been protesting for the better part of an hour. She wanted to go someplace quiet, get a sandwich, a carafe of iced tea and relax. Alas, it was not to be. When the phone sounded again, she threw her purse and briefcase on the desk chair and picked up the phone. It was Detective Nick Carey.

"Marion," he blurted out. "I think we might have something."

Marion felt a surge of adrenalin. "Talk to me."

"A guy walked through the lobby a few minutes ago and he just didn't fit, you know what I mean? Like, this is a pretty ritzy joint. Lots of snooty people walkin' around like they own the place . . . if you catch my drift."

"I've been to the Hilton before," Marion said. "So what was so strange about this particular guy?"

"Well, this guy looked like he would be more at home in a trailer park or lounging in a plastic pool than hob-knobbin' with the rich folk. So I asked the manager did he ever see this guy before? And he says no, he didn't recognize him. So I figure he might be our boy."

"Keep him there," Marion said. "I'm on my way."

When Jake Leighton stepped out into the hallway, he was wearing an Armani suit, red tie, and black Oxfords. A pair of wire-rimmed shades had replaced his mirrored sunglasses. His face and head had both been shaved clean. In his left hand, he carried his belongings in a medium-sized suitcase.

He spotted a neon sign at the end of the hall past the elevators that read, STAIRS. He hurried towards them. As he drew near the elevator, the bell sounded and the doors opened. Jake felt his heart skip when the man with the buzz cut, two uniformed police officers and a woman in a pantsuit stepped out into the hall. Jake eased to one side of the hall, smiled and let them pass. He waited by the elevator watching Buzz Cut and his group move down the hall.

The entourage was about halfway down the hall when Buzz Cut stopped and slowly looked back. He reached into his top pocket and removed what appeared to be a photograph. Glancing at it, his eyes went wide. He took another look at Jake and yelled, "It's him!"

The uniformed officers went for their guns.

Jake pulled his Beretta and put a bullet through the chest of one of the officers before the man could pull his weapon from its holster. Buzz Cut pushed the woman behind him and fumbled for his weapon. The second uniformed officer pulled his gun and raised it. Jake dropped him with one to the head at the same time he saw Buzz Cut take aim.

Jake leaped into the elevator as Buzz Cut's gun popped a round. The bullet hit the wall at the far end of the hall with a crack. As the elevator doors closed, he could hear Buzz Cut cursing. Jake laughed aloud. "Amateurs!" he shouted.

"What did you think you were doing?" Marion bellowed, pushing Nick away from in front of her. "I could have nailed him."

Nick did not answer. He knelt by one of the downed officers, felt for a pulse and then shook his head.

Marion grabbed the radio from her belt and clicked the "ON" button. "Charlie, Berry!" she shouted. "Officers down. I repeat, officers down. Leighton is on his way down in the elevator. Don't let him get away!"

Nick stood up, turned and looked at his partner. "I was just trying to—"

"I know what you were trying to do! I'm not some teeny-bopper schoolgirl who needs your protection. I'm a police officer. And if you have trouble with that, then I think it's time I ask the captain for a different partner."

"You're overreacting," Nick said as he started towards the stairs.

"Geeze," Marion said as she followed. "I really hate this male chauvinist crap."

The elevator reached the lobby. Jake rushed out, gun in hand and headed straight for the front door. An elderly woman saw the gun and screamed. The suits that had been milling about earlier jumped to their feet and rushed towards him, guns drawn. The two officers who had positioned themselves out front rushed through the front door. Jake turned and headed in the opposite direction. At the far end of the hall he saw an exit sign and took off running. From behind him he heard the words, "Stop! Police!" Jake dropped, rolled and took aim. He popped off three shots, dropped one officer and sent the other diving for cover behind a wall. Jake jumped to his feet and hit the exit door full stride. He ran down a back alley, listening for sounds of pursuit, but no one came. When he reached a busy street, he holstered his weapon, hailed a cab and climbed in.

(35)

Brian eased along the slow lane heading towards home. He once again found himself questioning his abilities as a police officer, a habit that was beginning to leave a bitter taste. It seemed so long ago when he had enthusiastically walked through the doors of the academy with idealistic delusions dancing through his young mind. Five partners, a half dozen shootings and a lifetime had gone by since then and many things had changed, not the least of which was Brian Fogarty.

When he reached the intersection of Scottsdale and Camelback, instead of heading straight home, he swung right and headed towards the east Phoenix address of Frank Westbrook; the last name on the list. Perhaps Westbrook could shed some light on the subject. Perhaps it was another dead end. There was only way one to find out.

Fifteen minutes later he pulled up in front of a brown brick ranch-style home in desperate need of a gardener. The lawn and trees were dying and the paint along the eaves was peeling away, exposing dry, split wood.

Brian parked on the street, went up to the front door and tried the bell. He was surprised when it worked. When the door opened, Brian found himself looking not at Frank Westbrook, but at an elderly woman with thick, white hair. She had two chins, drooping eyelids, and her cheeks were red from too much blush. A pair of dark rimmed glasses hung from a black nylon string around her neck.

"What do you want?" she asked.

Brian showed her his badge. "Detective Fogarty. I'm looking for Frank Westbrook. Does he live here?"

She looked Brian up and down as if he was a piece of meat and she was from the F.D.A. "What do you want with Frankie?"

"I just need to ask him a few questions," Brian said.

"You just missed him," she said.

Brian bit his lower lip, rubbed the back of his neck. He was getting nowhere fast and the frustration was beginning to wear on him. "Do you know where he was going?"

"You should know. Two of your officers just took him away."

"Why?" Brian queried.

She shook her head with obvious disgust. "Because the stupid shmuck didn't learn nothin' in prison but how to be an even bigger idiot than he was before." She inspected one of her bright red fingernails, made a ticking sound.

"What was he arrested for?"

"Armed robbery. They said he held up a pawnshop right after the guy handed him a gun. I guess that means he's going back inside."

"More than likely." Brian pulled Jake Leighton's picture from his pocket and showed it to the woman. "Have you ever seen this man before?"

She straightened up, put on her glasses, and studied the picture with a deep crease in the middle of her forehead. "No," she said, removing the glasses and letting them drop to the end of the cord. "Doesn't look familiar."

"Thank you for your time." He handed her his card, turned away and headed down the weed-infested path towards his car.

"Wait a minute!" the woman called out. "Can I see that picture again?"

Brian turned around, hurried up the path and handed the picture to her.

Stepping out of the doorway onto the front stoop and returning her glasses to her nose, she looked at the picture again. Brian waited. He could feel his pulse quicken. A wasp hovered around a nearby bush.

"You know," she finally said, "I have seen this guy before . . . a couple weeks ago out at the track. He was coming out of one of the offices and nearly bumped into me. I remember he had piercing eyes, almost made me shiver when he excused himself. He was real polite, though, a real gentleman."

Yeah, Brian thought, *a real gentleman.*

"Which track?" Brian asked.

"Desert Downs, where else? Only good racing in the city."

"Thank you again." He reached out and shook her hand. Her skin felt cold and dry. "You've been very helpful."

"Why you looking for him?" she asked.

Brian scratched his chin. "Let's just say I owe him."

(36)

A block away, Brian dialed Marion and got her answering machine. He left a message as to his findings and then tried her cell phone; it was busy.

He felt compelled to share his newfound information and get Marion working on it. Vince Decker, the owner of Desert Downs, had been a thorn in Brian's side ever since he took over the operation three years earlier. Although Brian knew the track was a front for organized crime, he and Gabe had been unsuccessful in digging up anything that would stick. They always seemed to be one step behind the criminals.

But now with this latest information, a piece of the puzzle seemed to drop into place. He finally had a connection. Vince Decker and Jake Leighton were tied together somehow. Although the pressure Gabe and Brian had applied to Decker over the last few years had been minor in Brian's mind, perhaps Decker had decided it was time to rid himself of a festering problem. Question after question raced through his mind as he tossed around different ideas. Some seemed highly possible while others bordered on the bizarre. But if he had learned anything over the years, it was to overlook nothing and investigate everything.

Halfway home he pulled up to a traffic light and stopped. Rumbling hunger pains sounded from his stomach like distant thunder. He picked up the phone and called Christine.

"Hi, honey," Brian said. "Are you all right?"

"Except for a serious case of the nerves, I guess I'm all right." The pitch of her voice was higher than normal and had a slight waver.

"Well, I'm on my way home. I should be there in about fifteen minutes. Is the officer Captain Fernandez sent over still there?"

"No. He left a few minutes ago."

"Have you eaten?" Brian asked.

"No. I don't think I could eat. My stomach's tied in knots."

"You have to eat. I'm on my way home. I'll pick up something quick."

"Okay," Christine replied. "But make it something light."

"How about a grilled chicken sandwich from K.F.C.?"

"Actually, that sounds good."

"Should take me about forty minutes. Call me if you need me."

After he hung up, he checked the rearview mirror and spotted a dark blue van. He hadn't given it much thought when he'd first seen it shortly after leaving the station, but now, as the driver tried to stay several cars back and blend in with the traffic, it was beginning to concern him. He strained to see the driver through the tinted windows but all he could see was a reflection of the sun. A couple of quick detours proved he was not just being paranoid. The van was still behind him, persistent as the Arizona sun.

He decided to stop by the station. The fact he had been unable to reach Marion by phone concerned him. He wanted to talk to her, see if anything new had developed. He found her at her desk typing on her keyboard. She wore a white blouse, tan slacks, and a pair of white Reeboks with mauve stripes. Nick was nowhere in sight.

When she noticed Brian beside her she looked up with wide eyes. "We had him, Brian."

Brian felt his heart race. "Leighton?"

"Yes. We had his hotel staked out and Nick spotted him sneaking in looking like a tourist. He called me and I rushed

203

right over." She paused, lowered her eyes, and took a deep breath. "But we let him get away. I'm so sorry."

"How could that be?"

"It was crazy." Marion spun around in her chair to face him. She placed both hands on the arms of her chair and tightened her grip. Her knuckles slowly turned white. "He killed three officers and disappeared out the side entrance. The guy's possessed, I swear it."

Brian sighed and shook his head. He leaned against the side of her desk. "You don't have to tell me."

"You left a message on my machine earlier, but I couldn't make it out; too much traffic noise I think. What did you want?"

Brian took a few minutes to fill her in on Vince Decker and his connection to Jake Leighton.

"I'll get a man on it right away," Marion said. "This is good. Now we're getting somewhere."

Brian thought about bouncing some of his theories off of her but decided against it. He wanted to do a little more digging on his own before he would feel comfortable laying out his thoughts. If he was wrong, he might come across as a man on the edge, looking for conspiracies around every corner, which was not far from the truth. Besides, he wanted to prove himself wrong.

"I need you to do me another favor," Brian said.

Marion sat back in her chair and smiled. "Oh, yeah?"

Brian felt his face warm. His first thought was to go with it, to make a comment about her hair or her face or the way the light reflected in her eyes. Or maybe even something about the curve of her hips. There were a hundred different directions he could have taken the conversation. But, for reasons he couldn't quite grasp at the time, he went on with his question as if he hadn't caught the sexual overtone. "I've picked up a tail. I need you to run the plates. I'd do it myself but I'm not even supposed to be here."

"I know." Marion sighed. "What's the number?"

He gave her the plate number and waited while she did a search through the computer. The room seemed unusually quiet. No phones rang. No loud conversations. No hard soled shoes clacking on tile. But the hum from the overhead fluorescent lights seemed louder than he remembered.

"Is it a 1987 VW bug?" Marion asked staring at the computer.

"No, a dark, blue Chevy van."

Marion removed her hands from the keyboard and spun in her chair. "Then the plates are stolen."

(37)

After leaving the station, Brian stopped off at KFC and parked by the front door. The blue van was nowhere in sight. Still, he felt uneasy. Removing his service revolver from his shoulder holster, he checked the cylinder; it was fully loaded. Then, just to be on the safe side, he removed his spare .32 revolver from the glove box and shoved it inside his boot. He opened the door, climbed out of the car and went inside.

A rather chipper young lad with short maroon hair greeted Brian enthusiastically. Brian watched with amazement as the young man quickly and efficiently gathered up the order, stuffed it all in one large sack and set it on the counter. "Have a really great day, sir. And drive carefully." Brian left the counter chuckling, with no doubt in his mind that this kid was destined for sales or politics.

Outside, he opened the passenger side door, placed the sack on the passenger seat and closed the door. From behind him, he felt something solid jam him in the ribs. Then a giant hand grabbed him by the collar, spun him around and removed his revolver from his shoulder holster in one practiced motion. He found himself staring face to face with two men who could have easily played middle linebacker for any number of N.F.L. teams. They both had long hair and skintight shirts. The one pressing a .357 into Brian's ribs had a small, diamond shaped birthmark across the side of his nose.

"The boss wants to have a word with you," Birthmark said.

Brian's first thought was how to disarm the man. A quick elbow to Birthmark's forearm would do the trick, but his partner would likely drop Brian where he stood. As his heart hammered in his chest, he struggled to remain calm. Behind him he could hear traffic rumbling up and down Hayden Road. As he listened, it suddenly occurred to him that if the man referred to as The Boss had wanted him dead, it would have been over by now. Maybe The Boss had some information to share. Perhaps he was the missing link to the puzzle. Brian's curiosity was aroused. Still, deep inside, his flight or fight mechanism raged the eternal war. Common sense told him going along with these two Neanderthals was pure insanity. On the other hand, it might shed some light on the situation. He bit his lower lip. Questioning the logic in his next move, he looked up at Birthmark and said, "The boss have a name?"

Birthmark smiled at his partner. "Yeah, The Boss."

Brian sighed. "How silly of me."

"Let's go."

Feigning a smile, Brian said, "Lead on, McDuff."

The dark van that had been tailing him earlier was sitting at the far end of the parking lot under the shade of a huge mulberry tree. When the sliding door opened, Birthmark pushed Brian in and climbed in behind him. The other man took a seat behind the wheel. He started the engine, tromped on the gas and pulled out into traffic.

"Where are we going?" Brian asked.

"You weren't paying attention." Birthmark shook his head. "We're going to see the boss."

"I didn't catch his name."

"Didn't give it."

Twenty minutes later they pulled up behind a long, black limo and parked. Birthmark helped Brian from the van, walked him to the limo and opened the door. "Get in," he said.

Inside, Brian found himself face to face with Vince Decker who was sipping a glass of what appeared to be champagne. He was dressed in white shorts, Hawaiian shirt and sandals. If there had been a little more hair on his head, he might have looked a little like Don Ho.

Seated next to Decker, sweating profusely and wearing a look of grave concern, was Brian's good-for-nothing, brother-in-law Eric. He had on a blue and white-checkered sport shirt with the tail out, a pair of cut-off blue jeans, and Birkenstock sandals. An inch-long gold earring hung from his right ear.

Brian had more than a few questions, but he thought it best to wait until Decker was ready.

"Detective Fogarty," Decker said. "We meet again."

"Always a pleasure, Vince. To what do I owe the honor?"

Eric sat forward, his hands on his knees, and looked at Brian. "Brian, I —"

"Young Eric here," Decker cut in, "finds himself in an uneasy situation."

"How much?" Brian asked.

"Fifty grand and change," Decker said and sipped his champagne.

Brian shook his head, turned his sights on Eric. "You just don't learn, do you?"

"Brian, I —"

"There might be a way to resolve this situation peacefully," Decker cut in again.

Brian raised an eyebrow. His palms were sweating. "I'm listening."

Decker smiled. "Perhaps you could see your way clear to . . . shall we say, relieve Eric from his burden."

"What makes you think I would have that kind of money?"

"Sometimes people of your obvious intelligence, make sound investments. Sometimes they inherit valuables from a rich relative that can be turned into cash with relative ease. Or maybe they just sock away every spare dime they have until one day, *voila*, those pennies have transformed themselves into a healthy retirement fund."

Brian thought about it a moment. He could feel anger swelling inside him. He not only hated the fact that Eric had managed to lose over fifty-thousand dollars, he hated that he owed it to a low life, two bit shyster like Vince Decker. But then Eric had never been overly bright in anyone's eyes except his own.

Brian turned to Eric and asked him to step outside the car. Eric looked stunned. He fidgeted in his seat, looked at Decker then back at Brian. "Where do you want me to go?"

"I don't want you to go anywhere," Brian said. "I just want you to leave Mr. Decker and me alone so we can come to some sort of an arrangement."

Eric opened the door, climbed out, gave one last pleading glance, and closed the door. He wandered off down the sidewalk, glancing over his shoulder and talking to himself. The two Neanderthals leaned against the side of the car, their arms folded across their chests, watching him go.

Brian swallowed hard, cleared his throat. "Now," he began, his tone all business. "Let me tell you what you're going to do. You're going to forget this whole farce and renounce Eric's debt."

Decker smiled and tilted his head back in mock amusement. "Why would I do that?"

"You and I both know your races are fixed. And if I were to dig hard enough, something I haven't done up to now because I figured you just weren't worth the trouble, I bet I could find a disgruntled jockey or an unhappy stable boy who would be more than happy to testify that your whole operation is one big scam."

Decker twirled his champagne glass in his hand nervously. "You can't prove a thing and you know it."

"I don't have to. Once the word leaks out that your races are fixed, your customers will be as scarce as rainwater on the African plains. And I'll bet if I dig even harder, I might stumble across the fact that you're bringing in illegals from Mexico along with some very high quality pot, not to mention that pretty little mistress of yours. I'm sure the Mrs. would love to hear about her." Brian guessed at the mistress, but it was worth a shot. "And I'm sure if I dig real hard, I can find a connection between you and a professional killer named Jake Leighton."

Suddenly the glass snapped in Decker's hand. Blood began to flow from a cut on his palm. He pulled a monogrammed white handkerchief from his pocket, wrapped it around his hand then glared at Brian. "I don't know anybody named Leighton."

"That's a lie, Vince. You and I both know it. So let's cut the crap. Are we going to make a deal here or not? It makes no difference to me. Either way, Eric's debt is forgiven. It's just a matter of whether you stay in business after this meeting is over."

Decker put a closed fist against his mouth and coughed. "You know, Fogarty. People who push me usually don't live to regret it. My boys out there have been rather bored lately. They would love to get their hands dirty."

Brian lifted his pants leg, grasped the handle of his .32 revolver and made sure Decker saw him do it. "Your boys aren't quite as thorough as they could be."

"I can see that."

"Listen, Vince, I've had a bad couple of days. I really wouldn't mind taking you out. I could probably even convince homicide to sweep this one away. I don't think anyone would object."

Decker's gaze held on Brian. "We're talking a lot of money here. How's it going to look to my people if I let this slide? I could lose their respect. And if that happens, I lose control."

Brian snorted. "Frankly, I don't care how it looks; but if it helps you save face with your people and solves our problem, tell them I've agreed to pay you. They won't hear any different from me."

Holding his injured hand at this side and working his fingers gingerly, Decker stared out the window. The white handkerchief had turned a mixture of pink and red.

"And I want Leighton delivered directly to me," Brian added. "I've had enough excitement for one week."

Without turning from the window Decker said, "Do you have any understanding of loyalty, Fogarty?"

"As a matter of fact, I do. But I doubt our definitions are the same."

"If I do this," Decker said, inspecting his hand, wincing and then fixing his eyes on Brian, "what assurance do I have you won't go back on our deal and bust me anyway?"

The corners of Brian's mouth curved upward. He looked Decker square in the eye. "You don't."

Decker started to laugh. When he had regained his composure, he looked at Brian through stern eyes. "You ever want a job, stop by and see me. I could use a guy like you."

Forty minutes later, Brian and Eric were standing in the parking lot of Kentucky Fried Chicken watching the van drive away. Except for Brian's Taurus and a beat up old Chevy parked near the dumpsters, the parking lot was empty. The air smelled of grease and car exhaust.

"You're a piece of work, you know that?" Brian said.

"What happened?" Eric asked.

"I took care of it." Brian chose his words carefully. "And I told him I would see to it you never passed though the gates of his racetrack again."

A broad smile crossed Eric's face. He wrapped his arm around Brian's shoulder and shook him. "I can't thank you enough. I'll pay you back, I promise."

"Don't make promises you can't keep," Brian said, pulling away from Eric's grasp. "You've been lying to Christine and me all along. I guess I knew where you were really going when you had all those job interviews but I wanted to believe you were actually trying to change. Just another one of the many mistakes I've made lately." Brian started to laugh. "You're the one who should go into sales, not me. Anyone who could convince Vince Decker to keep loaning him money after he's thousands of dollars in debt could sell heaters in the Australian outback." Brian stopped, wiped the perspiration from his brow and shook his head. "But I'll tell you one thing, you need help. And I'm going to make sure you get it."

"What do you mean?" Eric asked.

"Tomorrow morning, I'm taking you to the company shrink. Maybe he can recommend a specialist."

"You make it sound like I got a disease or something."

"You do, Eric."

(38)

When Brian and Eric arrived home, Christine was sitting at the kitchen table drinking iced tea. She was wearing pink slacks and a white blouse. Her feet were bare. All jewelry and make-up had been removed.

Eric stormed through the kitchen without a word, tromped down the hall, and slammed his bedroom door behind him.

"What's the matter with him?" Christine asked.

"Later," Brian said. He grabbed a Coors from the refrigerator. It felt cold and refreshing going down.

"What took you so long?" Christine asked. "I'm starved."

Brian stood in the doorway, drinking his beer, leaning against the wall. His body ached; his mind exhausted. A good night's sleep would be welcome, if he could sleep at all.

"So what happened?" Christine repeated.

Brian let out a heavy sigh and sat down at the table. Rehashing the day's events would be like living them over again, and that was the last thing he wanted to do. Still, he owed Christine an explanation. She deserved it. So he told her everything, leaving out nothing with the exception of the heated conversation he and Eric had in front of Kentucky Fried Chicken. Christine listened intently. When he finished, he got up, snatched another beer and returned to his chair.

"Well," Christine said after a long silence. "You did the right thing."

Brian took a long sip off his beer. "I'm not sure *what's* right or wrong anymore. I crossed a very thin line today I swore I'd never cross. And once that line has been crossed, it's hard to go back."

"Don't be silly," Christine said. "You got Eric out of a big jam. You did what you had to do. You had no choice."

Brian was silent. He wanted to tell her he could have let Eric suffer the consequences of his own actions, but then that option had never crossed his mind until now. Besides, Eric had always been a source of uneasiness between them. He could do no wrong in his sister's eyes. Christine was the ever-doting older sister. She had been taking care of him ever since she was fourteen when her father ran off and left her mother with three kids. Perhaps that was one reason Eric had never grown up; he'd never had to.

"Look, honey," Christine said. She leaned her elbows on the tabletop and placed her chin in her cupped hands. "The last few days have been a nightmare. A lot has happened. I'm scared out of my wits that this crazy S.O.B. is going to come after us again. But we have to stick together. We have to see this through."

Brian reached out, took her hand, forced a smile and nodded. "I know."

"I'm going to go talk to Eric," Christine said.

"He's pretty upset with me." It came out before Brian realized he had even said it.

Christine dropped her hands and leaned back in her chair. "Why?"

If there had been any way out of this conversation, Brian would have taken it. Without a doubt, this would not go smooth. It never did. He cleared his throat, ran his finger across the side of the beer can and removed a half-inch long swipe of condensation. "I told him he needed help. His gambling is more of a problem than either of us thought. Tomorrow I'm going to talk to the department shrink and see if he can recommend a specialist."

"He's not a psycho!" Christine cried. "He just likes to gamble, that's all. Lots of people gamble. It's practically a national pastime."

"Not to the tune of fifty grand."

Slamming her hand on the table, Christine jumped to her feet. "You're always condemning him. Why don't you ever cut him some slack?" She turned and stormed out of the room. A moment later the bedroom door slammed shut.

Great, Brian thought. *What else could go wrong?*

(39)

Captain Fernandez leaned back in his desk chair, took a sip of bitter coffee from his Arizona Cardinals mug and perused the report handed him by Jerry Travers who was seated across the desk in a worn leather chair. When he felt satisfied the report contained nothing out of the ordinary, he gazed out over his reading glasses and stared at Jerry.

"I told you there was nothing going on," Fernandez said. His striped tie was loose and the top button of his white dress shirt was unbuttoned.

"It's my job to investigate all allegations concerning our police officers, Captain. You may not believe it, but I'm glad we came up empty." Travers' double-breasted suit was buttoned and his tie tight. His hair had been freshly cut.

Fernandez shot him a look that said he knew that was a lie. Travers was a self-serving, arrogant little weasel who would throw his own father in jail if it meant looking good to his superiors. The sight of Travers made Fernandez want to toss his pension aside and throw the piece of dirt out the window.

"But you have to admit," Travers continued. "There are still some unanswered questions regarding their activities."

"Like what?" Fernandez held up the report. "I see nothing in here that constitutes further investigation."

Travers folded his hands on his lap and took a deep breath. "Well, for starters, how is it that Bethencourt drives an antique Triumph TR 6, wears custom tailored suits and lives in a

216

two-story, six bedroom house in North Scottsdale on a detective's pay? And don't tell me he's some sort of financial wizard because I'm not buying it."

"He told me once," Fernandez said, "that he inherited some money from an aunt."

"We looked into that and could find nothing to substantiate such a claim."

"Well, then how should I know?" Fernandez barked out, throwing the report on his desk. "As long as my guys do their jobs, I don't care what they do on the side."

"Even if it's not legal?"

Fernandez felt his heart jump. His teeth were clinched so tight they hurt. There was a knock on the office door. "Enter!" Fernandez barked.

Jerry's partner, Marty Kirkland came into the room, walked over to Jerry without a word and handed him a 9x12 beige envelope. Kirkland wore an off-the-rack, gray suit and a yellow tie. His face bore a dark shadow.

"What's this?" Jerry asked.

"I think you should look at it, Jerry," Kirkland said.

Travers opened the envelope and removed the contents.

Fernandez eased back in his chair, trying to calm his churning insides, and took a sip of coffee.

Kirkland remained standing, fidgeted with his tie, glanced at his watch.

Jerry read the note, then looked at a photo and smiled. "I'm afraid our case may have just reopened itself, Captain." He tossed the contents of the envelope on the desk and looked up at Kirkland.

Fernandez picked up the photo and papers and inspected them. He could hardly believe his eyes. The photo was of two men sitting in a limo; and although there was a glare from the window, it was clear the two were Vince Decker and Brian Fogarty.

"This doesn't prove anything," Fernandez said tossing the photo on the desk. "Fogarty is a detective, for Pete's sake. It's part of his job to infiltrate crime organizations. It's how we *real* police officers do our job."

"And it's part of my job to investigate internal corruption. And in my opinion—in light of this new evidence—there's enough here to warrant continued investigation."

"Get out of my office!"

Travers' face turned a bright red. "I'll be sending some people to pick up both Fogarty and Bethencourt for questioning. If you see them before I do, I expect you to place them under house arrest and contact me immediately. I also intend to inform my superiors of your lack of cooperation in this matter." He turned and stormed out of the room with Kirkland on his tail.

When they were gone, Fernandez closed the door, picked up the phone and punched in a number. After two rings, Detective Bill Green of the special task force picked up the phone.

"Travers just left my office," Fernandez said. "He has a photo of Fogarty with Vince Decker. Now Travers is picking them up for questioning. I told you I wanted this thing wrapped up before IAD got too close. Now the whole thing is blowing up in our faces. We were nearly in the clear until this happened." Fernandez wiped a hand across his face. It came up wet. "Now it's too late. I put my career on the line over this, Green. You told me you could handle it."

"Stay calm. You're overreacting. Only you and I know of our activities over the last few weeks, so don't panic."

"We should have never tried to—"

"I told you, don't panic."

Fernandez paused, licked his lips. "What do we do now?"

"We lay low. Let the chips fall were they may. It's too late for us to stop it."

Without another word, Fernandez placed the phone on the receiver. He opened the bottom desk drawer and removed a full bottle of Jack Daniels. He poured a two finger shot into his Cardinals mug and downed it in one gulp. When he looked up, Detective Marion Bantor was standing at the door. She had on a green pants suit with black pumps. The corners of her mouth were turned downward. Her eyes inspected the carpet.

"How long have you been there?" Fernandez said curtly.

"Just walked up as you were finishing your coffee, sir."

Fernandez took the cup and bottle and shoved them into the bottom desk drawer. "What is it?"

Marion shuffled from foot to foot. "I have some bad news."

"Wonderful," Fernandez said waving his hand through the air. "Just what I need."

After Marion had explained what had happened at the hotel and had left, Fernandez clinched his fist tight under the desk. His entire body shook. For more than a minute he sat motionless, considering his options, listening to his stomach gurgle and churn. Then he hurled his coffee mug across the room and watched it shatter into tiny fragments against the far wall and rain down over his sofa.

(40)

Jake Leighton took a room at a dive little motel called THE ECSTASY. Initially, the desk clerk — a native Middle Eastern man with rudimentary English skills — had trouble comprehending that Jake required the room for the night and not by the hour. After the initial confusion, the clerk took Jake's cash and accepted the false name without a second glance.

Once Jake had settled into his room and found it adequate, he sat on the bed, removed his shoes and laid back. His thoughts turned to Brian Fogarty. No one had ever evaded Jake the way Fogarty had done over the last few days. He had made Jake look bad. Jake found this condition totally unacceptable. But the game was far from over. Brian Fogarty *would* die, of that Jake was certain. His only dilemma was to ensure his own survival once the game came to its inevitable conclusion. With his identity revealed, he would have no choice but to flee the country.

After a while, Jake realized he could not recall when he had eaten last. A rack of lamb with a bottle of Pinot Noir would do quite nicely, but it was doubtful a suitable restaurant would be in the immediate vicinity. Ah, sweet New York; he would miss it. Taking a glance around his room, he shook his head. "If dear old Mummy could see me now," he said aloud.

Deciding he would have to rough it just a little longer, he sat up on the edge of the bed, pulled a phone book from a rickety wicker nightstand, looked up the nearest Pizza Hut and ordered a large with everything.

"You have beer?" Jake inquired after a meek sounding boy had taken his order.

"I'm afraid not sir."

"I'll tell you what," Jake offered. "You stop on the way over and pick up a six-pack of Heineken for me and I'll throw in an extra twenty for your trouble."

A momentary silence hummed on the phone line.

"Your pizza and beverage will be there within thirty minutes, sir."

After he hung up, Jake climbed off the lumpy bed, stripped and climbed into the shower. He let the hot water run across his head and cascade down his back and felt the warmth penetrate his aching muscles and soothe his weary bones. He was getting too old for this line of work. Before leaving New York he had promised himself this would be his last job. It should have been simple. It had been anything but.

As he toweled himself off, a knock sounded at the door. Ever leery, Jake hurried across the room, pulled his Beretta, went to the door, and peered through the peephole. It was the pizza delivery boy. And unless Jake missed his guess, there would be some liquid refreshment in the closed sack the boy clutched under his right arm. Jake opened the door, slipped the boy two twenties, and sent him on his way.

Perched on the bed enjoying his greasy slab of cheese, tomato and dough, Jake found the remote, turned on the TV and flipped through all the channels twice. He settled on an old John Wayne western, turned the sound down low and cracked open a beer.

Half an hour later, his hunger satisfied, he folded his hands behind his head, closed his eyes and drifted off to sleep.

When he awoke, the room was dark. He felt for the light switch and flipped it on. He picked up the phone and dialed.

"Hutching, Morrison, and Blake," the woman said.

"Hello, Mary," Jake said. "It's me."

"Oh, Mr. Leighton. Are you enjoying your vacation?"

"How could one not enjoy the Virgin Islands? Temperature hovers at a balmy eighty degrees in the daytime and drops to a chilling seventy-two at night."

"Sounds lovely," she cooed.

"Could you get me Mr. Morrison, Mary? I need to speak with him right away."

"Sure, Mr. Leighton. I'll let him know you're waiting."

"Mr. Leighton," Harry Morrison said a minute later. "How's the weather down there?"

"Weather's great. Listen, Harry, I need you to do me a big favor."

"Anything you want, Mr. Leighton."

"I need you to cash in everything I have that's liquid and have a check waiting for me when I get back. And arrange to have the remainder of my assets transferred to a bank abroad. As soon as I make the necessary arrangements, I'll call you with the account numbers."

There was a long pause on the other end. "Are you in some kind of trouble?" Harry Morrison asked.

"No, no," Jake lied. "I've met a couple of young English gentlemen down here who have made me a business proposition that's too good to pass up. But it requires me to move to Europe for a couple of years. Besides, New York is beginning to be a bit of a bore. I need a change."

"I'd really hate to lose you as a client, Mr. Leighton. I believe our firm has handled your money very well over the last eleven years; and I see no reason not to continue our mutually lucrative relationship. Our international division would be glad to handle your account and any concerns you might have. It would make your transition much smoother to stay with a firm with which you already have a working relationship."

"That is a thought, Harry," Jake said. "We can discuss that when I get back. But in the meantime, if you would be so kind as to do as I ask, I would appreciate it."

An hour later, Jake waltzed into the office of Vince Decker. The office was full of leather and glass encased paintings of

English hunting scenes. He walked up to a middle-aged woman with graying brown hair and a bad overbite sitting at the receptionist counter and asked to see Mr. Decker.

"And you are?"

"Tell Mr. Decker it's his cousin from Minneapolis."

She looked at the appointment book on her desk and frowned. "I don't show you on his schedule."

Jake smiled. "Just tell him I'm here. I'm sure he'll see me."

She picked up an inner office line, announced Jake's arrival, informed the listener she was making the post office run, and hung up.

"He didn't sound happy," she said, "but he said to send you back."

"I thought he might."

"Third door on the left," she said, pointing down the hall. She stood, gathered up an armload of letters, envelopes and packages, and headed for the front door.

Jake headed down the wide hallway lined with photos of racehorses, his stomach churning. Someone was going to pay for this fiasco, maybe everyone. He entered Decker's office and took a seat in a visitor's chair opposite a large mahogany desk.

Decker looked up from the computer and said, "What are you doing here?" His Hawaiian shirt was unbuttoned past his chest. A large, oval shaped, gold medallion lay nestled among his dark chest hairs like an egg in a bird's nest.

"I need the name and address of the guy that arranged this whole mess."

"No way. That was not the arrangement. You were to work strictly through me."

Jake clinched his teeth. "Things change."

Decker was quiet, his fists clamped together under his chin. "If I give you what you want, a very sweet and lucrative business arrangement will go right down the tubes."

"Your business arrangements are of no concern to me. I want the guy's name and address that arranged this thing; and while you're at it, I want the other parties' addresses as well. And I want them now."

"I can't do that. I should never have gotten involved in this. You're on your own. And as of now, our association is terminated. If anyone asks, I've never heard of you. Now get out."

"Apparently, you're not listening."

At the same time Decker reached under his desk, Jake heard the faint sound of a buzzer in the adjoining room. He pulled his Beretta and gripped it tight. An instant later, Decker's two thugs barged in the office, guns drawn. Jake put a bullet in each of the two thugs brains as they came through the door. He stood, took two steps towards Decker and stuck the end of his silencer to Decker's forehead. "Listen to me very carefully. I've had about all I can take of this God forsaken hellhole of a city and everyone in it. You're going to give me the information I want, or you're going to find out what pain really is."

"Okay, okay," Decker sputtered. "Take it easy. We can work this out."

"That's better," Jake said. "Start talking."

(41)

Marion and Brian were walking past a fountain made from pieces of scrap metal and formed to look like a flock of migrating geese. Silently, they strolled down the concrete walk, past the outdoor amphitheater, until they could no longer see the stationhouse. They took a seat on a lattice wooden bench under the shade of a towering elm.

Brian had on a short sleeve shirt, tan slacks, a wide brimmed straw hat and dark glasses. Marion, still dressed in her green pants suit, sported a pair of large, round mirrored sunglasses.

"What was so important you couldn't tell me over the phone," Brian asked.

Marion looked up at the sky with her hand cupped over her brow. "I know I should have mentioned it before but I wasn't sure of what was happening until a few minutes ago." She put her hands on her lap and turned to Brian. "But now I'm sure. And this isn't something I wanted to say over the phone."

"Talk to me."

"Ever heard of Jerry Travers?"

"Rings a bell."

"It didn't to me. How do you know him?"

"I don't really know him. I've only heard the name. I noticed this Caddy outside Elaine's apartment the other day and ran the license plate. It's registered to Jerry Travers."

"Well, that makes sense. Do you know who he is?"

"No. I've been so busy I haven't had a chance to follow up on it."

An elderly couple in matching t-shirts and shorts strolled past holding hands. They smiled, said "Hello," and hurried down the path.

"He's I.A.D.," Marion said.

Brian felt a sudden twinge of fear.

"I didn't know who he was at first, but I saw him come out of the captain's office twice and he didn't look happy either time. So you know me—Ms. Curiosity. I asked around and found out he was I.A.D. I've never been involved with I.A.D. and it made me nervous, so I dug a little deeper."

"He's investigating me," Brian said.

"Yes. You and Gabriel."

Brian shook his head. "I knew this was going to happen."

Marion pulled off her glasses, revealing a set of wide eyes. She looked at Brian as if his teeth had just turned blue. "What do you mean you knew this would happen? What are you involved in?"

"Indirectly, I've crossed one too many lines lately. It has to stop." His foot bounced up and down on the pavement so fast his knee was a blur.

"What are you talking about? What's going on?" Brian looked around. The elderly couple was gone. Several joggers in bright garb bounded down a nearby path and a group of skateboarders were doing tricks across the clearing. "Are you familiar with the name Vince Decker?"

"Sure. He owns Desert Downs and runs a string of hookers. Why? Does he have something to do with this?"

"A few years ago," Brian began, nodding. "Gabe and I got a tip that Decker was bringing in a shipment. We were all ready to take him when Gabe told me the shipment was delayed and wouldn't arrive for another week. So we postponed the bust. It was all a lie. The next day Gabe called in sick. I went about my regular duties thinking everything was fine. The following day, Gabe tells me he was wrong and the shipment did come in the night before and we missed it. Over the course of the next several months, I noticed similar patterns when it came to Decker. I figured Gabe was padding his bank account with Decker's money. So I confronted him."

Marion was leaning close to Brian, her mouth hanging open like her jaw weighed more than she could stand. "What did he say?"

"He denied it, of course. Acted insulted that I would even suggest such a thing. But the evidence was there. I should have done something about it at the time, but Gabe's my partner and my friend. I just couldn't bring myself to turn him in."

"I can't believe what I'm hearing," Marion said. She slapped both hands on her thighs, leaned against the bench back, and looked straight ahead. "You know a cop is taking payoffs and you do nothing?"

Hearing it in that particular tone only compounded Brian's realization that he had made a huge mistake. "I know, Marion. Like I said, sometimes you cross a line and don't even realize it. Then, before you know it, the line that was once so impassable, seems to fade . . . and eventually, it disappears all together."

They were quiet. The skateboarders moved on to another location and the joggers grew less frequent. Birds chirped in a neighboring tree. A squirrel scurried across the lawn and disappeared among a clump of oleander bushes. The fountain hissed in the distance.

"What are you going to do?" Marion finally asked. "I think Travers is arranging to have you two picked up for questioning."

"I'm going to talk to Gabe. He needs to understand the party's over and it's time to come clean. Unless he tells the truth, it's going to be hard to convince I.A.D. that I wasn't directly involved. Either way, my career is over, not to mention the possibility of a nice little stretch of jail time. I deserve to be reprimanded—even fired—for holding back information; but I don't intend to do jail time." Brian stood up. "I'll walk you back to the station and talk to Gabe while I'm there."

Marion stood. "He's not at the station. He's been on sick call for the last three days. I assume he's at home."

"That's interesting. Then I'll pay him a visit at home and see how he's doing."

Brian looked into Marion's eyes. He could see her disappointment and strangely, it hurt him. He respected and admired Marion. She was a good cop, a straight cop. And for the first time, Brian realized, he was not.

"Why don't you turn me in yourself?" Brian asked.

Deep creases formed on Marion's forehead. She doubled up her fist and punched Brian in the arm. "You idiot. If you don't know the answer to that, then Nick's right; I really have been wasting my time."

The elevator doors opened. Brian and Marion walked out into the detectives' room. Brian spotted Nick across the room seated at his desk with the phone pressed to his ear. His eyes were wide and he seemed excited. About the time Brian turned to Marion to say goodbye, Nick looked up and saw them. He waved them over.

"He's got something," Marion said. She took off at a fast clip and Brian followed.

They pulled up next to Nick as he hung up the phone and sat back in his chair, smiling. "That was a courtesy call from Detective Ramirez with the Phoenix Police Department."

"What happened?" Brian asked.

Nick gave Brian a sideways glance that could kill and turned his attention to Marion. "Ramirez knows we've been after Vince Decker for years and thought we'd like to know what happened."

"What happened?" Marion asked.

"Vince Decker's secretary just found him and his two bodyguards in his office; and, it would seem, someone was apparently very unhappy with the latest race results."

"I don't like this at all," Brian said. "I have to get home."

"Go," Marion said. "I'll keep in touch."

* * * * *

Jake Leighton eased his car past the address given him by Vince Decker, pulled to the curb and parked two doors down. He smiled to himself at the quaintness of the homes with their towering palm trees, tangled orange trees, and lawns in desperate need of water. They were a far cry from the compact and towering buildings of New York City.

He checked his gun under his suit coat, climbed out of the car, and strolled down the sidewalk towards Fogarty's house. A woman across the street came out of the front door, turned on a sprinkler attached to a hose, and waved at Jake. He smiled and waved back. The woman went back inside and closed the door.

Parked in front of the house was a battered Volkswagen with a crumpled front fender. Jake walked up to the door and rang the bell. He could hear activity inside as he waited. A moment later the door opened and a young man with blonde hair, wearing shorts and a tank top stood before him.

"Whatever you're selling," the young man said. "We don't want any." He started to close the door.

Jake reached out a large hand, placed it on the door and pushed it open.

"I said —"

"I'm afraid this isn't going to be your day, young man." Jake pulled his gun, pushed his way through the door and closed it behind him.

(42)

As usual, the traffic on Scottsdale Road loped along at the pace of a ninety-year-old marathon runner. Brian pulled off and took the side streets. Ten minutes later, as he drove down his street, he noticed a tan Buick sitting in front of his house. He recognized it immediately. As he drove past he saw Captain Fernandez sitting behind the wheel. Brian pulled in the driveway, parked and climbed out of the car.

The captain met him in the middle of the drive, wearing a wrinkled tan suit and scuffed brown shoes. He had dark bags under his eyes and the skin around his jaw seemed to be sagging. "You hear about Decker?" Fernandez asked.

Brian reached out and shook the captain's hand. "Yeah. Just a little while ago." He was troubled by the captain's appearance and the strong odor of bourbon on his breath.

"Just got the call on it over the radio while I was waiting for you. That's a few tax dollars saved."

"If you just heard about it, that's not why you're here."

Fernandez looked over his shoulder and inspected the neighborhood. Then he put an arm on Brian's shoulder and said, "I need to talk to you. Can we go inside? This heat's about to kill me."

"Sure, come on in. I'll fix us some iced tea."

Once inside, Brian noticed a handwritten note on the table that read: Went to a movie with Margie, back by five. Christine.

He felt relieved. For the moment, she was out of harm's way. He started to fix the tea.

"You have anything stronger than tea?" Fernandez asked taking a seat at the kitchen table.

Brian's eyes went wide. "I thought you gave it up."

"It would seem only temporarily."

In the cabinet were two bottles of wine, a half-empty bottle of bourbon, and a bottle of vodka; the refrigerator held three beers. "I'm fresh out of liquor, Captain. Sorry."

Fernandez looked at Brian through sagging eyes and forced a smile. "You're a good man, Brian. I've always liked you."

Brian poured two glasses of iced tea and joined the captain at the table. "You've always been good to me, Captain." He noticed tears forming in the captain's eyes and realized the sight was as foreign as a sunny December day in the city of Seattle.

"I'm an old man, Brian." Fernandez ran his hand across his face. "Two years from retirement. And you know what I have to look forward to? Nothing. Not a thing. My wife is gone. My kids won't even talk to me. Hell, I don't even know them anymore. Spent too much time working, and not enough time being a father. The only thing I've ever known was the job. Put everything I had into it. And now it's all crashing down around me."

"What's happened?"

"You know you were my protégé. I was always proud of you. And now . . . " He let it trail away as a single tear dripped down his cheek. The man, who had been known around the station as "The Rock" was beginning to crumble. Brian felt his throat tighten.

Brian suddenly realized he had not only betrayed himself with his actions, but he had let down the one man who had been like a father to him since he moved to Phoenix; the one man who had cared for and nurtured his career and saw to it that every opportunity was presented to him. And how had Brian repaid the captain's trust and kindness? By looking the other way when a fellow officer turned bad. He hardly knew what to say, but he owed the captain an explanation.

Brian stood, walked to the counter, poured two more glasses of tea and sat back down at the table. "I don't know what to say, sir. I should have done something sooner and maybe I could have avoided this mess. But I just couldn't bring myself to turn him in. He's my partner."

Fernandez looked up, his eyes wide; his eyebrows rose high on his forehead. "Partner? What are you talking about?"

Brian was puzzled. "What are you talking about?"

"I'm talking about you and Gabe taking kick-backs from Vince Decker. You think I didn't know?"

Suddenly it all made sense. Why wouldn't the captain think they were both involved? Partners knew everything about each other; or they were supposed to. "I know about the I.A.D. investigation, Captain."

"I couldn't keep Travers out of it," Fernandez said. He doubled his fist and clenched it so tightly his knuckles turned white. "When Nick Carey initially told me you guys had turned, I didn't believe him. In fact, I threw him out of my office. After I thought about it for a couple of days, I decided not to take any chances and asked Bill Green from Special Forces to look into the matter; he owed me a favor, and I asked him to keep it quiet. I wanted to keep it within the department, so to speak. I needed to find out for myself what was going on. I figured if you guys were really dirty, I didn't want it going on my record, or yours, for that matter. I would have asked for your badges, had you resign, stating personal reasons, and you would have gone out quietly and squeaky-clean. But then Carey went to I.A.D. and Travers showed up."

"Captain," Brian said, "I think I'd better fill you in on the facts."

Fernandez took a sip of tea, frowned, and leaned back in his chair. "Better late than never."

Clearing his throat, Brian said, "You remember the shipment that got by us out at the airport a while back?"

"Yeah. You had some bad information on the date and time."

"No. We had it right. But Gabe told me the shipment had been postponed."

"It wasn't?"

"No. And we missed it. The plane landed out in Carefree, instead of P.I.A. By the time I found out about it, the dope was gone, probably in ten different directions. That's when I began to suspect Gabe had turned. I can't prove anything, but I think Gabe has been taking Decker's money in exchange for information regarding our investigations into Decker's operations."

"And you didn't do anything."

Brian shrugged. It sounded just as bad coming from the captain as it had from Marion. He wanted to explain the loyalty he felt for his partner and their long friendship. But there was nothing he could say, no justification that could excuse allowing a ton and a half of heroin into the country. He lowered his head. "No sir, I didn't."

Fernandez leaned forward, placed his elbows on the table and produced a broad smile. "Frankly I'm relieved."

"Relieved? I don't understand."

"Relieved that you weren't directly involved. And although I don't condone your actions, I do understand them. Don't forget I'm the one who lectured you about loyalty and a code of ethics within the department. What goes on within the department stays within the department. That's always been my philosophy, and that's why I resented Travers sticking his nose into our business." He paused a moment, sipped his tea. "Travers showed me a photo that looks rather incriminating. Perhaps you'd care to explain it."

"What photograph?"

"A photo of you and Decker sitting in his limo."

Brian pursed his lips and nodded. "I can explain."

"I figured you could."

"You know my worthless brother-in-law, Eric?"

"I've met him."

"To say he has a bit of a gambling problem would be an understatement. He was into Decker for over fifty grand. I, shall we say, was working out an arrangement that would get Eric off the hook."

"What kind of an arrangement?"

"I suggested it might be in his best interest to let Eric's debt slide. I told him I was sure I could find some people that would testify to his illegal activities." He hesitated. "I even suggested his wife might find out about his extra-marital affair."

"Was he having an affair?" Fernandez asked.

Brian shrugged his shoulders. "Don't know. But I wouldn't be surprised. It was a calculated gamble."

Fernandez nodded. "I like your style. That's something I might have done, back in my earlier days."

Brian felt his mouth crinkle in the first smile he'd had in some time.

"Ironic, huh? If you'd have waited a day, you wouldn't have had to bother," Fernandez said. "With Decker out of the picture, Eric's debt problem seems to have been resolved."

Brian was thoughtful. Had Decker really hired Leighton? And if so, what did he have to gain? And why would he go through the trouble of setting up a meeting with Brian in the hope of convincing him to pay Eric's debt if he planned to have Brian eliminated? Perhaps he'd planned on killing two birds with one stone, as the saying goes; collect the money from Brian, then get rid of a sore spot. But it just didn't make sense. There had to be more.

"If you hear from Gabe," Fernandez said, breaking Brian's train of thought. "Tell him to turn himself in to me. It'll go much easier on him if he does." He tipped back his glass and drained the rest of the tea.

"Before I found out about Decker, I was about to head over to Gabe's house and talk to him. But I thought it best to come home and check on Christine, given the circumstances. I'll call him tonight, after I'm sure Christine is safe, and talk to him."

"Good. But if he won't listen, I'll have to issue a warrant."

"I'll convince him," Brian said wondering exactly how he was going to do it.

"It won't be easy convincing Travers of all this, you know. He sees this as his shot at a promotion. He's liable to be very disappointed."

"Breaks my heart. I'll explain it to him real slow so he'll be sure to understand."

After the captain had left, Brian went into the living room and checked his messages. There were three. The first one was a recorded voice informing him he had been selected for a special, once-in-a-lifetime offer, and he had to call before five today. The second was Christine's office informing her of the Wilson's decision to purchase the McCutcheon home. And the third was from Gabe. His voice sounded shaky and slurred:

"Brian, this is Gabe. I screwed up royally this time, buddy. Got in way over my head. I'm so sorry. I tried to call it off, I really did, but it's gone too far. Call me at home, please. I'll be waiting."

As soon as the recording finished, Brian felt a chill run up his spine. He didn't want to believe that his friend and partner for over seven years had actually hired Leighton to kill him, but it fit perfectly into the theory he had been formulating over the last few days. And much as he feared discovering the whole truth, he knew he had to. There was no turning back.

He picked up the phone and dialed Gabe's number. There was no answer.

Then from down the hall, he caught a whiff of a strangely out of place yet familiar odor. He recognized it instantly — it was burned gunpowder. Reaching down into his boot, he removed his .32 and grasped it firmly in his right hand. Easing down the hall, the smell grew stronger and seemed to be coming from Eric's room. Brian's heart raced as he crept towards the door. Once inside, he gasped for air. Across the room, seated in his favorite chair was Eric . . . with two bullet holes through his head. His eyes were staring straight ahead, and his mouth was gaped open.

Brian's stomach churned, and he fought back the urge to vomit. Dead bodies were sometimes part of the job, but he had never grown used to the sight. And seeing Eric sprawled across his chair, murdered in his own home, was more than Brian could stand. He threw back his head, shook his fists in the air and shrieked.

It occurred to him Leighton might still be in the house. He dropped to one knee, his gun out in front of him. Wiping the tears from his eyes with the back of his hand, he went to the closet and opened the door: no one. Although he was sure of the outcome, he rushed to Eric's side and checked his pulse, but Eric's skin was cold and no pulse existed. Then Brian noticed the note pinned to Eric's shirt. It read:

Sorry I missed you, but when the cop pulled
up out front I thought it might be best to leave.
By the way, your partner sounded upset. I think
I'll see what I can do to help. See you soon.

Brian ripped the note from Eric's shirt and threw it to the floor. He rushed out into the kitchen, phoned Marion and filled her in.

"Stay right there," Marion said. "I'll make the necessary calls and meet you there."

"No. I have to get over to Gabe's. I think Leighton is headed over there, and I don't want what happened to Eric to happen to Gabe."

"You shouldn't leave the scene, Brian. It would look bad."

"It's a chance I'll have to take. And listen, Christine should be home soon. I don't want her seeing Eric this way. Do me a favor and post an officer out front to make sure she doesn't come in. Then take her to the station and keep her safe until this is over."

"But, Brian—"

"Just do it, Marion. Please."

The line went quiet. Just as Brian was about to hang up, Marion said, "Be careful."

"Always."

He snatched his keys off the counter, ran to the car, and laid rubber down the street. His sole thought was reaching Gabe before Jake Leighton did.

(43)

Jake Leighton pulled his rented Lexus up to the curb and parked across the street from Gabriel Bethencourt's house. He turned off the engine and checked the area. It was an older neighborhood with towering trees that shaded the entire street. The homes were old and looked expensive.

When he felt confident no one had noticed him, he climbed out of the car and strolled up to Gabe's door. He knocked three times. No answer. Then he tried the doorknob. Locked. He glanced over his shoulder at the quiet neighborhood and smiled. He stepped off the front porch, walked around back and tried the back door. It was also locked. From his back pocket, he extracted a small pouch and removed a long silver instrument. Inserting it into the lock, he twisted until he felt the gears click free. He pulled his gun from inside his coat and eased the door open. It squawked from lack of oil. The constant drone of the air-conditioner was the only sound that immediately drew his attention——that and the smell of cheap aftershave. He crept through the kitchen, inspected the living room, and eased down the hall into each bedroom. No one seemed to be home. When he had made his way back to the kitchen, a deep male voice came from behind him.

"Don't move!"

Jake kept his back to the voice, slipped his gun into the front of his pants and pulled his coat over it.

"Drop the gun."

Jake held up his hands and turned around slowly. Gabe stood in the hallway—his .38 police special pointed at Jake's chest. Bethencourt's hand shook. His face was gaunt and pale. He wore a pair of khaki Dockers and an unbuttoned floral shirt.

"So, Mr. Bethencourt," Jake said. "We meet at last."

"How did you find me?"

Jake shrugged. "In Vince's defense, he was not overly eager to tell me your whereabouts, but in the end he was quite cooperative."

"This has to stop!" Gabe demanded. "I made a mistake. I don't want you to go through with it."

"It makes no difference to me if I finish the job or not, as long as I get paid."

Gabe motioned towards the kitchen table with his gun. He licked his lips. "The money's on the table in the grocery sack. Take it and go."

Jake glanced at the sack on the table and smiled. It would have been simple to pick up the money and leave, but simple was not the way of the world. Too many people had seen his face. Life as he knew it was over. People would have to pay for this, and Decker and his thugs were just a down payment.

"May I?" Jake asked, motioning towards the table.

"Slowly." Gabe grasped his gun with both hands.

Jake walked over to the table, picked up the sack, counted the money, and slipped it into his inside coat pocket. As he did so, he jerked the gun from his pants dropped to one knee and leveled the gun on Gabe.

Brian pulled his Taurus into Gabe's driveway. He was trying to figure out what to say. He and Gabe had been friends for many years. This would not be easy, but he had to know the truth, no matter how much it hurt.

Easing his car down the long drive that led to the back of the house, he pulled up next to Gabe's Mercedes and turned off the engine. As he climbed out of the car, he noticed the back door standing open. Hurrying towards the door, his eyes searching the area, he spotted something that made him stop. On the cement, trailing away from the door and down the drive was what appeared to be blood. Brian pulled his weapon and crept towards the back door.

Once inside, he found more blood scattered across the kitchen floor. He knelt down and took a closer look. The blood was fresh. Whatever had happened had occurred recently. After a slow, careful search revealed an empty house, he ran outside and followed the blood until it stopped. There were scuffmarks on the drive not too far from the corner of the house. Someone had been dragged out back and loaded into a car. Brian had a queasy feeling.

Trotting back to his car, he picked up the cell phone, called Marion and filled her in on what he had found.

"You were right to call me, Brian. Now get out of there. When Travers got wind of the shooting at your house, he went ballistic. He and his men are heading to both of your houses to bring the two of you in. It won't look good for you if you're there when they arrive."

"Did you intercept Christine?"

"She's at the station. But she's not exactly a pillar of cooperation, if you know what I mean."

Just then Brian heard sirens.

"Too late," Brian shouted. "They're here."

He tossed the phone on the seat, fired up the engine and started down the drive. He could hear Marion yelling his name through the phone on the seat.

Two marked police cars pulled up in front of the house and blocked the drive. A dark sedan squealed to a halt behind them and Jerry Traver's partner, Marty Kirkland, emerged from the car wearing a broad grin. Four officers jumped out of the marked car with their weapons drawn. Brian had no choice. He stopped the car, climbed out and placed his hands on the top of the car. "I'm a police officer," he shouted.

"Keep your hands on the car," one of the officers said.

(44)

The knock on the door startled Captain Fernandez. He slipped a nearly empty bottle of Jack Daniels into his bottom desk drawer, wiped his lips with the back of his hand and started shuffling through the paperwork piled on his desk.

"Enter," he said.

Jerry Travers entered the office looking as dapper as a Hollywood superstar. He had on a double-breasted pinstriped suit with a red silk tie and matching handkerchief.

Fernandez felt the urge to crawl out the window and find the nearest bar. The last thing he needed right now was this arrogant jerk prancing around the office like a stallion out for stud. He took a deep breath and leaned back in his chair.

"What is it now, Travers?" Fernandez shuffled through some files on his desk.

Travers took the chair across from the captain and crossed his legs. "We have a new development, Captain."

"Great."

"As you know, I sent my people to pick up Fogarty and Bethencourt for questioning."

"Yeah."

"We found Fogarty at Bethencourt's house, alone."

Fernandez shook his head. He hid his shaking hand under the desk. His head was pounding like a two-ton jackhammer. "Would you get to the point? I have work to do."

"We've arrested Fogarty on suspicion of murder."

Fernandez came out of his seat. "What?"

"Bethencourt is missing. There's blood all over the house, and Fogarty was in the process of vacating the premises when we arrived."

"You don't seriously think Detective Fogarty killed Detective Bethencourt, do you? You must be delusional. Did you ask Brian . . . " He caught himself. "I mean Detective Fogarty. Did you ask him what happened?"

"Of course, Captain. He gave me some cock-and-bull story about Detective Bethencourt being involved in the recent attempt on his life. Said he received a phone message from Bethencourt to come over to his house immediately and when he arrived, he found the place just as we did."

Fernandez was finding it difficult to hide his mounting contempt. But at the moment, he just didn't care. He had had about all he could take of Travers. A drink was sounding awfully good. He tried to focus. "Did you check out his story?"

"I have a full crew going over the scene as we speak and another crew at Fogarty's, including the coroner."

"Coroner?" Fernandez frowned. "What happened? Who's been killed?"

"A young man by the name of Eric Aberst was found at the Fogarty residence. Shot twice through the head."

"And you think Fogarty did this?"

"The evidence points in that direction, Captain."

"Travers, you are an idiot."

Travers stood up, his eyes wide. "I resent that remark, Captain. You have no right—"

Fernandez waved a dismissive hand, stood up, grabbed his coat and headed for the door.

"Where are you going?" Travers asked.

"I'm going to find out what happened."

Brian sat on the edge of a hard metal cot staring through the bars of a six-by-six cell in the Scottsdale City Jail. In the outer room, he could hear people talking, phones ringing, and computer keyboards clicking.

Sprawled across the cot against the opposite wall was a smelly man in desperate need of a bath snoring loud enough to knock the plaster off the walls. Brian sighed and wondered how things had got so out of hand?

He was drawn from his thoughts when Captain Fernandez marched through the door, followed by an armed guard.

"Brian, what's going on?" Fernandez demanded when he reached the cell.

"It's a long story, Captain."

The guard inserted a key into the lock and opened the door.

"Let's go," Fernandez said. "We need to go over to your house and get the recording Gabriel left for you. I believe that's your ticket out of this mess."

Brian lifted his aching body from the cot and walked towards the cell door just as Jerry Travers stormed through the outer door.

"What are you doing?" Travers demanded.

"We're going to Fogarty's house to get the tape. You can follow us in your car."

"This is my bust, Fernandez! You can't waltz in like this and take him out. There are procedures to follow. Bail needs to be posted."

Fernandez whipped around and glared at Travers. "It's Captain Fernandez to you Detective Travers. And I *have* waltzed in here and had Fogarty released. If you have a problem with that, you can go on over to the courthouse and talk to Judge Masterson."

The guard, a pudgy man with a couple extra chins who had remained silent during the exchange, handed Travers a sheet of paper and took a step back.

"I'm sure," Fernandez continued, "if you read that form carefully, you will find everything in order. He's been released to my custody."

Travers glanced over the release form. "My superiors are not going to be pleased about this. You're exceeding your authority. When I get through with you, you'll wish you'd chosen a different line of work."

Fernandez frowned, crinkled his brow. "Too late."

Travers wheeled around and stormed out the door.

Brian smiled. It was great to see the old captain back in action.

"I guess," Fernandez said, "that means he won't be joining us."

"Be a lot quieter ride that way."

They arrived at Brian's house to find a half dozen police cars, an unmarked brown Buick, a paramedics van, a coroner's wagon, and roughly twenty officers scurrying in and around a string of yellow crime scene tape. Brian parked two doors down and they climbed out of the car. As they crossed the front yard, a male and female officer were standing by the front door smoking cigarettes and laughing.

"You two find this situation amusing?" Captain Fernandez asked.

Upon recognizing the captain, the officers snapped to attention. "No sir," the male officer said. "We were just —"

"I know what you were doing." Fernandez stopped, looked at their nametags and continued on.

Brian smiled. Vintage Fernandez.

They went in through the kitchen door. Several uniformed and plainclothes officers were milling about, writing in notebooks, talking and pointing. A female officer was dusting the kitchen doorknob for prints. Out in the living room, Brian could hear laughter. A heavyset man with a camera strung around his neck lumbered down the hall and into the kitchen. He approached two somber looking gentlemen and told them he was done.

Brian crossed the living room and, without touching it, he checked the tape player. The tape was gone.

"Looks like they've already bagged it, Captain."

Fernandez looked around. He zoomed in on the man Brian knew as Detective John Miller and walked over to him. They spoke for less than a minute and then Fernandez returned to Brian.

"He said they've already dusted the machine and the tape is in the evidence bag on the kitchen table," Fernandez said.

In the kitchen, Fernandez slipped on a pair of plastic gloves, rummaged through the bag and pulled out the tape. Back in the living room, Fernandez shoved the tape into the player and pushed the button. They listened to Gabe's frightened voice three times through without a word. When the tape had finished Fernandez turned and looked at Brian.

"You have a blank tape around here?"

Brian smiled and retrieved one from the stereo stand.

After they had copied the tape, Fernandez put the original back where he found it and the duplicate in his pocket. He stripped off his gloves and tossed them in the trash. Then he thanked Miller for his cooperation, commended him on his thoroughness, mentioned the two idle officers out front sharing a laugh, turned to Brian and said, "Let's go."

Brian was impressed. The captain was back.

As they walked back to the car, Fernandez said, "You know Gabe's probably dead, don't you?"

Brian considered this. "It's possible. But something tells me he's still alive and Leighton is going to use him in some way to get to me."

They were quiet until they reached the car. Once inside Fernandez said, "You know what bothers me most?"

"What's that?" Brian switched on the ignition.

"It's that once we nail Leighton," Fernandez paused, turned and looked at Brian. "And we will get him, Brian." He turned his attention back to the road as Brian pulled away from the curb. "He'll probably get off. Some lawyer will find a way to convince a jury of Leighton's insanity and they'll send him to an institution for a couple years."

"Insanity is hard to prove."

"True. But if history proves anything, it's that jury's are unpredictable. And if a smart lawyer digs enough, he can find some precedent that will introduce enough doubt to get his client off. Then they'll send him to a hospital for a couple years of rehab. After that, they'll release him back into society stating he's made a miraculous recovery. Then Leighton will withdraw whatever money he has stashed in some foreign account, move someplace warm and tropical, and enjoy the rest of his life laughing at our incompetence."

Brian shook his head. "I think this job has worn us both down, Captain. Maybe it's time we both considered a change."

"Past time," Fernandez said. "Way past time."

Again, they had to park several houses away from Gabe's house and weave their way though an assortment of busy detectives scurrying about taking pictures, dusting for prints and questioning the crowd of onlookers. As they ducked under the yellow crime scene tape, Brian looked over his shoulder at a group of reporters relentlessly jamming microphones into the face of a nervous-looking public relations officer and firing questions in rapid order.

"I'm going inside to find Kirkland," Fernandez said. "I want to straighten this out right now." He turned and walked through the madness into the house.

Brian started to follow but stopped short when his cell phone rang. He picked it up and hurried away from all the noise. "Fogarty," he said.

"Brian, it's me, Gabe." Gabe's voice sounded rough and strained.

"Where are you? Are you all right?"

"Listen, Brian. Are you alone?"

"Yes," Brian lied. His heart was pounding.

"He's going to kill me if you don't do exactly what he says."

"Leighton?"

"Yeah."

Through the phone line Brian heard Gabe gasp for air.

"Gabe, what's happening?

"He says for you to shut up and listen."

Brian waited, adrenaline pumping through his veins like an Indy driver on the final lap.

"There's a construction site on the corner of Pima and McKellips," Gabe said. "He says to meet us there at nine o'clock tonight, and to come alone. If you don't do as he says, he's going to kill me."

Brian knew the place. It was a large, twelve-story office complex going in that had been controversial due to its size.

"Let me talk to him, Gabe." Brian said.

There was a long pause while the phone line hummed. Brian could hear traffic in the background and the pounding of his heart. The late afternoon sun beat down on him, increasing his anger.

Leighton's haunting voice came over the line. "The time has come, Fogarty. It's just you and me. And may the best man win."

"You arrogant son —"

A deep, resonate laugh came through the line. "So articulate, Fogarty. I'm impressed."

Brian felt his grip tighten on the phone. "I'll be there, Leighton."

"Come alone, or your partner will die very slowly and very painfully. Do you understand?

"Oh, I'll be alone," Brian said. The line went dead. *I don't want any witnesses for this one.*

(45)

"So what's your theory?" Fernandez asked as he drove Brian back to the station.

"About what happened to Gabe?" Brian asked.

"That and why he would try to have you killed."

Brian decided to come clean. "I got a phone call while you were in the house. It was Gabe."

Fernandez slammed on the brakes, hung a right at the next corner and angle parked in the first available slot. He jammed the gearshift into park, tromped on the parking brake and turned to face Brian. "Why didn't you tell me this earlier?"

"I also talked to Leighton," Brian added.

"You better fill me in on the details right now."

Brian told him word for word of the phone conversation with Gabe and Leighton. When he finished, he rolled down the window to get some air. It suddenly felt very warm inside.

"We don't have much time to get organized," Fernandez said. "But I can get a few men—"

"No! He'll see it coming, kill Gabe and escape again. Then we'll be right back where we started. We have an opportunity to finish this, here and now. We have to do this his way."

"It's a set-up! He'll pick you off the moment you step out of the car."

"I don't think so," Brian said. "It's gotten personal. I've damaged his pride. He'll want to see me up close and watch me die. I can use that to my advantage."

Fernandez sat still, his face turning dark red. "I could order you not to do this, you know. I could throw you right back in the tank until this is over and do it my way."

"Yes, sir. You could."

They were quiet for what seemed to Brian an eternity. Self-doubt swarmed over him like a tropical heat wave. Was he doing the right thing? Perhaps the captain was right. Maybe he should stay out of it and let a sniper take Leighton out. Or was it possible Brian's own motivation was revenge? After all, Leighton had killed Pete Williams—one of Brian's oldest friends—attacked and terrorized him and Christine, hunted them through the woods like animals, murdered Eric under Brian's own roof, and had now held Gabe hostage in an attempt to lure Brian to the kill. The anger swelling within him intensified. His pulse quickened and he knew what he had to do. And regardless of how Fernandez handled the next few minutes, Brian was going to do it.

"All right," Fernandez said. "I didn't ascend to my position without learning the ability to compromise. Do you have something in mind?"

"As a matter of fact, sir, I do."

"Surprise, surprise." Fernandez pulled the gear lever down into reverse and backed out of the parking slot. "Fill me in; I'm all ears."

By the time Brian had finished relating his plan to the captain, they had arrived back at the station and were on their way up the elevator to the second floor. When the doors opened, Jerry Travers was standing there.

"Captain," Travers said. "I insist on . . ."

Captain Fernandez held up a hand to stop him.

"Come with me," Fernandez ordered, pulling the tape from his shirt pocket and holding it in the air. "I think we can clear this up once and for all."

"What are you talking about?" Travers asked.

Fernandez grinned, motioned Travers to follow and headed towards his office.

Brian watched them march across the squad room and into the captain's office. He smiled, wishing he could listen in on that conversation.

Then he surveyed the squad room searching for Christine. Instead, he spotted Marion sitting at her desk eating pastrami on rye and rummaging through a stack of papers several inches thick. She would know Christine's whereabouts. Hurrying over, he took a seat at Nick's cluttered desk. "Where's Christine?"

Marion looked up. She had a piece of red meat hanging from her lips. Placing her hand over her mouth, she chewed for a moment then swallowed. She wiped her mouth with a blue paper napkin. "She's in the lobby downstairs waiting for you. I'm surprised you didn't see her when you came through."

"We took the elevator up from the parking garage."

"Well, she's waiting, but I wouldn't say patiently. We practically had to handcuff her to her chair."

Brian shook his head. "Does she know about Eric?"

"She didn't hear it from me, but I can't say someone hasn't slipped." Marion picked up a 20 oz. Styrofoam cup and took a drink. "Everyone is talking about it."

Brian stood up. "I'd better get down there."

Marion shoved the rest of her sandwich into her mouth. Her cheeks puffed up like a squirrel.

Brian couldn't help but find the sight amusing. "You really should eat a variety of foods to stay healthy," he teased.

"Oh, shut up." She wiped her hands on the napkin, put her hand over her mouth and finished chewing. After she had swallowed she said, "Where have you been anyway? I heard Travers had you arrested but when I checked with the jail, they said you had been released."

"The captain can be a great ally. He's straightening Travers out on things as we speak."

Marion sat back in her chair. "I'm so relieved. Things have been wild around here lately."

"It's going to get worse."

Marion frowned. "What do you mean?"

"I got a call from Leighton." He told her of the construction site, the meeting time, and the plan he and the captain had manufactured.

"Excellent," Marion said. "How do I fit in?"

"I don't want you involved. It's going to be dangerous. I'm only telling you because . . . " He let it trail away. Why was he telling her? What did he hope to gain? Was he trying to say goodbye? Did he want her — in some strange way — to mourn for him should it end badly? He shook his head. Perhaps he didn't even know. Perhaps his feelings were deeper than he realized. So many emotions had run through his tired body recently, he didn't know what to think. He loved Christine, but their differences outweighed their likenesses. Christine's obsession with gathering wealth coupled with Brian's lackadaisical attitude towards the matter and the loss of Brian Junior had put a strain on their marriage they had struggled to overcome. It had been a difficult and emotional road.

But Marion was different. In the past she had listened to his problems with unwavering compassion and genuine concern. And like Brian, she was a cop. She understood what the life was all about. How it got under your skin, and how it could almost possess a person until the job became like life itself. At forty-three, Brian found himself at a crossroad, and the decision as to which path to take stood before him like Mount Everest: seemingly insurmountable, yet somehow possible, if only by taking one step at a time and having the determination to forge ahead, regardless of the uncertainty of the outcome.

"No," Marion said, shattering Brian's thoughts. "You can't do this on your own. This isn't some Wild West movie. You can't go racing into this like some vigilante. There are rules, and we have to follow them. If we don't, we're no better than the people we put behind bars."

The last statement hit home. Brian realized she was right. Regardless of recent events, he was still a cop and there was a right way and a wrong way to handle this. The choice would be his.

"You're right," Brian said.

"Of course, I am." She smiled and sipped from the Styrofoam cup.

"I'm supposed to meet him at nine. We know Leighton's a smart guy, so he'll be expecting us to set a trap. We'll have to make it good. One or two people at the most. Any more, and we'll give ourselves away."

"Nick and I can handle this." She wiped her hands on the napkin, wadded it up into a ball and threw it into the wastebasket. "No one else needs to know."

Brian was quiet a moment. "I'm not so sure —"

"I'm coming, Brian. And there isn't a thing you can say that will change that. As for Nick, I'll admit he has a few issues that need attention, but he's a good cop."

"He's still a jerk."

"No argument there," she said. "But he's also the jerk who took first place last May in the annual shooting competition; and, if memory serves, the three previous years as well."

"So he's a jerk who can shoot well."

"Jerk or not, if I was in your shoes, that's the kind of person I would want on my team."

She was right, of course. "Okay. I need to get down to Christine. I'll call you later and we'll work out the details."

"I'll be here," Marion said.

Downstairs, Brian found Christine pacing the floor of the lobby biting her nails and talking to herself. When she saw him, she said, "Where have you been? These idiots won't tell me anything."

"Let's get out of here," Brian said taking her arm and leading her towards the elevators. "I'll explain everything in the car."

On the ride home, Christine was staring straight ahead, chomping on her nails and tapping her foot like she'd consumed a week's worth of caffeine in an hour.

"It gets worse, honey," Brian said, choking back the words.

She turned and looked at him with watery eyes. "What do you mean?"

"It's Eric."

Christine swung sideways to face him. She put her hand over her mouth as tears flowed freely. "No . . . not Eric."

"Leighton was at the house looking for me. He found Eric."

Christine cupped her hands over her face and sobbed. Her chest heaved as she gasped for air. At one point she took her hands away from her face and glared at Brian with a look of hatred. She screamed, hit the window with the back of her hand, and then cupped her hands over her face again and wept.

Helplessness washed through him. It was a feeling he'd experienced all too often lately. What could he say?

He reached out and put a hand on her shoulder. What she did next startled him. She jerked her hands away from her face, tossed his hand away and turned on him with venom.

"This is all your fault!" she screamed.

Shaken, Brian felt his mouth drop. Words escaped him.

"This guy was after you, not Eric!"

Anger suddenly swelled within him. "Are you saying it should have been me?" The moment the words came out, he regretted it. She was distraught, angry, frightened — all natural reactions in a crisis of this magnitude. He was not handling this well.

"Just take me home," Christine said.

Calming himself, Brian drove the rest of the way home in silence. As he weaved his way through traffic, his thoughts wandered to Eric and Pete and how they had paid the ultimate price for being in the wrong place at the wrong time. He thought about Vince Decker and his two thugs, about Betty Applegate and her non-stop smoking, about Melissa and sweet, innocent Elaine and her worthless half-brother, Mark Taberhaun. He thought about the captain and his ongoing battle with alcohol and about Gabe and the unimaginable set of circumstances that had brought him to take out a contract on his partner and best friend.

Then suddenly, things began to click. The theory he had been formulating over the last two days made sense. He could see it all in his mind with alarming clarity; and it terrified him. *Dear God*, he thought. *Please tell me I'm wrong.*

(46)

Captain Fernandez had just finished filling in Jerry Travers on the situation at hand and now stood by the window gazing out across the city. He felt tired, weary, and suddenly very old. Perhaps retirement wouldn't be such a bad thing after all. Maybe he could take a trip up to Prescott and surprise his daughter, Martina, and his two grandchildren. It just might be possible, if he made the first move, to ease back into their lives. The fact he had been a lousy father would never be disputed, and he could never make up for the lost years of his children's youth; but the past was the past and could not be changed. He could only change the future; and he suddenly felt a deep, resounding need to try.

"I want to be informed the second this is over," Travers announced.

Fernandez turned away from the window and faced Travers. "I'll phone you the moment we have Leighton in custody."

"And I intend to prosecute Detective Bethencourt to the fullest extent of the law. His conduct has been deplorable. He doesn't deserve to wear the badge."

"And what of Detective Fogarty?" Fernandez asked. "He had no proof of Detective Bethencourt's activities, only suspicions."

Travers smiled. "What is it with you and this guy?"

Fernandez shook his head. "You wouldn't understand."

Travers stood, straightened his tie and adjusted his suit coat. "I tell you what I'll do. We won't pursue charges against

Detective Fogarty—although I could charge him with any number of violations—if in the future you extend my office a little more courtesy should the need arise."

Fernandez gritted his teeth. "Done," he said.

Travers smiled and walked out of the office.

"I hate that man," Fernandez said as he strolled over to the office door and closed it. Then he went to his desk, opened the bottom drawer and removed the nearly empty bottle of Jack Daniels. As he swirled the caramel colored liquid around in the bottle, he clenched his teeth together and swore under his breath. What was it about this vile tasting liquid that made him crave it so? It was like some sordid love/hate relationship. And most of the time he hated it, but like a bad marriage, it was hard to leave the familiar behind. He popped the top, tipped back the bottle, drained it and then tossed the empty bottle in the wastebasket. Easing into his chair, he stared out the window at a group of gathering thunderclouds and promised himself he would never touch another drop.

(47)

After he made sure Detectives Bantor and Carey were in position, Brian eased his car past the HARD HAT AREA sign and through the construction gates; a severed lock dangled from the chain link fence. His tires crunched and crackled as he crept through the debris that seemed inevitable around construction sites. Up ahead on the right were three large dumpsters illuminated by a high intensity light attached to the corner of a single-wide construction trailer. Beyond the trailer, a towering metal shell stretched into the night sky like something from the apocalypse. Several dump trucks, a front-end loader, and an industrial size cement mixer were scattered about in no apparent order.

As he drew up next to the dumpsters, the light from the construction trailer blinded him and his heart began to race. Feeling exposed, he pushed on the accelerator. It seemed to take forever, but when he finally emerged from the light, he stopped the car and waited for his eyes to readjust. When they did, he noticed a small vehicle parked up ahead on the right; the size and shape were unmistakable. Reaching for the gun lying on the seat next to him, he grasped it in his moist hand and eased his car forward. When he was close to the vehicle, he stopped the car and rolled down the window. For more than two minutes, he sat in the car, waiting, listening. In the direction of the metal skeleton, he could hear something flapping in the breeze; and off to his right, the sound of traffic on McDowell. Then something clanked in the direction of the tower.

With extreme trepidation, he climbed out of his car and crept towards the familiar vehicle. When he was close enough to get a good look at it, his suspicions were confirmed; it was Gabe's Triumph TR6. Holding his gun out in front of him, he surveyed the area. If this was a trap, he was walking right into it. But he had come too far to stop now.

Staying low and holding close to the side of the Triumph, he slid along its side and peered inside. There were several bloodstains on the front seat but no body. That meant Gabe was probably still alive. Breathing a sigh of relief and keeping as low to the ground as possible, he worked his way back to his car, picked up the radio and called Marion. "I'm going in."

"Copy," Marion's voice replied. "We're ready."

After he signed off, he crept through the construction site until he reached a set of metal stairs leading to an elevator attached to the outside of the building.

Just then a haunting, guttural laugh echoed though the construction site that sent a chill through Brian's body. From somewhere in the darkness, out in the direction of the tower, Brian heard a now-familiar voice.

"Poor Fogarty," Leighton taunted. "Have you lost someone?"

More laughter produced a rage that shot through Brian's veins like a swift-moving forest fire. His gun clenched tight in his quivering hand, he trotted in the direction of Leighton's voice.

"That's right," Leighton teased. "You're getting warmer."

Brian fought back the urge to scream.

Leighton laughed again. "Warmer."

Then Brian heard a different voice, a strangled voice, in obvious pain. He recognized it immediately. It was Gabe.

"Brian," Gabe moaned. "Help me."

"I'm afraid your partner has had an unfortunate accident, Fogarty. It would seem his arm is broken and he has sustained several rather nasty cuts and bruises. And I doubt solid food will be in his immediate future—a shame, really. The pain must be excruciating." He laughed.

The voice had come from somewhere in the darkness. Brian struggled against the urge to vomit. His hands shook as he forged ahead.

Nick and Marion were sitting in an unmarked police car on a side street across from a temporary chain link fence separating the construction site from the surrounding businesses. Nick was drumming his fingers on the steering wheel. Marion was watching him.

"This is insane," Nick said, and opened the door.

"What are you doing?" Marion asked. "We have to stick to the plan."

"Hang the plan. That idiot Fogarty is going to get himself and his partner killed if we don't take charge of the situation." He started jogging across the street towards the construction site.

"Nick, wait." But it was too late. He'd disappeared into the darkness.

Brian moved through the gloom with careful precision. His dilated pupils took in whatever light the half moon provided, searching for his quarry. He stopped, straining to hear something other than the sound of his labored breathing. Then it came.

"Oh, don't stop now," Leighton said, his voice a little stronger. "You're getting really hot, and your partner's fading fast."

Brian remained quiet and pressed on. He felt like he was exposing himself to a deadly virus with no hope of a cure.

Then he heard Gabe scream.

Leighton laughed. "Better hurry, Fogarty. He's running out of time."

Brian's whole body shook as fury swelled within him. From somewhere deep inside, a voice urged him to rush Leighton and take a shot. The voice howled for revenge, cried for blood.

Brian fought off the urge and shook his head. He had always been a logical man, a careful man, afraid of the consequences of a wrong decision. The only hope he had of bringing Gabe out of this alive was to act wisely. With this in mind, he eased himself to the ground and crawled on his stomach towards the voice. If he could get close enough to identify his target, maybe he could put a bullet in Leighton before he had a chance to further harm Gabe. It seemed logical. But was logic the best course of action with someone as illogical as Jake Leighton? Time would tell.

All of a sudden, Gabe's frightened and strained voice called out, "Brian, it's a trap!"

Next came another agonizing scream and then silence.

Gabe's voice had come from off to Brian's right, not more than twenty feet away. Sweat flowed from every pore of his body. Unblinking eyes strained through the darkness.

Suddenly, he could see them: two silhouettes against the streetlights beyond, one standing upright, and the other kneeling beside him. Brian leveled his gun and aimed, but stopped short of pulling the trigger. A voice from the past called to him: *Know your target.* It was the voice of his father and a phrase he'd heard often as a youth. He reached for the flashlight he had clipped to his belt. His intent was to hold the flashlight off to the side, turn it on, roll and shoot whichever one was really Leighton.

Then, from somewhere behind him out of the darkness, a shot rang out. The upright silhouette let out a loud grunt and toppled to the ground. With his ears still ringing from the gunshot, Brian watched the crouched figure roll left. Fire belched from his gun. About twenty feet behind him, Brian heard another grunt and a body tumble to the ground. He prayed to God it wasn't Marion.

In the distance, sirens blared.

"It's over, Leighton!" Brian called out. "You can't get away!"

Again Leighton laughed. Another shot rang out and ricocheted off a metal pillar directly on Brian's left. He remained still, frozen like an ancient fossil, afraid to move.

The sirens grew louder.

"You're a worthy adversary, Fogarty. You going to see it through?"

Off to Brian's left, a moan came out of the darkness. He craned his neck in the direction of the sound. It had to be Gabe. He wasn't dead. But he soon would be if Brian couldn't finish this and get Gabe some medical attention.

A few feet away, Brian could hear movement. Leighton was drawing closer. Making each motion count, Brian slithered along the ground towards the sound. Grit and pieces of sheered metal tore at his forearms. The dirt reeked of oil. His heart hammered within his chest.

When he had gone just a few feet, he could see a dark shadow where none should be. *Know your target.* He raised his gun and shouted Leighton's name. Fire belched from the shadow. Brian felt instant pain shoot through his arm. Without conscious thought of the pain, he wrenched himself from the ground and scurried towards the metal pillar and what he hoped would be safety. In the distant light of the construction trailer, he could see three police cars fly through the open gate, sirens blaring. They came to a stop near the edge of the tower and switched on their floodlights. Six police officers emerged from the vehicles, guns drawn.

"Officer down!" Marion shouted from the darkness.

Brian breathed a sigh of relief. Help was on the way.

The officers were shouting orders as they gained positions. A shot rang out.

On the far side of the construction site, opposite the police cars, Brian spotted a dark figure emerging from the construction site and running towards McDowell Street. It had to be Leighton.

Brian jumped to his feet and started after him.

As he reached the edge of the construction site, he heard Marion shouting at him from behind, but the words were unintelligible. He didn't slow. His eyes were fixed on Leighton who had reached McDowell and was negotiating traffic in an attempt to cross the street. He pushed himself on despite the pain in his arm and his heart threatening to explode. His legs felt like putty.

He reached McDowell just as Leighton made the other side and trotted off through a greenbelt leading to a small business area. Brian knew he had to catch him. There was too much at stake to stop now. He had to finish it.

Brian dodged the traffic and made it across the street safely. In the distance, about a hundred yards ahead, he saw Leighton pull up next to an abandoned Circle K, the cracked and broken parking lot filled with weeds and shattered bottles. Leighton bent over and placed his hands on his knees. Then he looked up and saw Brian coming.

Brian ran towards him, gun held out in front of him.

Without leaving his crouched position, Leighton brought his gun up and aimed. The gun popped.

Brian heard the shot whiz by off to his left. A wild shot. Leighton was tiring. Brian thought about taking a shot himself but decided against it. He wasn't close enough to be sure his shot wouldn't go wild. When he did shoot, he wanted it to be sure and true.

Leighton straightened up, turned away and trotted towards the alley between the convenience store and a run down Texaco station with a single car at the pumps and both bay doors closed. He was obviously running out of steam, and Brian felt himself narrowing the gap.

When Leighton disappeared into the alley, Brian felt his heart jump. Now he was on the defensive again. He drew up next to the side of the Circle K and crept along the building's edge. When he reached the corner, he stuck his head out and peered towards the alley. A shot rang out at the alley entrance. The bullet clipped the side of the building and sent plaster cascading down on Brian's head.

Brian darted to his right, dove and rolled towards a Nissan Sentra parked in the back lot. He came up on one knee, his pistol out in front of him, his eyes searching the darkness. Then he heard the sound of footsteps pounding down the alley and knew Leighton was moving again. Brian took a deep breath, jumped to his feet and thundered towards the alley.

As he entered the alley, gray and black shadows mixed with scattered streaks of yellow from nearby windows. He struggled to focus. For a moment he stood still, listening. The footsteps were growing faint. His breathing had become short and labored. He could hear the sound of muffled freeway traffic a mile away and an air-conditioner struggling against the heat.

Slowly, his eyes began to adjust and shapes started to take recognizable forms. He could make out toppled trashcans, laundry dangling from invisible clotheslines, a gutted car resting on concrete blocks, and at the far end of the alley, the contour of Leighton as he disappeared through an opening in the fence.

Brian quickened his pace. His only thought was ending the madness. As he reached the opening in the fence, he thought about backup; procedure dictated it. But there had been no time. If he had waited, Leighton would have escaped and there was no way Brian was going to let that happen, not again. No, this had to stop now.

With his gun grasped in both hands and poised in front of him, he crouched low and peered around the corner of the fence. The streetlights were sparse, maybe one every hundred yards. Several parked cars lined the curb. Brian could hear music rising from one of the homes across the street. He leaped across the opening to the other side of the gate just as the right side of the fence where he had been seconds before exploded into splintered fragments. The second shot hit a concrete wall twenty yards to Brian's right, ricocheted, and whistled away. He frowned. What was going on? Then it occurred to him; Leighton had to be hurt and fading fast.

Leaping to his feet, Brian ran for cover behind a green Chevy Blazer parked in front of a white duplex. From the duplex behind him, a porch light came on and a man in boxer shorts stood in the doorway.

"What's going on out here?" the man shouted.

A shot shattered the picture window to his right. A second later, the man slammed the door and the porch light went out.

Sirens sounded from down the street, and Brian could see the flashing lights moving down McDowell.

"It's over, Leighton!" Brian shouted. "Throw down your weapon."

"Screw you!" Leighton yelled, his wheezing voice coming from somewhere across the street.

Brian repositioned himself towards the back of the blazer.

Another bullet penetrated the metal of the Blazer with a grinding thump.

Brian rose up just enough to lay his gun across the hood of the truck and take aim. That's when he saw Leighton leaning against the passenger side door of a small foreign number with a chrome luggage rack, bloodstains covering the front of his shirt. His head hung forward. Blood dripped from his chin.

In a blazing rage, Brian wanted nothing more than to put a bullet through Leighton's warped brain; poetic justice for what he had done to Pete, Eric, and the others. He felt his fingers squeezing the trigger and the hammer start to move. His heart pounding, teeth grinding, he focused solely on Leighton.

Suddenly, the realization of what he was about to do surfaced and startled him. He tried to shake off the intense hatred swelling within him. If he didn't stop now, he would be walking into Leighton's dark and evil world; the final line would be crossed. And once he did, there would be no turning back. No hope of reprisal. He eased his shaking, sweating finger off the trigger.

"I think I've had enough for one night, my friend," Leighton said, waving his gun through the air. He spit a wad of blood on the ground and tried to laugh.

"You need a hospital. Put down your weapon and I'll see that you get help."

Leighton chuckled. Blood spewed from his mouth and rolled off his chin. "Oh, I don't think that will be necessary. Just show yourself so I can get this over with. I have a plane to catch." He coughed again and blood started to flow freely from his mouth. His knees buckled and sent him sliding to the ground. The gun fell at his side.

Brian raced forward and kicked the gun away. Then he knelt down beside Leighton and looked into the man's wide, blinking eyes.

"Tell me who hired you," Brian demanded.

His back against the side of the car, his legs spread-eagled out in front of him, Leighton turned his head slowly and looked up at Brian. "You're a smart guy, Fogarty. You tell me."

Brian shook his head. The man was dying, and he still had time for games. "I have an idea. But I want to hear it from you."

Leighton gasped for air. His bloodstained mouth hung open and his eyes rolled around in their sockets. "You were going to be my last, you know." He winced with pain. "I was going to call it quits."

"An ambulance will be here soon. Hang on."

"I'll never see the inside of that ambulance, Fogarty, and you know it."

"Then give me a name before it's too late."

"Why don't you ask your partner . . . if he's still alive? You're not catching me at my best." With that he arched his back, gasped for air and slid over sideways onto the ground.

Out of the darkness, Marion appeared at this side. "Paramedics and two ambulances are on the way," she said. "ETA's about two minutes."

"Where's Nick?" Brian asked.

Marion shook her head. "He must have caught one of Leighton's bullets. I don't think he knew what hit him."

Placing two fingers on Leighton's wrist, Brian felt for a pulse. It was weak, but it was there. "He's alive. Let's make sure he stays that way. I don't want him getting off that easy. I want this guy to go away for a long time."

The paramedics and ambulance pulled down the street one after the other and parked next to the police cars that had arrived a minute before. Two men in white garb sprang from the cab of the ambulance, raced around to the back of the vehicle, swung open the doors, and pulled a collapsible gurney from inside.

The paramedics rushed to Leighton's side and started an I.V. and oxygen. Brian helped them put Leighton on the stretcher and load him into the ambulance.

Watching the ambulance drive way with sirens blaring, Brian's thoughts turned to Gabe. He looked around for a patrol car to take him back to the construction site and spotted Marion standing ten feet behind him, her eyes filled with tears.

"Are you okay?" Brian asked.

She shook her head, her shoulders heaving.

Brian moved towards her and put his arms around her. She wrapped her arms around his waist and held on, her head buried in his chest. Brian felt his own tears streaming down his cheeks and watched them drop into Marion's soft brown hair.

Back at the construction site, Brian raced to Gabe's side with Marion close behind. Two paramedics had him on his side trying to stop the blood flowing from a large hole in his back. As Brian knelt down beside him and inspected the wound, he found the bullet had entered through Gabe's left side, shattering ribs during the journey, and had exited out his back, with the exit wound roughly three times the size of where the bullet had entered. Brian gritted his teeth; it looked bad, real bad.

Brian placed a hand on the shoulder of the female paramedic and said, "What do you think?"

She pursed her lips and shook her head.

Gabe reached up and put a bloody hand on Brian's leg. "I'm sorry, partner." His voice was raspy and labored. Blood filled his eyes and trickled from the corner of his mouth. "It's all my fault. I wasn't thinking with my head again." He forced a grin. "You know me; always letting my John do the thinking for me."

Brian felt a twinge through his stomach that nearly made him gag. He had prayed his suspicions would prove false. Despite the struggle raging inside him, he posed the question that had been haunting him for days: "Why, Gabe? Why would Christine want to have me killed?"

From behind him, he heard Marion gasp.

Gabe flinched, swallowed hard and tightened his grip on Brian's leg. "Eric was in trouble. She needed money."

"Well, she picked a lousy way to get it," Brian said. "Besides, I convinced Vince Decker to forget the debt just before somebody killed him."

Gabe forced a grin. "I heard. That's when I tried to stop it. But he wouldn't listen." He coughed and spit blood.

Brian turned and called to a paramedic who was removing a gurney from the back of the van, "Hurry up!"

"All she wanted," Gabe continued, "were nice things. You could have funneled some of Elaine's money her way. What would it have hurt? It might have saved your marriage. It certainly would have kept her away from the likes of me." Gabe coughed again, forced a grin. His teeth were covered with blood. He looked up at Brian with glazed eyes, forcing a smile. "You always were a cheapskate."

Brian wanted to explain that the money Elaine's parents left her and had been entrusted to Brian's care, was solely for Elaine's custody. It was never intended for his personal use. How many times had he tried to explain that simple fact to Christine? But where money was concerned, Christine had a one-track mind. There was always a nicer house, a nicer car, another necklace or earrings to add to her collection. She was never satisfied.

He shook the thoughts away. With his friend and partner dying in front of his eyes, his most immediate concern should be for Gabe's life. "You're going to be all right," Brian said. "Just hold on. They're going to get you to the hospital and fix you up just like new."

"You never were a good liar." Gabe groaned. Blood flowed steadily from his nose and mouth, and he choked on it. His body shook and his wide eyes held a look of terror. Then he gasped, let out a faint cry, and his hand fell limp to the ground. His deep blue eyes, the same eyes Brian used to think were so full of life, now gazed out at some distant point only he could see.

Brian felt for a pulse. None existed. His knees buckled and he fell to the dirt. He cupped his hands over his face and began to weep. Then he felt a consoling hand on his shoulder; without looking, he knew it was Marion.

(48)

Marion was sitting on the ground beside Brian, her arm wrapped around his shoulder. As he looked into her pained eyes, he could see far beyond the uniform, and into the eyes of a loving, caring, and sensitive woman. And for the first time, he admitted to himself that he cared for this woman, and cared deeply.

Then he thought about Christine and realized things were far from over. He lumbered to his feet, helped Marion up and dusted himself off. "I have to get out of here," he said.

"No," Marion protested. "We have to stay here and give our statements."

"The statements will have to wait. I need to find Christine." He started out across the construction site.

Behind him he could hear Marion shouting her disapproval. "What about your arm? You need medical attention!"

"The bullet just grazed me. I'll be fine."

"You're going to get in big trouble for leaving the scene of a shooting."

Like I give a crap, Brian thought. With his entire world falling down around him, the last thing concerning him was a slap on the wrist from the Scottsdale Police Department for his failure to follow procedure. His wife had tried to have him killed. And at that very moment, it seemed far more important to find her and confront her than it did to stick around for hours answering questions and filling out reports. That would come later.

As he crossed the construction site and neared his vehicle, he wondered how long Christine and Gabe had been an item, and how long they had been planning his demise. Even more importantly, how he could have been so blind as not to see it? It saddened him to believe he'd been living with a complete stranger for so many years. He'd seen many horrible things in his years as a police officer, but none as horrendous as his own wife taking out a professional contract on his life. The thought tore at his very soul like nothing had ever done before.

When he reached the parking lot, he climbed into his car and sped away. Ten minutes later as he pulled into his driveway, he realized he remembered nothing of the trip: no traffic, no traffic lights, nothing. His sole concentration had been on getting home and the words he would use when he confronted Christine. But as he opened the garage door, his heart sank. Her car was gone.

Inside, he phoned his next-door neighbor, Marge McKeever, and was told she hadn't seen or heard from Christine since the morning they returned from Greer. If she hadn't been spending time with Marge, she must have been holed up at Gabe's house awaiting the news that her plan had succeeded. Then she would have likely spent a few weeks in mock mourning, and when all seemed safe, she would have contacted her lawyer, collected the money she'd sold her soul to acquire, and headed for parts unknown. And what would have happened to Elaine? The thought sent shivers through him.

It was then that he noticed the blinking light on his answering machine. He hurried over to the phone and punched the play button. Melissa's soft and shaking voice came over the speaker: *Brian, call me as soon as you get this message. It's urgent.*

Brian dialed Elaine's number and felt relieved when Melissa picked up the line.

"Are you all right?" he asked.

Melissa's normally clear and cheerful voice sounded shaky and frightened. "I think you'd better come over here, Brian. Right away."

"Why?" Brian asked fearing the answer.

"Ah . . . I'm having trouble with Elaine."

If it had been anyone but Melissa, he would have believed her in a moment. But Melissa was as unaccustomed to lying as Groucho Marx was to drama. She simply wasn't good at it, and it showed.

"What kind of trouble?"

"She's sick. She's asking for you."

"Stay calm," Brian told her. "I'll be right there."

He ran to his car, checked the bullets in his revolver, picked up his cell phone and called Marion.

"I could use your help," Brian said when she picked up the line.

"Of course. What's the matter?"

"I believe Christine is holding Melissa and Elaine hostage in order to bring me to her so she can finish the job herself."

"Do you think she'd really do that? She can't possibly believe she could get away with it."

Brian thought about it a moment. "You know, at this point I don't know how far Christine would go. She's not the woman I thought I knew."

"What can I do to help?" Marion asked.

"Do you know where Elaine lives?"

"I should. You've talked about it enough."

"Then meet me in the back parking lot. And come in quietly. I don't want to attract any attention."

"I'm on my way."

Brian fired up the engine of his Taurus and pulled out into the street as he dialed the station and asked for Captain Fernandez.

"You sit tight," Fernandez said after Brian had told him what was going on. "I'll have a SWAT team assembled and on the way in half an hour. Until then, you do nothing. Do you hear me?"

"I hear you, Captain, but I can't do that. This is my sister we're talking about here. I can't wait."

"You listen to me. You go rushing in there like John Wayne, and Christine will get her wish. And I will have lost two good officers today."

The fact that the Captain was omitting Gabriel from the list of good officers did not go unnoticed. It was a sad epitaph to his partner's career.

Brian's hands were shaking. He could feel the sweat dripping down his back and soaking his already drenched shirt as he pulled his car out into the midday traffic of Thomas Street.

"Don't you think a SWAT team converging on Elaine's apartment like World War III is going to attract just a little attention of it's own, Captain?"

There was a long silence on the other end of the line. Finally, Fernandez responded. "I'll issue a code two and have them surround the complex. We can go in quietly, break down the door and arrest her before she knows what's happened."

"You're talking about a cop's wife, Captain. Christine knows all the tricks. She'll be watching for it. And I can't take the chance she'll harm Elaine or Melissa. Frankly, the only reason I called you is so you can have some backup for me in case it goes bad. But I have to do this alone, Captain. It's important to me. I believe I can talk her out of it, and at the same time find out why she would go to such extreme measures."

"No," Fernandez said, his strained voice beginning to sound raspy. "If it were just you and Christine, I might agree to this but there are innocent bystanders involved here, and I won't have their lives on my conscience if this goes sour. Like it or not, this is a police operation, and we'll conduct it as such."

Brian was quiet a moment as he turned an idea around in his mind. It could work, if the timing was right.

"Listen to me, Captain. I have an idea that I think will make us both happy."

"I'm listening."

(49)

Brian and Marion were seated in the Taurus in the back lot of Elaine's apartment. Through the windshield, Brian watched a line of palm trees swaying in the hot wind, their browning palm fronds waggling like flirtatious fingers. At the base of one of the trees, a calico cat pounced on something and began to eat it.

"Are you sure this will work?" Marion asked. With the knuckle of her first finger, she wiped away the moisture gathering on the bridge of her nose.

"Elaine loves the fresh air," Brian said. "The arcadia door is always open, even in the winter. I'm always trying to get her to close it to save on utility bills, but no matter how many times I talk to her about it or close it myself, the minute I leave, she opens it again."

"What if Christine has closed it?"

"The back of Elaine's apartment faces the street. I checked when I pulled in and it's open. We can only hope it stays that way."

They were quiet for a moment.

"So," Marion ventured. "You about ready?"

Brian sighed heavily. "Ready as I'll ever be."

Marion picked up her radio and punched the button, "We're ready, Captain."

"We're in position," Fernandez came back. "I'll give you two five minutes, no more. If I don't get the all clear by then, we're coming in."

"Understood," Marion said.

"Okay then," Brian said. "Let's do it."

As Brian rapped on the door of Elaine's apartment his heart was pounding furiously. He had run everything he wanted to say to Christine through his head a thousand times, but at the moment, he could recall none of it. His mind was blank.

When the door opened, Melissa stood in front of him, her red face streaked with tears. Forcing a smile, he mouthed the words: It'll be okay. Melissa stepped aside and opened the door wide as a tear flowed from her eye and dripped from her cheek. From the doorway, Brian could see Elaine sitting on the sofa; her hands, feet and mouth were bound with duct tape. Nearly overcome with fury, Brian pushed through the doorway and into the apartment.

He stopped a few feet into the room as the door closed behind him. Christine was seated at the kitchen table, Brian's spare .32 caliber revolver — the one he normally kept on the top shelf of the bedroom closet — clutched in her hand and pointed directly at Brian's chest. As Brian looked into her eyes, he saw a stranger.

"You're a piece of work," Christine said, spitting out the words with intense rage. "You can't do anything right, not even die."

Brian stood in the doorway, his hands shaking at his sides. "This is between you and me. Let Elaine and Melissa go, and we can work this out."

Christine laughed, her eyes blazing. "Oh, come on, Hostage Negotiation 101? Really, Brian, you never cease to disappoint me."

"What is it you hope to accomplish here, Christine?" He worked to keep his voice steady.

"What I started out to do."

"You know you won't get away with this. We know everything."

Her mouth twisted in a malicious sneer. "Oh, but I will get away with it, and you're going to help me." She stood, and keeping Brian covered, she walked to the arcadia door, closed it and locked it.

Brian felt a sudden sense of panic. He removed his hands from his pockets and rubbed his right thumb in his left palm.

When she turned to him, her sneer was arrogant. "You must take me for a fool, Brian. Don't you think I know there's a SWAT team outside? Do you think for one minute I actually believed you would be man enough to come here and face me alone? You're not human. You're not even a man. You're a cop, heart and soul. I doubt two minutes went by before you were on the horn to Fernandez screaming for backup. I don't know why I ever thought I could change you."

"Then how were you planning on pulling this off?"

Her eyes narrowed to tiny slits. "It's really very simple." Her words were cold, icy. "You give Fernandez whatever signal you two have cooked up, then get on the horn and tell him we need a van at the front door in five minutes. Then all of us are going to walk right out of here, get in the van and drive away. If anyone follows, I shoot someone."

Brian stared at Christine. Her face was pale and gaunt; and her hair, matted and greasy. She wore wrinkled tan slacks and a white blouse unbuttoned past her bra. The polish on her nails was chipped and flaking. As he studied her, Brian tried to determine if she was really capable of pulling the trigger and taking a life. True, she had tried to have him killed, but she had hired it done, the way one would hire someone to pump a septic tank; it was something that had to be done, but doing it yourself was a whole different ballgame.

Now that the arcadia door had been closed and locked, his entire plan, such as it was, had been flushed down the toilet. He was on his own. He had to make a move and soon.

"Christine," Brian said, shaking his head. "Why? How in the world did things get this out of hand?"

Christine took a step towards the table and slammed her hand down on the Formica top. Tears began to flow down her cheeks.

"You really don't have a clue, do you? I've been hounding you for three years now, trying to tell you I needed more from you than a part-time husband. I hate that you put your job before me. I hate that you love a job that pays nothing, has lousy hours and is dangerous. Do you have any idea how many nights I've laid awake all night worrying about you, wondering if you'll come home at all? If anything drove me to this moment, it was you. You and your righteous attitude, your black and white mentality, and your lack of ambition."

Brian bit at his lip. "Why does it always have to come down to the money? Would we have avoided this moment if I had gone to work for Bob in his stuffy furniture store? Or would we just have postponed the inevitable? What dollar amount do you put on happiness, Christine?"

Christine clenched her eyes shut and screamed, "Stop!" She stormed across the room, stopped three feet in front of Brian and held the revolver at arms length directly at his head.

Melissa shrieked and cupped her hands over her mouth.

Elaine struggled against her bonds.

Christine's hand shook. Tears streamed from wide eyes as her finger applied pressure to the trigger. Her chest heaved in and out.

Brian stared past the gun into Christine's eyes. He could see the pain, the frustration, and the anger. And, despite the moment, he felt a deep sorrow for the obvious agony he had so inadvertently caused.

Behind Christine, through the arcadia door, Brian could see Marion climb over the terrace railing and onto the porch.

In the distance he could hear footsteps pounding up the stairs and the familiar clank of heavily armed officers. He had to hurry, time was running out.

When he returned his line of sight to Christine, she seemed not to have noticed his momentary flinch of the eyes. Her own eyes had lowered and were now staring at Brian's chest, tears flowing freely, her hands trembling, her bottom lip quivering.

At that moment, Brian knew exactly what to do. Christine's resolve had faltered. He could see the agony on her face. She simply couldn't follow through, no matter how much a part of her wanted to.

With his heart pounding and his knees ready to buckle, he raised his hand slowly, grasped the barrel of the gun, and eased it out of Christine's hand.

When she realized what had happened, Christine dropped her arm, burst into heaving sobs, and crumbled to the ground. She curled up in a ball on the floor, gasping for air.

Brian's throat tightened and he had an overwhelming urge to join her. But the time for tears would come much later, in solitude, where individual grief recognizes no partner and only time can heal the wounds.

From the corner of the room where Melissa had been hovering through the entire ordeal, she rushed to him and embraced him in tearful relief. After a moment she released her grip, went to the sofa and began to pull the tape from Elaine's mouth.

Brian heard the sound of pounding feet outside the apartment. He rushed to the door and swung it open just as the SWAT team reached the top of the stairs. Unclipping his badge from his belt he held it high enough for all to see and said, "It's over. Stand down." The SWAT team stopped abruptly. The officer in front removed a radio from his belt and gave the all clear.

Back inside the apartment, Brian crossed the room to the arcadia door, unlocked it, and slid it open. Marion walked into the room and stopped. Her mouth hung open. She stared at Brian as if he had antlers growing from his head.

"That was the most amazing thing I've ever seen," Marion said, her head shaking from side to side.

Brian said nothing. At the moment everything around him seemed amazing, almost dreamlike.

Marion placed an arm on Brian's shoulder. "Are you all right?"

Brian thought about it. No, he wasn't all right. His wife had taken up with his partner and best friend, and together they had tried to have him killed. Gabriel Bethencourt, Pete Williams, Nick Carey, Eric Aberst, Vince Decker and his two bodyguards were all dead. Jake Leighton was on his way to the hospital. If he survived his wounds, he would in all likelihood, go to prison, but for how long? And what of the corruption investigation? Was it really over? Would Brian's name be cleared, or would he be drummed out of the force. A week ago he had planned to resign, now he would probably be fired.

He watched with deep sadness as two officers lifted Christine off the floor and helped her from the room; her hands cupped over her eyes. The last thing Brian heard as they made their way down the stairs was the beginning recitation of the Miranda Act.

"No," Brian said as he turned and looked at Marion. "I'm not all right." And despite his best efforts, his own tears began to flow.

(50)

Brian smiled as the morning sun peeked over the treetops. He cupped his hands around his coffee mug, took a welcome sip of the warm liquid and rocked contentedly on the porch. A cool, westerly breeze caressed his face with a hint of autumn. It was a welcome change from the intense heat of the *Valley of the Sun* and a sensation that reminded him of better times.

In the distance he could hear a vehicle rattling down the six mile rutted road that led from the main highway to Brian's cabin. He checked his watch: it was almost six a.m. They were right on time. Easing out of the wooden rocker his father had built, he went inside, removed two coffee mugs from the cupboard and filled them with his strong brew.

"You'd better get dressed," Brian called out. "They're coming up the road."

Elaine emerged from the bedroom wearing a bright red Cardinals sweatshirt, a pair of baggy, pink slacks and a huge straw hat with a multi colored hatband that read, Puerto Vallarta. She could hardly contain her excitement. "I'll get the ice chest out of the shed and fill it up," she announced and darted out the back door.

Brian put the coffee mugs on a small tray, walked outside, placed them on the railing, and watched a dark blue Toyota Camry pull in the drive. Although he didn't miss the bustle of the big city, he did miss his friends, and the time had come to reestablish old ties and, perhaps, salvage what was left of his sanity in the process.

When the car stopped, Captain Fernandez and Marion climbed out into the cool morning air. Brian almost chuckled. Both were wearing Khaki pants with pockets on the side, red flannel shirts, and fishing vests that looked as though they had never seen the outside of a sporting goods store until today.

Marion stretched, breathed in the air then looked over at Brian, smiled and waved. Brian jiggled his fingers at her and then felt embarrassed by the pubescent gesture.

"Coffee's on!" he called out.

While Marion lingered at the car fiddling with something in the back seat, the captain walked across the gravel drive and up the wooden steps to the porch. Brian shook his hand and pointed at the two mugs on the tray. "Strong and hot, Captain. Just like you like it."

Fernandez shot Brian one of his approving nods, took the cup in his hands, breathed in the aroma, and took a sip. His eyebrows raised and he smacked his lips. "Strong is being kind. You could market this stuff as rust remover."

Brian laughed loudly. It was the first time in a long time he had been able to suppress the depression brought on by Christine's conviction, the divorce, and the loss of Gabe; it still lingered just below the surface waiting. But now, with his old friends coming to share the weekend, he felt renewed, like it was genuinely possible to leave the past where it belonged and move forward, with the hope of better times ahead.

When Marion finished at the car, she walked across the drive carrying a small cardboard box. She climbed the steps to the porch, set down the box, and laid a hug on Brian that both startled and excited him. They held the embrace for what seemed an eternity. Deep inside Brian hoped it would never end. It was good to feel the caress of a woman again. He'd forgotten what a marvelous sensation it could be. When Marion was finished with the embrace, she took a step back, put her hands to his face and smiled. "It's good to see you, Brian. How've you been? Are you okay?"

Brian nodded. "I'm doing good; thanks to the arrival of some old friends."

At that moment, he noticed a glimmer in her eyes. It made him shiver. He'd seen the look before, but not in a long time. Turning his attention to the captain he asked, "So how's retirement?"

Fernandez sipped his coffee, pursed his lips and nodded. "It takes some getting used to, but I'm starting to get the hang of it."

"He's taken up golf," Marion said. "Can you believe it?"

Brian looked at him with amusement.

Fernandez wrinkled his brow and glared at Brian through one open eye. "Don't even say it."

Brian sipped his coffee. Marion inspected the sky.

"So," Fernandez said. "You about ready? I don't want to keep the trout waiting."

"Poles are loaded and ready to go," Brian said. "Elaine's out back filling the ice chest. All we need to do is load it up and we're on our way." He glanced inquisitively at the box at Marion's feet.

Marion smiled, leaned down and picked up the box. "A little housewarming present," she said and handed him the box.

Brian cocked his head to one side and grinned. "What's this?"

Marion shook her head and nibbled at her lower lip. "Open it."

Inside, Brian found a highly polished wooden plaque of birch wood. Inscribed in the wood were the words: WITH THE FUTURE COMES HOPE, AND WITH HOPE, ALL THINGS ARE POSSIBLE.

"It's from both of us," Marion said, wringing her hands together.

Much as he tried to fight back his emotions, he could feel his throat tighten and his eyes moisten. "Thank you. It's beautiful." He reached out and shook the captain's hand and hugged Marion even longer than before.

"So," Marion said. "How is Elaine doing up here, anyway? Is she getting along all right?"

"You know, I wasn't sure how she would do, but everyone around here has been just great. When she's not over at Eddie's house helping Millie with her morning baking, she volunteers at the library or she's bugging Harley over at the parks department to let her cut the grass at the ball field. And that's on top of her helping me out at the lumberyard and snapping pictures of everything that moves." Brian smiled. "She's really quite remarkable."

Marion shuffled her feet and peered through the open front door. "You said Elaine is out back?"

Brian nodded.

"I think I'll go help her with the ice chest." She turned and headed towards the back of the cabin.

After she had disappeared through the back door, Fernandez smiled and leaned close to Brian. "She's been talking about this trip for weeks."

"Oh, yeah?" Brian said. He was pleased to hear it. "I've been looking forward to it, too. It's good to see you guys again." He placed his hand on Fernandez's back and patted it gently.

"You know," Fernandez said. "I have to go back Monday afternoon, but I understand Marion took the whole week."

"You don't say." Brian felt his heart skip.

"Yup. And if I were in your shoes, I think I'd invite the lady to stay on a few extra days after I leave. Maybe have a heart to heart and see what happens. It just might be your ticket over the hump."

"Sounds like good advice," Brian said. "I think I just might do that."

Fernandez turned and looked out across the clearing towards the mountains in the distance. "It's beautiful up here. I can understand why you love it."

"It's home."

Fernandez turned and fixed his eyes on Brian, a look of fatherly concern etched across his face like a weathered tattoo. "I worry about you, you know."

Brian stuffed his hands into his front pockets and nodded. "I'll admit it's been hard since the divorce, Captain. But I think I'll be all right. I'm getting settled in here. The job at the lumberyard is just perfect and everyone in town has been great." He paused, felt his cheeks rise and widen into a full-blown grin. "You know, I almost forgot how remarkable people can be." He tapped his stomach with the palms of his hands. "I've never eaten so much pie in all my life, not that I'm complaining. Everyone seems to want to take care of me."

"They sound like good people."

"The best."

"Sheriff Condolora still bugging you to sign on as his deputy?"

"Oh, yeah, almost every day. I've thought about it, but I think I'm happy where I am for now. Eddie's been a good friend in a time of need and for that, I'll always be grateful; but I think my days as a cop are over."

"What about Christine? You still going over to the prison?"

"No. After she refused to see me six weeks straight, I finally gave up. The hardest thing I've ever done was sign the divorce papers she filed. It was finalized three months ago last Tuesday." Brian paused, looked up towards the sky, and watched a flock of geese fly overhead in a perfect V formation. "You know, once I got used to the fact it was over, I felt a strange sense of relief. I guess I was clinging to something that just wasn't there anymore, a memory really. Much as I wanted to fix it, I simply couldn't do it alone. So I had to accept the fact that it was over. And once I did, I found it easier to move on."

"That's a hard thing to do," Fernandez said, gazing across the clearing towards a distant group of mountain peaks. "I've had a little trouble with that myself. It was really hard on me when Alice died. I thought I couldn't go on. But I did; and from the sound of it, you will too."

Brian bit at his lower lip and fought back the heaviness in his chest.

They were quiet a moment, sipping coffee, taking in the clean mountain air. A cool, gentle wind blew out of the southwest. The grass in the clearing swayed and rustled. Trees creaked and moaned. Orange, brown and yellow leaves twirled and danced in the breeze. Dark clouds gathered on the horizon, transformed, and moved closer. The air smelled of rain. In the distance, behind the cabin, the call of the river rose up over the knoll, like a mother beckoning her children home.

"I've been dry for over three months," Fernandez suddenly offered.

Brian nodded, sipped his coffee. "I'm glad to hear that. It's a big step."

"Well, it hasn't been easy, I'll tell you that. I'm taking it one day at a time."

"Aren't we all," Brian said. "Aren't we all.

ABOUT THE AUTHOR

Gary Carmody grew up in Scottsdale, Arizona. Many of his weekends were spent exploring the numerous small mountain communities in the northern and eastern part of the state. Drawing from these experiences and his love of the mystery genre, he fashioned the novel you just read. He currently lives in Colorado with his family and makes his living as a Freelance Copywriter.

If you enjoyed this book, please visit the publisher,
Grace Abraham Publishing
at http://www.graceabraham.com
to read about additional mysteries in the
Dark-N-Stormies line.

Printed in the United States
23422LVS00001B/37-45

9 780974 109022